When the Dogwoods Bloom Again

by

Robert Hays

When the Dogwoods Bloom Again

Copyright 2025 by Robert Hays

Published by Thomas–Jacob Publishing, LLC

info@thomasjacobbooks.com

This book is a work of fiction. While some of the places referenced may be real, characters and incidents are the product of the author's imagination and are used fictitiously. Any resemblance to events or persons living or dead is purely coincidental.

Title font Tangerine.

Library of Congress Control Number: 2025935225
1. Fiction/historical/general 2. Fiction/war and military 3. Fiction/war and romance
ISBN-13: 978-1-950750-57-3
ISBN-10: 1-950750-57-4
Thomas-Jacob Publishing, LLC, Deltona, FL USA

"This is the truth the poet sings, that a sorrow's crown of sorrow is remembering happier things."

—Alfred, Lord Tennyson

To Alan and David, who carry my spirit into another generation.

1

THE OLD JOHN DEERE struggled, like it was feeling its age. But it kept crawling forward and slowly dragged the deeply set two-bottom plow up the hill toward the row of trees that marked the northern border of Bennett land. The young tractor driver rocked back and forth on the unpadded metal seat and pushed hard against the steering wheel with both hands, as if he thought his added physical effort might help.

"Come on, old boy!" he urged. "Come on. You can do it. This is the last round of the day."

Another thirty yards brought the struggling machine to the edge of the cultivated ground. The freshly turned soil was still damp and virtually glistened in the slanting rays of the afternoon sun. The driver stopped the tractor under a lopsided catalpa tree in the overgrown fencerow and moved the gearshift into neutral and pulled back the throttle lever until the engine idled. He was almost desperate to get his feet on the ground and stand, straightening his pained bent knees after four hours in the tractor seat without a break.

Today, he had plowed straight through the afternoon, not willing to take even the shortest time out for anything else. He wanted to be back at the house as early as he could to get ready. Tonight, he had something special to do.

He climbed down onto the tractor drawbar, gripping the back of the seat so as not to risk a fall. From there he jumped off onto the soft plowed ground. He felt a wave of satisfaction. This had been an unusually productive day. He was not expected to finish plowing this outlying forty acres before sundown and the sun still was high above the clouded horizon.

From this high ground he could see fields all the way to the Ohio River several miles to the east and it looked as if spring plowing on most of the farms was well under way. He looked toward Lake Emily to the south. Nearly all the trees in patches of woods scattered about the landscape already were in full leaf. The dogwood and redbud trees were blooming beneath the tall oaks and hickories in Soloman's Woods along the ridge. Before him lay a fresh green world he never would find monotonous.

This landscape was, in fact, one he dearly loved. He felt a great kindred with this place, this natural environment in which his life was deeply anchored. Yes, there had been times he wondered what the rest of the world might offer and he thought he might like to see an ocean someday but this was where he had spent his entire existence and as far as he was concerned the Bennett farm would always be home.

Change would come, of course. Mostly because he wanted to please Annie, he had tentatively agreed to take over her grandmother's farm. But as Mother White herself would say, it was "right down the road." He would only be expanding his boundaries.

Even if he always had found almost complete satisfaction here, though, Gilbert Bennett's usual state of contentment was absent. His mind was awash in recollections from his past and worries about his future—the known and familiar and the fearful expectations of what might lie ahead. His tranquil life had been turned upside down and the only certainty in his future was that he was about to go to war.

For the first time ever, Gilbert Bennett was not confident that sunrise in the morning would mark the beginning of another good day. And for the first time ever, Gilbert Bennett was afraid—not afraid he might be killed or suffer physical injury in combat, but afraid he faced the most painful circumstance he could imagine, a long separation from those he loved. Yes, he would miss his mother and father, but he was a grown man now and would not expect to live with his parents much longer, anyway. He would miss Aunt Gloria and a great many friends. But he would miss Annie most of all. Annie was his first love and deep in his heart he knew she would be the one great love of his life.

The draft notice was not unexpected, and he would have had time to prepare if he knew what he was preparing for. Since as far back as two years or more, most informed Americans had worried that things happening on the European continent ultimately would lead to a wider conflict the United States would be drawn into. The Japanese attack on Pearl Harbor had erased even the smallest fragment of doubt that the country's able-bodied men soon would be in uniform.

Gil Bennett was not among the first wave of draftees called into service. He was too young. But as the conflict grew to a magnitude that surely affected most of mankind, it was a given that the men his age would not be spared. President Franklin D. Roosevelt was straightforward in his reports to the American people and radio newscasts brought the war into their homes. The voice of United Press reporter Walter Cronkite became all too familiar as they sat and listened in their living rooms at night, wondering what might come next.

Gil's father never went to bed without catching the latest war news and his mother expected to be brought up to date at the breakfast table the next morning. Gil, himself, had tried to ignore it and pretended it didn't matter.

Aunt Gloria had been the first to voice an expectation that Gil would be called soon. It was almost like she had inside information, as his notice had come a week ago and his mandated time to report was close at hand.

And now, Gil Bennett felt a sense of urgency he never had felt before. Things that in the past he might have been in no hurry to get done needed to be handled at once. The most important of these would be taken care of tonight and he had spent the day in nervous anticipation.

He unhooked the plow and disconnected the trip rope and climbed back up on the tractor and settled himself again in the hard steel seat. He sat for a few minutes more and looked over the freshly plowed field and the world beyond like a convicted man about to face his executioner knowing this was his last view of something precious. He might have felt that way, except that something he was about to do was even more precious and it was time for him to get moving.

The rough ride back down the slope took very little time and he soon guided the old tractor back into the barnyard. His father was in the workshop hammering on a red-hot piece of steel on the flat surface of an anvil. Hot coals smoldered in a nearby forge. He looked up when Gil walked in, his surprise evident.

"Please don't tell me something broke down," he said.

"Nope. I finished."

Jake Bennett lifted the hot steel from the anvil with long-handled tongs and plunged it into a bucket of dirty slush water. The hot iron caused a small eruption of steam. When this subsided he dropped the iron into the bucket and put aside the tongs. He wiped his hands superficially on a shop towel and turned back to his son.

"Boy, you sure didn't spare the horses," he said. "I didn't think you'd be done for at least a couple more hours. It's good to be finished with the plowing, but I swear it seems too early."

"Oh, Dad, you always say that," Gil answered. "You look like the village blacksmith without his apron. What's that you're working on?"

"Your mom wanted me to make a brace of some kind for that sagging kitchen cabinet. Come on, let's get to the house and see what's for supper. I'm getting hungry."

Gil fell in step beside him. The two men's strides were remarkably similar and they were close to the same size, just over six feet tall and slender. Their pace was not hurried.

"I don't think we're having supper here," he told his father. "I think we're supposed to go to Aunt Gloria's tonight."

"Oh, yeah. I forgot about that. Well, we better get in and get cleaned up, then."

Aunt Gloria, his mother's younger sister, was one of Gil's favorite people in all the world. She had coddled him as a child and, having three daughters but no son, had virtually treated him as her own. She had been more emotional than anyone else in the family when she heard the draft had caught up to his age group and he would be going to war.

Tonight's gathering was in his honor, he understood, and she would have invited a good number of friends and relatives. That part he would have gladly skipped.

Yes, these were the people he knew he would miss and dreaded to leave, but he never had been really comfortable in a crowded room and there was no reason to expect tonight to be any different. And as the honoree he wouldn't be able to hide in the kitchen or plop himself on a couch in the living room and listen to the radio. But there was one thing that mattered more than all this: Annie would be there. It seemed like weeks since he had seen her.

When they arrived at Aunt Gloria's house a little later, they could see that she had outdone herself. Her table was loaded with a holiday style dinner that would have to be served buffet style because there were too many guests to be seated. When Gil and his parents walked in, she clapped her hands for attention and announced that the guest of honor had arrived. Everyone applauded and someone took up a chorus of "For he's a jolly good fellow."

Gil found it all embarrassing, but he also was proud. Who could ask for more than a gathering of people who cared for him and had come to offer their best wishes. He tried hard not to show emotion, but by the time everyone grew quiet he could feel tears about to well up in his eyes. His mother squeezed his hand as a signal of support.

Someone yelled, "Speech!"

Aunt Gloria raised her hands to signal quiet. The room was instantly silent. Her face showed a mixture of pride and sadness as she addressed him: "Gil, honey, would you like to say anything?"

To his own surprise, Gil found his voice and was able to express his gratitude. He needed only to say what was in his heart. He finished with a personal vow he thought was appropriate for the occasion.

"You all know I'm not one to go looking for a fight," he proclaimed. "And, heck, I don't even join you guys squirrel hunting in Soloman's Woods. But I swear to you here and now, I will do my duty. America is the greatest country that ever existed and if it takes a war to defend our way of life, well then I can promise you this is a war we will win. I will be proud to defend America."

The well-wishers who encircled him burst into a rousing and long-lasting round of applause. Aunt Gloria pumped a fist in the air and his father put a hand on his back and whispered, "That was great, son."

Pastor Ernie Maxwell of the Walnut Creek Church was the first to front him directly. "Gilbert," he said, "I want you to know that my prayers and those of all the Walnut Creek family will be with you every hour of every day. I have no doubt God will look after you and bring you home safely. But we're sure going to miss you!"

As they shook hands, the pastor put his left hand on Gil's shoulder. He started to move away, then reached his arms around Gil's shoulders and pulled him into a tight embrace. "You be safe, boy," he whispered, and Gil saw he was misty eyed.

Charley and Rachel Erikson, whose farm was adjacent to that of the Bennetts, pumped Gil's hand vigorously and wished him the best. Charlie then turned to his father and offered congratulations to "the man who raised a boy like this." Gil could tell his father was bursting with pride. This was more gratifying to him than his own feelings.

As the guests began to mill about, some filled plates at the table and others came and offered him their personal best wishes. He knew their words were honest expressions of their sentiments, not things they would say simply because they fit the occasion. These were his friends and neighbors and he knew these were good people.

Annie's mother hugged him and said all the right things. She told him Annie was having a hard time facing it all and was holding onto her grandmother for support. Annie and Mother White were the last to approach him.

"Gilbert, we just want you to come home safe," Annie's grandmother said, squeezing his hand tightly. "I hope you know this bunch of people wouldn't be here if they didn't care about you."

"Yes, ma'am. I know."

"Well, then, I'm going to get me something to eat and leave you two young folks to yourselves."

Gil reached for Annie's hand and motioned with a slight tilt of his head that he wanted to go outside. They slipped out quietly. A bedroom window on the back side of the house was open just wide enough they could hear music from a radio inside. Even though the sound was muffled, there was no mistaking the velvet tones of Bing Crosby singing one of his currently most popular songs, "People Will Say We're in Love." Annie usually would have commented on this as appropriate irony, but tonight she was consumed with the thrill of being with Gil while she still could just as he was with the nearness of her.

A little way farther and they reached the edge of a narrow wooded strip that separated the house and yard from cultivated fields. The sweet aroma of honeysuckle and wild roses filled the night air. They felt as if this was their own little universe, empty of all humanity except for them.

Annie's voice trembled with emotion. "I'm going to miss you so much," she said softly. "Don't know how I can stand it. My life will be empty without you, Gil."

Gil dropped to one knee. He held both her hands in his.

"Annie, will you marry me?"

She threw herself into his arms as she gave her answer. "Oh, yes! Oh, good heavens yes, Gil. I love you so much. Of course I want to be your wife."

They lifted themselves up and stood in a tight embrace. Neither felt a need for further words. There was no time and place, no concern for past or future. There was only the pair of them together, a man and a woman deeply in love having vowed to be as one for the rest of their lives. Stars could have fallen from the sky and they would not have noticed.

After a time they reluctantly accepted the fact they had to go back inside. Their absence surely had been noticed by now. Mother White and probably Aunt Gloria would be looking for them, as would anyone who might have missed their turn at offering Gil their personal hopes for his safe return. They made their way back to the house slowly, clasping each other tightly around the waist and walking in lock step.

"Gil," Annie said almost timidly, "can I tell them?"

"Yes. I would like to shout it to the heavens, myself. 'Hey, people, Annie has consented to be my wife! I'm the luckiest man in the world!' And after you've made your announcement, maybe I will."

He didn't, although this would have been an honest expression of his happiness. Annie did. With her brightest smile, she told those assembled to honor Gil that she was to become Mrs. Gilbert Bennett. This brought a new round of celebration that was little short of raucous. It transformed into a whole new party and it went on well into the night.

2

ANNIE HAD EXPECTED the move to her grandmother's house to be a routine change in her living quarters but little else. She was a grown woman and had felt for some while it was time for her to move. She loved her mom and dad and she and they got along well, but they were of different generations and she never had expected to live with them this long. She loved Mother White, too, and was confident they would be comfortable together. Theirs would not be the parent/child relationship and she would feel a great deal more independent.

But despite her positive expectations, Annie found the actual leave-taking from the home she had lived in all her life to be an emotional experience. When her mother called attention to her high school prom dress in the back of a closet, she almost could have changed her mind. She had roots here that never would release their hold completely.

Now that the move had taken place and she had been with Mother White for a while, though, she was quite happy with the choice she had made and grateful for the support she'd received on both sides. And as her grandmother emphasized several times, she hadn't moved a hundred miles away but only a few minutes' drive from that former home.

Life with Mother White brought no big changes, but there was one little one. Annie had never lived with a pet in the house and Elmo, Mother White's especially handsome and intelligent

orange tabby cat, was an ever present fixture in her new surroundings. He treated her with snobbish indifference in the beginning but quickly came around. On her third night he slipped
into her room and joined her on her bed. He woke her early in
the morning, nuzzling her face. She wasn't sure whether this
was a show of affection or a plea for her to get up and get him
some breakfast.

"You have to get along with Elmo," Mother White declared.
"He and Gil are best buddies."

"Oh, Gil's a pushover. A rag doll could get him to be a friend.
But speaking of Gil, I'm getting awful scared, Grandmama. He's
going off to the war and I know he might not come home. How
did you deal with it when Grandpa White was in the war?"

Mother White laughed. "I had it pretty easy," she said. "He
never left the States."

Annie had expected her grandmother to be easy to talk to
and was not disappointed. They carried on conversations as
equals, one woman to another. This was a relationship she never
had enjoyed with her mother. She couldn't remember ever having anything even close to a personal talk with her father so in
this regard she hardly missed him. At a different level, though,
there was no substitute for the comfort she'd always found in
his presence. When she was little she had been certain he would
protect her from all the dangers she imagined.

Annie's daily routine hardly changed. It was understood
that providing companionship for Mother White benefited the
whole family. For her, though, it was an alternative to looking
for a paying job. She would have no income but would be sup-
ported for as long as she cared to stay.

She had given no thought to the changes in her social life
working might bring. As it stood now, her only regular social activity was attending services at Walnut Creek Church.

She had tried to get her grandmother to go, too. It had been a good many years since Mother White had attended church regularly and when Annie asked if they might go together she declined. But she made it clear that Annie was free to use her old Dodge any time she wanted, so Annie was able to go.

With Gil to be leaving soon, she confessed to her grandmother that going to Walnut Creek could be hard from now on. "I'll always have a feeling Gil should be sitting there beside me," she said. "Sometimes I wonder if I should go to church someplace else, or maybe just stop going."

Mother White's sympathy was evident, but she had no advice to offer. But Gil wasn't gone yet. Annie had looked forward to another Sunday for the joy of sitting with him and his parents and now it was here. She would see him again tomorrow. Even as she talked about church with her grandmother she laid out her clothes for the next day.

In the morning, she put on her best dress and was ready to go, but deliberately lingered to see if Mother White might be tempted to go with her. When her grandmother showed no interest, she went on quickly so she wouldn't be late. It was only eight miles to the church and she got there in just a few minutes. She saw her father's dented and rusty Ford pickup truck as soon as she turned into the parking lot. Her parents had arrived just ahead of her and were getting out of the truck as she parked beside them.

The three exchanged greetings and hugs appropriate to a long absence. Annie's father said since she had a car, he hoped she would visit them once in a while. Her mother laughed and reminded him that no matter how much they'd missed her Annie hadn't been gone all that long. Annie laughed, too, although his welcome made her feel good. Gil was waiting on the front steps. He joined them and they took seats in a pew near the middle of the church. This was where Annie and her parents had sat through services for a great many years. Fellow churchgoers might have assumed nothing had changed. The minister knew, though, and made a point of greeting Annie as if she were a visitor.

"You can count on Preacher Maxwell to always know what's going on in his flock," Annie's father whispered after the minister moved on. "That's why he's so good for us, I suppose. If anybody needs him he's there before sundown."

As regular churchgoers had come to expect and looked forward to, the pastor often opened his sermon with some light-hearted story from recent personal experience. He claimed, and most of them agreed, that it was good for everyone to hear how others faced problems they had, themselves, but thought nobody else did. But very often he only sought to be entertaining.

"We did a little missionary work in Indiana last week," he began this time. "Had the pleasure of seeing a distant cousin for the first time in years. I think we all have distant cousins we barely know or don't know or maybe don't want to know."

A small ripple of agreement went through his congregation. He smiled in appreciation.

"Well, I asked my cousin what our chances were of seeing a real Hoosier and he didn't know. So I spent a lot of my time watching for one and think I may have seen a couple of them. And you know what? Hoosiers look just like us."

This brought a rousing roar of laughter, his congregation's hearty approval. They liked his stories, which probably were among the evidence they would cite that he was "as common as an old shoe" in his personal relations with the members of his church.

Neither Annie nor Gil could have repeated the pastor's story nor anything he said in the long sermon that came next. Their only interest was their togetherness and his words might as well have gone unspoken.

When services were over, Gil said he had to go home and

take care of something he had neglected for too long, but he didn't say what. Annie had hoped to have more time with him and was disappointed, but at the same time grateful for the time they had.

Annie and Gil presented entirely different fronts when it came to their coming separation. Annie could count on Mother White's sympathy, and mentioned the dwindling number of days Gil had left every day at breakfast. But Gil pretended he wasn't concerned. He went about his daily routine mechanically, almost as if in a trance. He got up early in the morning and did the work he was expected to do to help get the planting done and took care of any other chores that were his responsibility.

But all he really wanted was to see Annie, to be with her as much as he could in the time he had left. His pretended lack of concern could barely mask his painful awareness that in ten days he would be inducted into the United States Army.

Gil had a fatalistic view of his future. He would be in the war and he might not come back but he had no control over whatever happened. He was careful not to reveal his doubts, though, and managed to keep up a false front of confidence. If someone brought up the subject, he talked about his return and life with Annie after the war.

Gil knew that Annie had had mixed feelings about moving in with her grandmother. She had been very positive when she first told him about it, then a week or so later had confessed that she was having second thoughts. She seemed happy with the move after she'd been there for a few weeks, and now that they were to be married the move seemed exactly the right thing because of his plan to take over the management of Mother White's farm.

Counting down his days, Gil would have called Annie every night if he could have. But Mother White had no telephone. He had done nothing but sit home and read for the last two nights when his father finally prompted him to act.

"Aren't you going to see Annie, son?"

"I want to, but now that she's living with her grandma can I just show up at the door like I was invited? Old people like Mother White have different ideas about what's proper and I don't want to be rude."

Jake Bennett had a hard time not laughing at his son's naivete. This boy had lived a much too sheltered life! But he loved Gil's honest effort to do the right thing and willingness to sacrifice rather than do something he was afraid might embarrass Annie or get him off to a bad start with Mother White. He knew, too, that if Gil waited too long and lost much of the time he could be with Annie he would regret it terribly later.

He told Gil, "I don't know how old her grandmother is, but if she's really old fashioned she'll remember when it was proper for young men to 'come courting' as they used to say. Don't think you have anything to worry about."

He did laugh when he saw Gil's obvious relief.

"See, the old man's still good to have around," he said.

"Yeah, I'm glad you know so much, Dad. I'm going to see Annie right now."

A few minutes later he was out the door.

Showing up uninvited not only was acceptable to Mother White, but also proved to be a real boost to her already high opinion of Gil. She viewed the situation exactly as Gil's father had said she might. She had been disappointed when a couple of nights went by and he did not come to court Annie.

Now that he was there, she was almost as excited by his presence as Annie was. She also was conscious of the young couple's need for privacy. With the nights still too cool for them to be comfortable on the porch, she excused herself soon after Gil's arrival and left the living room all to them. And Gil stayed very late.

Gil's mother had made little effort to hide her despair over his going to war, but his father had tried hard to take it in stride. He made a "family announcement" that Gil no longer had any obligation to do farm work and encouraged him to feel free of needing to do anything at all.

Gil was accustomed to having work to do and felt guilty not doing anything, but rationalized that this was what his father wanted. And, well, it was his good fortune that it was what he wanted, too. During the days he had left his time would be Annie time.

This meant getting to Mother White's house about one o'clock in the afternoon and either picking up Annie and going somewhere or spending the next ten hours or so there.

"Grandmama wonders if you could come tomorrow in time to have lunch with us," Annie told him on the third afternoon. "I think she likes the idea of cooking for a man again."

Gil quickly said he would. It wasn't the meal he was particularly interested in but the chance to spend more time with Annie. His spirits were beginning to sink with the realization that time was running out. And when he had to leave her, how long might it be before he saw her again?

Mother White made what Annie recognized as a marvelous lunch but Gil hardly noticed. He knew it was good, but he was almost totally focused on the young woman sitting across the table. He was careful to praise the delicious meal to Mother White, though, and was rewarded with a proud smile.

After they had eaten, the young couple sat and talked with Mother White for a while then went on the porch and sat in the swing. Gil could have been content to sit here forever, holding hands with the girl he loved. Words would hardly have been necessary.

"Grandmama said they built this house here because of the view," Annie told him, recognizing that he was gazing across the meadow at the high ridge beyond the creek.

It was much too early for the ironweed to be in flower along the stream, but here and there a small splotch of brilliant purple showed that ironweed could be impatient, too. The delicate flowers of the redbud trees on the ridge were mostly gone but many of the dogwoods still exhibited their full beauty. Annie hadn't seen them yet, but her grandmother had told her that when the catalpas bloomed some of them were so massed with white flower they were like a crown across the brow of the hillside.

"Gil," Anni said softly, "why do you love plants and trees so much?"

He had to think for a minute before he tried to answer. Even then, he was uncertain.

"I don't know if I can explain it," he said. "Maybe it's because they show me the continuity of life. Do you know what I mean?"

"I'm sorry, honey, I don't think I do."

"Look at it this way. In the wintertime almost all of the trees and plants on the ground look dead. They have no leaves or flowers, no signs of life. If that's all you saw, you'd guess that none of them were living. But guess what? Not only are they alive, but they have been reproducing themselves, making seeds or growing new bulbs or stems underground.

"And then one day, almost like it happened overnight, it's spring and they all show life again. And we see it like new life, but it's not. It is a continuation of the same life that was there all along. And either way, whether it really was new life or we know it is the continuation of life already there, it gives us hope. Generation after generation, life goes on."

Annie snuggled closer, feeling the warmth of his body against hers. "That's beautiful," she said. "Almost religious. But do you think this only works in plants? Do we humans have everlasting life?"

Gil laughed. "Now you are getting religions," he said. "I don't know. I guess from a technical or physical standpoint it wouldn't be the same. But I do believe there is a form of continuation of human life, too. I think the spirits of your parents—"

"Whoa! Spirits? You mean like ghosts?"

Gil laughed and threw an arm around her and pulled her to him, in a quick move like a wrestler. With her head on his chest, he fluffed her hair.

"I don't think I can explain what I mean," he said. "No, not like ghosts. More like view of life or something. Let's say Mother White was a happy, contented kind of woman who liked being with people and your mother was like that and now, you are. That's more what I'm talking about. You got some of your mother's spirit and she got some of her mother's. A little bit of the parent is passed on to the child. Am I making any sense?"

Annie dug an elbow into his ribs and squirmed out of his hold. "Gilbert Bennett," she proclaimed, "you always make sense. Our little boys are going to be just like you!"

After Gil went home that night, Annie's glow still was so apparent Mother White couldn't help but notice. It made her happy to see her granddaughter so happy.

"Gil's a fine young man," she said. "He makes you happy and that means he's right for you."

"I love him so much," Annie told her. "And guess what? I'm just finding out how smart he is!"

Gil and Annie shared one thing they had not mentioned to one another. Every day when they woke in the morning they consciously counted the days of freedom Gil had left. And now they had run out. The Army—the *war*—was waiting and he had to go.

Annie rode along as his parents drove Gil to Evansville to catch a train that would carry him on the first miles of a journey no one wanted. After the formal induction process, he would go to Fort Jackson, South Carolina, to begin basic combat infantry training.

The Louisville & Nashville Railroad's big steam locomotive still was moving fast when it pulled into the station and only braked fully as the last passenger car came alongside the boarding platform. The car door opened and three people got off the train, one of them carrying heavy luggage. As soon as they were clear, a uniformed conductor stepped out. He was about to shout his customary "All Aboard" call but saw the little group surrounding Gil and lifted his cap and said in a normal speaking volume, "You can board now, as soon as you're ready."

Gil had to force himself to pull away. He gave Annie one last kiss and got on the train.

3

BASIC TRAINING WAS easier on Gil than it was for most of the other men in his company. He was strong and agile and able to handle the rugged physical action with little trouble. He was used to hard work. He could tell that many of the new soldiers around him had led softer civilian lives than his. But none of this mattered now. Being inducted into the United States Army was a great equalizer and once they were in uniform individual identities almost ceased to exist.

Gil had found South Carolina a bit exotic and simple discoveries of new things in the natural environment helped ease the stress of life in the Army. He never had seen palm trees before. There were few hardwoods in the patches of forest on the base, only pines growing taller than he'd ever imagined. Mimosa and crape myrtle, scarce in southern Illinois, grew like weeds here. His mother would love all the flowering shrubs and there were vines he couldn't identify.

On his first guard duty, his post was in a wooded area just off the rifle range. As he walked it in the middle of the night he imagined himself back in Soloman's Woods, probably walking with Annie. Just as he missed people, he also missed places. Soloman's Woods most of all. In his mind he went back to that special place, remembering those times he had gone there seeking and finding solitude, almost as if in another world. And he still could laugh at the jokes about the place's name. No one seemed to know where it came from, but there always were wise cracks like, "It was named after a king," or "It obviously was named by a very wise man."

The weather was miserably hot compared to what he was used to and the drill sergeants made sure the new soldiers took salt tablets twice a day when they were in the field. The heat also figured into another dire warning that became a threat in the mouths of training cadre dedicated to molding individual egos into a common lot.

"We'll sweat that baby fat off your lily-white asses so fast you won't even know it's happening," a foul-mouthed sergeant barked as Gil's Company A stood in the first early morning formation. And for any doubters, "That's gonna start right now!"

His threat came to fruition immediately as they were marched by platoons some four miles to a training area in the sand hills common to Fort Jackson. At the end of the march they were seated in bleachers for weapons demonstrations with a ten-minute break every hour to stand up and stretch and "smoke 'em if you got 'em." Gil didn't smoke but he welcomed every chance to stand and move around. After three hours of this they marched back to the company area to eat in the mess hall.

Every man was drenched in sweat by the time they got there. Gil saw two men drop from heat exhaustion on the first day, and heard there were as many as a dozen others.

The Army's training pace at Fort Jackson was hectic. Company commanders seemed almost manically determined to rush the trainees through and prepare them for whatever roles they would play in the war. And regardless of what that role might turn out to be, the training regimen assumed they would be in combat and was designed to make sure they were ready. Any doubt about this was quickly erased by long hours of demonstration and practice in hand-to-hand combat and bayonet fighting.

The Company A commander, Captain Virgil Roland, made a point of this urgency to the assembled recruits.

"They need you at the front today, not next month!" he bellowed. "And in short order I'll have a whole new bunch of pussyfooting greenhorns like you meatheads to get through all this fun and games. So don't let me catch you dragging your asses like you're not in any hurry! Do I make myself clear?"

And they had learned early on that when the captain asked this question they were expected to yell in unison, "Yes, sir!" If they didn't, they might be given an extra jog or two around the parade field holding their heavy M1 rifles over their heads.

Although unit designations were nothing more than an administrative formality, the officers tried to drum up a spirit of competition among them as an incentive. Gil and the other men in Company A heard constant taunts from those in Company B challenging them on rifle range scores and any other training activity that could be quantified. It was funny at first, but soon became an irritation. Captain Roland demanded that they fight back.

"You damned well better give as good as you get!" he shouted. "I'd better not hear any of those yahoos in Company B claiming my guys are a bunch of old ladies! Do I make myself clear?"

And the required response, "Yes, sir!"

"Let me hear you! Do I make myself clear?"

And again, as forceful as they could manage, "Yes, sir!"

It had taken Gil only a week or two of training to realize his blind and unquestioning acceptance of orders and protocol, no matter how foolish they often seemed, made military life much easier. Some of the complaints he heard from other men made him wonder if they had faced even the ordinary discipline of home and school as civilians. He had become keenly aware of the great variety of cultural backgrounds represented even in the small-sized unit that was his company. His southern Illinois accent fit well with that of men from the Southern states and men from the North "talked funny."

There was little free time for conversation and talking in formation was strictly forbidden. This made it hard to feel like he knew any other trainees. He had developed a modest friendship with Jeff Bartlet and Henry Burnett, not because he and they had found common interests but because they were one-two-three in their alphabetically formed rifle squad lineup. Burnett was from Philadelphia, which to Gil might as well have been a foreign country, but Jeff Bartlet was a farm boy from southern Indiana. They figured their home areas were no more than a hundred miles apart as the crow flies.

Lying in their bunks after lights out, he and Jeff talked about the transition to military life. Both had found it easier than expected, but recognized this wasn't true for some. They agreed that for the new trainees even modest resistance was the surest route to trouble.

"I wouldn't say my dad was particularly strict," Jeff said, "but if he told me to do something I knew he expected me to do it. I never tested him so I don't know what kind of punishment I might have faced if I didn't."

Gil proclaimed a similar background. He lay on the thin top mattress of their tiered bunks and had to lean over the side to make himself heard without being too loud. "How about school?" he asked. "You ever have a real tough teacher?"

"I don't think so, but I probably thought they were all tough at the time. How about you? Any horror stories from the classroom?"

Before Gil could answer somebody yelled and demanded

they shut up and let everyone get to sleep. They knew this was good advice; a drill sergeant would come storming through the barracks at five in the morning blowing his whistle and demanding they be out of bed and dressed and standing outside in formation in ten minutes. Anyone who didn't make it would get an extra work detail on the weekend.

"Well, good night, Gil," Jeff said softly. "Hope we have something real fun to do tomorrow."

Gil lay silently, a wide smile on his face. It was just as well he couldn't start the story he would have told because it was rather long and a bit complicated. Yes, maybe a "horror" story about one day in school, but one with a happy ending. It was something he might have forgotten long ago except that it involved Annie and Annie was always on his mind.

A simplified version would merely relate that in high school he and Annie decided to skip classes one afternoon and got caught by the principal as they slipped down a back stairway. They were threatened with punishment, but in the end the principal had more or less just laughed it off when they promised to get back to class. *And that was just one of a lot of times I could have got her in trouble.* Thinking back over the years, he realized he often had taken advantage of Annie's trust. He felt guilty. If there was one person in the whole universe he didn't want to hurt, it was Annie. He went to sleep hoping he would see her in his dreams.

He did. Vividly and so realistic it might have been actually happening. When he woke it was almost as if he had just left Annie after a beautiful walk in the moonlight in Soloman's Woods. In the moment before he was fully alert to his surroundings he might have been about to get up and make ready for a day on the Bennett farm.

His pleasant morning went downhill fast from there, with a drill sergeant's arrival and the chaos that followed. As usual, his dream world and the real world were a million miles apart.

Company A spent the day on the rifle range. The first thing they learned was that when you fired an M1 rifle you got a powerful kickback in your shoulder. The second thing was that rifle range cadre seemed to enjoy making fun of them when they proved to be poor shots. Gil eventually recognized this to be phony, a routine part of the training that apparently was supposed to make you more determined. That didn't work with him, but it looked like it did with Henry.

Gil and Jeff were learning that Henry had what he called "street smarts" they were lacking. His big-city environment had taught him things they never would have needed to know. They enjoyed a good example that night when the company was back in the barracks.

One of the drill sergeants they had not seen a lot of and whose name Gil didn't remember came in just before lights out and called all the first-floor dwellers together. His stern manner and obvious sense of urgency demanded their attention. He motioned them into a tight circle around him.

"One of your Company A buddies needs your help," he announced, speaking in a low voice. "I guess he slipped off base and went into Columbia and got drunk, but I'm not sure what happened after that. Anyway, that doesn't matter. He's locked up in the city jail and he'll be AWOL when he doesn't make formation in the morning."

The sergeant had Gil's rapt attention. He was impressed, though surprised, with the sergeant's obvious concern.

"You know what happens if he's AWOL," the sergeant went on. "He'll be court martialed and might even end up in the stockade. His only hope is if I can get him out and get him back here in time to avoid that. And I can. If I can get together fifty dollars bail money, I can go get him out right now. I know you guys will want to help, and if you'll just chip in a dollar apiece I can do it."

Gil and several other men were reaching for their wallets. Henry held up his hands and got their attention.

"I don't believe we got this poor guy's name, sergeant," he said. "I'd sure want to know if he was in my squad."

The sergeant appeared to be momentarily flustered, then said he didn't remember the name right off the top of his head but had it written down on papers in his car.

"Guys," Henry said, "he doesn't know the name because the poor man doesn't exist. This is one of the oldest scams in the world. I'll bet the captain will be interested to hear about this in the morning. Right, Sergeant?"

The sergeant was out the door before anyone got his name. Henry had saved them from being taken in.

The following Sunday was one of the rare days the trainees were allowed to leave the Company A area. Gil got out as early as he could and went to the main post service club. He wanted a quiet and peaceful setting where he could write Annie, and anyway he needed stationery and a postage stamp and could buy them there.

He wasn't sure how long it had been since he'd written Annie, but it had been longer than he liked. Even if he had nothing new to report he wanted to tell her how much he missed her.

The service club was crowded. This didn't matter to Gil, because it still was a welcoming place. After barracks and mess hall, designed to be functional with no regard for aesthetics, lounge areas with overstuffed sofas and chairs and reading lamps and music in the background would have made for a pleasant outing if he'd done nothing more than walk through them. He wanted to buy a cup of coffee and sit and drink it slowly and enjoy the home-like atmosphere but money was too scarce.

He was surprised to find a USO outlet in a corner niche of a busy commons area. It was only a table with literature and posters overseen by a pretty young woman volunteer, but one of the posters offered free writing materials and postage stamps "so you can send that letter to the folks at home."

The young woman welcomed Gil's inquiry with obvious enthusiasm. She gave him what he needed and said if he wrote a letter he could bring it back to her and she'd get it in the mail faster.

He took what she offered and went looking for a place where he could sit and write. As he climbed the stairs to the second floor another soldier got up from a small table by a window and Gil slipped in after him. As he settled in the chair, he gazed out the window. There was a thick stand of tall pines just beyond the parking lot and he had an urge to go down and walk into the little woods. But first he must write the letter.

How could he tell her all the things he wanted to say? *For God's sake, man, just tell her how much you love her! Say what you'd say if she was sitting there beside you!* He began to write:

"I keep thinking how wonderful it will be when we are married. And I promise you two things. First, and the one that tops everything else, is I will never stop loving you. And second—you can hold me to it—when it comes to running our household you will be the boss! I'll just do whatever you tell me to."

He wondered if she hadn't thought about all the times he had taken advantage of her easy-going nature, but he had, and it was time to make clear this was all in the past. And even if she hadn't thought of it—well, this was a commitment he needed to make, anyway.

"They have a sound system here playing music," he wrote, "and right now it's like they put a record on just for me—for us. It's Dick Haymes singing 'You'll Never Know.' Have you heard it? I'm pretty sure they play it on the radio a lot. Listen the next time you hear it and pretend it's me singing to you. You can believe it when you hear the line that says you ought to know how much I love you because I told you a million times or more. Well, if I haven't, I have wanted to."

He wrote on both sides of the three sheets of paper the USO woman had given him. He tried to tell her about infantry training and Fort Jackson and the hot South Carolina weather. He told her the food was good, and they were served plenty of it.

"But a lot of the guys complain, like it's not good enough for them. Maybe they are used to something fancy and I'm not. Of course, it couldn't be any better than Mom's chicken and dumplings we had a lot of the time on Sundays nor one of her out of this world cobblers when we picked blackberries."

He was afraid all this would be awfully boring to Annie, and it wasn't important to him, either. So just about every other paragraph he came back to how much he loved and missed her. He was careful to make this the last thing he wrote. He folded the letter carefully and put it in the envelope and was about to seal it when he remembered there was a stamp inside. He rescued the stamp and put it on the letter and addressed it to Annie at Mother White's.

The young USO woman accepted the letter from him and offered a pleasant smile.

"Looks like it's going to a girl back home," she said. "I don't mean to be nosey. It's just such a terrible thing the way this war has separated you young men from loved ones. I see it all the time." He voiced his agreement and she wished him good luck in his tour of duty.

When he left the service club, he walked straight to the small wooded area he had seen through the upstairs window. Pine forest was vastly different from Soloman's Woods, and yet in many ways the same. This felt like a familiar place and here, among the trees, he was at peace with his world. He raked together a mat of pine straw to sit on and leaned back against a tree and forgot the U. S. Army and dismounted drill and bayonet training and barracks life in general. He relished this time as his alone and wished it might last forever.

When he left the woods an hour later, Gil had shed the built-up mantle of futility that was a natural outgrowth of the regimented life demanded by Army training. The renewal was welcome. Once again he was ready to take whatever was to come and move on and do his duty in service to his country.

Some combination of this lingering spirit and knowing now what to expect in day-to-day activities helped him maintain an unusually positive attitude as Company A approached the final weeks of training. He was able to joke freely with Henry and Jeff and, occasionally, some of the men not in his rifle squad.

For Gil and his friends, every element of training had become routine. Henry had been counting the days until they finally were allowed to get passes and go into town. They would be able to go into Columbia and Henry vowed to find a good tavern, which he defined as "any tavern," and drink beer until he went broke.

Jeff allowed that unless he had funds rolled up in a sock in his footlocker this wouldn't take long, given their pitifully small Army pay.

"What? You haven't heard of the Burnett fortune?" Henry asked him, apparently in all seriousness.

"No, but now that I have, Private Burnett, I will be real happy to match you beer for beer, all at your expense."

Gil wondered how far they would carry on this exchange, and soon found out. Two hours later they entered a tavern on Main Street in Columbia. It was a comfortable establishment with a long bar and several tables, as handsomely decorated as a first-class restaurant. Men were sitting at three of the tables and six men in U. S. Navy uniforms sat at the bar.

Gil and his friends took a table up front, close to the bar, and ordered bottled beer. Jeff soon started again the pretense that he expected Henry to pay for his beer. But he promised not to run up a large bill because he was not really much of a beer drinker.

"And I guess, being a rich man from Philadelphia, you will want to pay for Gil's beer, too. Right?"

Gil protested. He didn't really like beer very much but he had ordered and paid for one bottle, which he expected to last him all night. He had become interested in and a little nervous over the game going on between Jeff and Henry. It looked like Jeff, obviously joking in the beginning, had decided to go ahead and see what Henry would do. Henry would have to either admit he did not have money or come off as stingy. Henry did not like to be bested on any front.

And he wouldn't be. Gil couldn't tell whether it was to call Jeff's bluff or he actually was being generous, but he said sure he would buy.

"And I want to pay for yours, too," Henry said to Gil.

Now it was Jeff who protested. "Nah, Henry. I was just joking, man. I don't expect you to pay for my beer."

One of the Navy men at the bar overheard their exchange. "Hey, we're safe now!" he exclaimed in a deliberately loud voice. "The U. S. Army's here! How the hell can we win the war with geniuses like them? Can't even figure out who's paying for their beer."

The other uniformed men at the bar all laughed and there was a flurry of derogatory remarks about the Army in general and Gil and his two squad mates in particular.

"Guess you hadn't heard," another sailor said, "the Army claims manpower, not brainpower."

"Yeah, well, we better get them bright young troopers onto one of our good ships and get 'em over there and show 'em the difference between a Kraut and a Frenchman."

There was more laughter among the Navy men, who were looking toward the three in Army uniforms now in a way to make it obvious they were making fun of them. Gil pushed his beer bottle to the middle of the table and pushed his chair back, ready to leave.

"Come on," he said to Henry and Jeff. "We don't need this. Let's get out of here."

Jeff was ready to go, too. But Henry wasn't.

Henry stood and walked casually over to the Navy contingent at the bar, directly behind the man on the end who had begun the mockery. In what looked like one swift move, he grabbed the back of the sailor's collar, jerked him backward off the bar stool, and smashed him in the face with a closed fist.

"Anchors away, my boy," Henry said loudly as the sailor fell backward to the floor.

Henry turned back to Gil and Jeff and yelled, "Come on, let's get out of here!"

He snatched a chair from a table near the door and wedged it in the door opening and slammed the door against it as they ran out. It would be a temporary barrier to slow down the Navy men who were making ready to give chase.

Gil was near to complete panic and he could see that Jeff was, too. Henry still seemed to be perfectly calm.

"This way," Henry called, as he ran to the nearest alley. "Back here, out of the streetlight."

In no time they were behind the building housing the bar, in nearly complete darkness. Henry pointed out that there would be lots of Fort Jackson men in uniform walking up and down Main Street.

"Those Navy jerks will realize pretty quick they couldn't pick us out of a crowd and give up the chase," Henry said. He spoke calmly, as if he had full confidence in what he had told them and no worries they might encounter the Navy men again.

They got back to the post with no further incident. The only loss was that Henry had not had much beer. At his first opportunity, Gil started to write Annie and tell her all about his first in-town experience. When he read what he had written, though, he decided not to send it. He wanted to tell her about Henry's daring action, but she could see it as a report on a bar-room brawl and that was the last thing he wanted.

He re-wrote the letter, stressing that his time at Fort Jackson would be ending soon. He told her he was confident he and the other men in Company A were fully prepared for whatever lay ahead.

4

ALMOST BEFORE GIL realized it was happening his company finished training and was aboard a troop transport ship churning its way across the Atlantic. Company A was intact, except for the officers and training cadre, who stayed at Fort Jackson to start all over again with a new batch of trainees.

As they had been from the beginning, Gil, Jeff, and Henry were together. They would be the only ones to address one another by first names; to everyone else they were Benett, Burnett, and Bartlet. Jeff suggested they call themselves the "Three Bees" and let the world know they were ready to sting.

Henry thought this was a great idea and clearly regretted not having thought of it himself. "Absolutely!" he exclaimed. "The Three Bees will go hang Hitler on a light pole. Eh, Gilbert?"

"Sure thing," Gil said. He was coming to accept Henry's boisterous style, which in the beginning he had found irritating. He remembered his father telling him once when he was little that, "We need the fools to make us feel better about ourselves." Henry was no fool but there had been times when he got carried away with his own efforts to be clever and sounded like one.

With no training activities and much time to kill, Gil wrote Annie every day. He knew none of his letters would get into the mail until they docked in England, but he tried to describe to her how it felt to be crossing an ocean and told her about the devastating sea sickness. He asked about things on Mother White's farm and told her he couldn't wait until he and she took it over. The land eventually would be hers and the White farm would become another Bennett farm.

And by the way, did she see his parents often and did they seem to be doing well? He knew the house could burn down and his mother, determined not to send him any negative news, wouldn't tell him about it. His letters from home were brief and predictable.

Picking up the worry expressed in Annie's letters to him, he tried to reassure her. He rationalized his company's situation as virtually immune from danger. The war had been going on for a good while now. The Allied forces had landed in France and would be pushing forward well ahead of whatever place he ended up in. Yes, he was in an infantry company but the whole U.S. Army had been through infantry training, and this didn't mean anything.

In answer to her questions, Gil promised he was well prepared to handle such war as he might get into. He had scored just below marksman status on the rifle range, gone through a fair amount of hand-to-hand combat training, knew how to handle explosive devices, could fight with a bayonet, and could dig a foxhole as fast as any man in the Army. He expected her to realize he was writing all this a bit tongue-in-cheek but had second thoughts. He need not remind her of the possible dangers he faced. He crumpled up this letter and threw it over the ship's rail into the sea. And so once again he would fill his letters with talk of love and missing her.

In his own mind, all those things he had told Annie were true. Army training methods were effective, and he had full confidence he was prepared for whatever came. He didn't want to get into combat, of course, but he took pride in his uniform and his small role in serving his country. He had taken an oath to defend the Constitution of the United States and he'd learned in civics classes in school how the Constitution was emblematic of the American way of life. If he had to fight, it would not be for himself. It would be for Annie, his parents, Mother White, and Aunt Gloria, and the freedom of generations to come. He was ready to do his duty.

There was a certain level of comfort to be found in being at sea. This was "travel time." No time devoted to most of the military protocol Gil found most tiresome. But this was not nearly adequate compensation for the discomforts. He had yet to develop the vaunted "sea legs" he had been promised and he was more than ready for the end of this voyage and welcomed word the ship was coming into port.

He and hundreds of other newly trained American soldiers crowded the deck as their huge Liberty ship churned its way slowly into the harbor. Before them lay England or Great Britian or whatever official designation was the Army's current favorite. As far as Gil was concerned, it could be Mars as long as it was dry land.

Taking no chances on potential last minute foul ups, the few Army officers aboard were getting their instructions from the Navy and already had formed up the men in their respective units. It looked as if the Navy wanted them off its hands as soon as a gangplank was down. Gil's Company A was among those on the rail in a position to be one of the first units off. They stood at ease, packed duffel bags at their sides.

"Wish they'd punch this big old fishin' boat up a little and get us to the docks," Jeff said. "I can't wait to find out where we're going."

Henry scoffed, but good naturedly. "I'll bet we don't know that for a week," he said. "They got to set us down right here for at least that long so we all can do a shift or two of KP and get another layer of polish on our boots. It's still the same old Army, you know."

A man standing somewhere behind Henry picked up on that idea and added his own. "Yeah, I'll bet they have whole rows of grease traps just for us to clean."

Gil had been so eager simply to get his feet on dry land he hadn't given much thought to where they might go next. Now it struck him that the rest of his life was in play; he might be on his way to a combat zone, or he might not. Had he been overconfident that he was ready to fight? He had felt himself prepared for war, but all war was not the same.

"So, what do you figure the chances are we're going to be shooting Germans pretty soon?" he asked, not directing his question specifically to either Jeff or Henry. "Either of you guys feel especially heroic?"

"Hey, we're the Three Bees," Jeff responded. "Fightin' for freedom and all that. Pity the poor German that gets in our way!"

"Yeah, keep that spirit alive, my good buddy," Henry said. "I want to see that fight for whatever still alive and well when the first Kraut uniform pops out of the woods! We're not talking about squirrel hunting or whatever it is you country cousins like to do."

Gil never had a chance to get his clever comment in. At that moment, for what reason they never knew, the ship's shrill whistle blasted loud and long, leaving the troops on deck holding hands over their ears. They would have been forgiving if it meant they actually were landing, but it was another full hour before the ship finally docked and Company A and the four hundred or so other new infantrymen were on solid ground.

Even though all were in organized units, it was something of a mad scramble moving them away from the waterfront. They had to carry their heavy duffle bags on their shoulders, which made it hard to march in tight formations. The rows of trucks they eventually came to were a welcome sight.

"Man, I'll take wheels to fins any time," Gil said as they took seats on a side bench in the back of one of the trucks.

Jeff voiced his agreement. "But I'll tell you what. Right now I wouldn't care if it was an Eskimo dog sled as long as I could sit down for a while."

The trucks finally started to move and they rode for what had to be several miles. From inside the canvas canopied truck bed they could not see their surroundings. Nothing was visible until the trucks stopped and they unloaded. Rows of barracks made it clear they were on a military base, but this was all they would know. They could have been back at Fort Jackson. Companies A and B still were neighbors in a new home environment that offered no obvious changes.

Henry claimed he expected to see Queen Elizabeth. He practiced what he said was the proper way to greet royalty, bowing to Gil and Jeff and pretending to doff his hat. They tried to make fun of his effort but actually were slightly impressed.

"Just be sure to give her my best, too," Jeff told him. "Tell her we are all in this together and the U. S. Army is proud to be fighting alongside the British. Or, the English, or whatever we're supposed to call them."

"Probably will be the first time she's heard that," Gil said.

When they were called out early the next day they learned that this was not their new station, but merely temporary housing. And tomorrow they would be in France. Whatever was to come next, the war suddenly was close at hand. Gil was eager to write Annie and let her know what was happening but now faced the limitations posed by the Army's censorship. He was no longer free to tell her much of anything.

Company A soon was broken up. Gil's rifle squad was separated from the unit and told they would have orders by afternoon. The rest of the company was moved out as part of a large multi-battalion unit of rifle companies headed for the front lines. Henry heard rumors they were needed desperately to replace casualties.

"Can't let Adolph down," he said. His tone dripped with sarcasm. "If he wants Americans to shoot, we have to keep them coming."

Gil sympathized with that sentiment. "Just glad we got pulled out," he told Henry. "But I wonder what they plan to do with us."

5

THE THREE BEES were still a team. And now what? Being separated from their organizational parent had given them hope for a better fate than getting sent to the front to replace casualties and they were nervously waiting for an answer to that most pressing question. They soon got it and it was what they hoped to hear. They were not headed for combat.

The officer who approached them was young and struck Gil as a bit cocky. "Are you the men from Company A?" he inquired.

They responded in unison, "Yes, sir."

"I'm Captain Ron Daniels," he told them. "I may or may not be your commanding officer permanently, but for now I am. You men are the core of a new reconnaissance squadron that is going to play a critical role in our advance across France and right into the heart of Germany. You will be on French soil before dark. That's all you need to know for now."

Without calling them into an organized marching formation, he led them along the docks to a waiting boat that from all appearances was a common English fishing vessel. But once aboard, they found it to be something quite different. The cabin was roomy, with built-in seating more than adequate for the dozen members of the squad. A ladder in an open stairwell led to an active communications center below the main deck, where four radio operators were busy at a bank of sophisticated broadcasting equipment and receivers. It sounded as if there were both incoming and outgoing messages.

"Well, men, we were fortunate to have this little luxury liner available to get you across the Channel," Captain Daniels told them. "Only thing is, we don't have life jackets. I hope you're good swimmers because if we happen to get torpedoed you are on your own."

Henry almost panicked. "Sir," he said in almost a shout, "I can't swim!"

There was a murmur of voices from other squad members, and Gil was relieved that he didn't have to add his voice to alert the captain that he couldn't swim, either. Captain Daniels threw up both hands and broke into a loud laugh.

"It was a joke, men," he said. "Just wanted to make sure no one tried to mutiny. Don't worry, we have life rafts and enough preservers to go around." Then, to Henry, "What's your name, soldier?"

"I'm Private Henry Burnett, sir."

One of the radio operators from below deck, who had climbed to the top of the stairs, caught the captain's attention. He held out a folded sheet of paper which the captain took, opened, and read. When he finished, he turned back to Henry.

"Well, Burnett, I think you spoke up as an act of desperation, but I commend you for it. I've just been assigned to this elite outfit as commanding officer, and I want soldiers who will stand up for themselves. As of today, men, you are a brand-new unit, the 2nd Platoon of B Troop, 4th Infantry Reconnaissance Squadron. You don't need to remember all that, because you will not be writing home about it! And don't worry about the top unit designation, because it doesn't matter. You serve the whole damned United States Army.

"If you are going to get along with me, you are going to show me the two things I demand: loyalty and dedication. By loyalty I mean you understand and accept the fact that this is a *team*. We're all for one and one for all. And by dedication, I mean you work your ass off to do your job. Do I make myself clear?"

In unison, "Yes, sir!"

Their boat apparently had hit rough water and began to toss up and down. Captain Daniels, who had been standing ever since they pushed off from the dock, took an empty seat between two of the squad members. "Everyone relax, we might as well be comfortable," he said. "I'll take this opportunity to fill you in on what we're all about. But first, I want to get acquainted."

He was looking straight at Gil and asked his name.

"I'm Private Gil Bennett, sir."

"No," Captain Daniels responded, "you are *Sergeant* Gil Bennett. I forgot to tell you, each one of you begins duty with your new intel platoon with a promotion. That work for everybody?"

This time, the "Yes, sir!" was shouted out in a rather jovial manner.

The captain called on each of the others, in turn, to introduce themselves. By the time he finished Gil was relaxed and comfortable with their commander. He came across as having a real desire to know them individually and show he was a member of the team, too. Gil sensed that the other men felt the same way he did.

Gil knew the names of the other rifle squad members, but sometimes confused names and faces. As he listened to them introduce themselves to Captain Daniels, he tried to link each name with some physical attribute of the man to help him remember who was who. Remembering names was something he'd never been very good at, but this was not a large group and he knew he could do it.

Not everyone offered an obvious identifying physical feature or personal characteristic. All had been nearly scalped by the requisite GI haircut and all would be clean shaven. They would not display exotic tastes in dress through gaudy shirts or unique footwear. Since the Army had gone to such great effort to make them all the same, Gil's options were quite limited. He would try to remember the names and learn to associate the faces over time. Besides the Three Bees, the rifle squad turned intel platoon was composed of O'Dell, Sampson, Elliott, Harris, Harrison, Jansen, Allison, Shelby, and Shaw.

Captain Daniels made use of the time it took to cross the English Channel to lay out their mission in simple terms, stressing its importance several times over. Essentially, they would be called on to get behind the German lines and report back on the location and strength of enemy forces in front of the Allied advance. Yes, it would be dangerous. Barring capture, though, they likely faced less danger than those troops in actual combat.

"Meaning if they don't see us they can't shoot us, right?" This query came from the platoon member Gil believed was Elliott. Captain Daniels said he had just hit the nail on the head.

"I could not have put it more succinctly," he exclaimed.

Jeff had a question, too. Would the whole platoon work as a unit, and if so wouldn't that make it harder to avoid detection? Once again, the captain said he was right on target. Yes, if they worked as a unit they were more likely to be caught but, no, most often they would not all be in action together. Usually, he said, he would expect no more than three men at a time to be sent on missions behind the lines.

"There's one thing I want you always to remember," Captain Daniels concluded. "You'll never get all the credit you deserve. But what you do will save the lives of Allied troops. You can make the difference in whether or not some guy goes home to his wife or sweetheart. Do your duty and you will be among the true unsung heroes of this war. And I think that's all I need to say."

Henry nudged Gil with his elbow. "Sounds like the perfect setup for the Three Bees," he said, speaking in a low voice he didn't want to be heard by the captain or any of the other men. The Three Bees weren't ready to go public just yet.

But nothing anyone else said at this point could have gained Gil's serious attention. The captain's words had struck hard. Yes, he had a sweetheart to go home to. A vivid image of Annie's sweet smile filled his mind's eye and for an instant left him almost breathless. He would do anything he could to help assure other guys got home to loved ones. But what mattered most was that he, Gil Bennett, return to the beautiful girl he loved more than life itself.

When their mock English fishing boat reached the French coast, a short convoy of Jeeps was waiting. The platoon was quickly loaded. With no assigned placement, the Three Bees all climbed into the same Jeep. Jeff gave the other two a wink and thumbs up. He had a smug expression like he thought they had done something sneaky.

Once they headed inland they immediately got a closeup view of war's destruction. Very few buildings had escaped at least some damage and burned-out German tanks were scattered here and there, along with occasional American vehicles. Craters from bombs and artillery shells pocked streets and highways and open fields alike.

"My God, the poor French people!" Henry exclaimed. "Can you imagine what they've been through?"

"Yeah, they've been through hell," Gil said.

They were barely a few miles inland when a flight of maybe eight or ten fighter planes roared over their heads, flying so low Gil could swear he felt the heat of their exhausts. The roar of their powerful engines was deafening.

"They got to be Thunderbolts!" Jeff yelled. "Now I feel right at home. Man, I love that Thunderbolt roar."

"How in the hell did you come to love something you never heard before?" Henry demanded.

"You're damned straight I heard it before. Back home we had Thunderbolts flying over all the time."

Henry was skeptical. "No way! Why would they be flying over the middle of nowhere?"

"Middle of nowhere, my ass!" Jeff told him, obviously a bit irritated. "They build the Thunderbird at Evansville, right down the road from where I live. Test pilots take 'em up as they roll off the assembly line and put 'em through their paces. Sometimes it was almost like we were under attack, if we hadn't known they were Thunderbolts."

Henry had no comeback. He slid down in the seat a little and looked off in another direction. Jeff looked at Gil and winked.

Gil rode in the front passenger seat of the second Jeep in line, next to a young corporal who immediately impressed him as a careless driver at best and at worst one who might be downright dangerous. He barely missed sideswiping a disabled gun carriage on the side of the road by a quick swerve that led to a short dash in the ditch. This led to another exaggerated jerk of the steering wheel that almost threw Jeff and Henry out of the back seat.

"Dammit, man, you're going to kill us before we even get to our unit," Jeff yelled.

The driver wouldn't be intimidated. "You want to drive, buddy? How many miles you put in behind the wheel of a Jeep? In case you don't know it, these things don't drive like your granddaddy's Lincoln."

Gil sensed that the driver didn't want to be confrontational. And it was true none of them had driven a Jeep. Maybe there was common ground.

"So, how about you?" he said to the driver. "Ever drove an old John Deere? And where are you from? Where's home, I mean."

The driver's response was exactly what Gil had hoped for. His questions had given the young corporal a link he could identify with,

"Old John Deere? You damned well know it! You must be a farm boy like me. I'm from Kentucky. How 'bout you?"

"I'm from southern Illinois—right across the Ohio from Kentucky. We're probably neighbors."

This brought a pretended rumble from the back seat. Henry and Jeff complained about the obvious collusion up front. Henry suggested that the next thing probably would be planning for a "down home" celebration that would not include him and Jeff. Jeff jumped in to declare that he would be included, but Pennsylvanians would not fit in. The tension had been broken and the Three Bees and the driver were having fun.

The driver got back to Gil's response.

"Well, you may be close to western Kentucky," he said, "but I live on the other end. You probably never heard of a place called Paintsville. That's where I'm from. Live just outside town on a little ole bit of a farm my granddaddy bought about a hundred years ago."

Jeff asked how far they had to go. The driver didn't know. He said only the lieutenant in the lead Jeep knew where they were headed and he and the other drivers had orders to follow. But he guessed it was still some distance because he understood there was to be a stop somewhere for fuel.

Gil had begun to wonder if he knew what he was talking about when, a long while later, they stopped in a field fuel depot and got gasoline in all the Jeeps. The depot was the first example of a U. S. Army field unit they had seen and he was impressed with the quick and efficient operation. He couldn't see much in the dark, but he could tell the whole installation was designed to be mobile.

It was several hours before they reached their destination.

They knew they were deep in France but had no notion how close they might be to the front. Gil found himself wishing he had taken his only high school geography class more seriously and maybe have learned more about France. At the very least he wished he had a better idea of how big it was. He remembered there were French Alps so there had to be mountains somewhere and he wondered if they were close. All he really knew was that France fit into Europe something like a very large state fit into the United States but he couldn't remember ever knowing how big Europe was.

Unit headquarters for 2nd Platoon turned out to be a dilapidated, unoccupied old French farmhouse situated a few hundred feet off a narrow rural highway and almost hidden by trees and bushes. The area between the house and the road was overgrown to the extent the front door was almost unreachable but the gravel driveway circled to the back where there was ample space for a parking lot between the house and an old machine shed.

They unloaded in the dark and watched the Jeeps that had brought them go back the way they had come. The vehicles quickly disappeared and Gil couldn't help but have a feeling of desertion, as if they'd been dumped in the middle of a sparsely populated wasteland and had no way out.

Henry claimed they were victims of the Army's intentional determination to keep them in the dark. For all they knew, they could be just ten miles outside Paris.

As the platoon stood waiting for the captain to give directions, he surprised them by breaking into a comedic "Welcome Home" pantomime including an impressive soft shoe routine in the pale moonlight. By the time they realized it was all in fun and felt at ease he was finished. The men all laughed and a couple of them offered applause.

Henry nudged Gil and whispered, "I think we got a CO we

can live with. This guy doesn't think he ought to be a four-star general." Gil was about to answer when the captain held up his hands to call for their attention.

"This place is supposed to be ready for us," he said, "whatever 'ready' means. One thing we probably will check out right off the top is the field latrine they are supposed to have dug behind the shed over there. As far as the inside goes, we'll find out soon enough. But I need to caution you that our survival here depends on our being invisible. That means no loud noise, no bright lights, no anything that might tip off the Germans to our presence. Now, if we're all clear on that hit the latrine if you need it and let's go in and make ourselves at home."

The whole platoon was more than ready for the latrine break and happy for the moonlight that let them find their way. It was several minutes before they all got inside the house.

Just enough had been done in the old farmhouse to make it functional as a place to survive and carry out their intel operations. There was a stack of unmarked boxes of supplies in the kitchen and enough mattresses on the floors, both ground level and upstairs, for each platoon sergeant to have his own bed. There was no bathroom but a hand pump over an oversized sink drew cold water from a deep well. The captain had a field-grade flashlight but said he didn't want to use it and told the men to claim a mattress and sack out till daylight.

"Then we will have an hour or so to check out our new quarters before we go to work," he said. "And, men, I want you to know it is my honor to be a part of this elite group. I hope I prove worthy and I know you will make me proud."

6

GIL'S LETTERS ADDRESSED to her at Mother White's gave Annie's move an element of permanency that had been lacking. When he finished basic training at Fort Jackson, his letters showed confidence he was prepared for whatever assignment came next. Reading between the lines, she took this to mean he expected to be in the fighting soon. Nothing he'd told her since had shed doubt on this and she lived in fear of hearing he was actually in combat.

It didn't help when he told her what he thought was a funny story about being on the shooting range and listening to a drill sergeant chew out the man next to him for getting his thumb cut by mishandling the bolt on an M1 rifle. To her, it simply was talk of shooting and it caused her to think of him being a target. Her worry was so persistent it led to a vivid nightmare in which she saw him lying on the ground with blood flowing from a wound in his chest.

Even so, she had relished his frequent letters and waited hopefully for every day's mail. When a new letter didn't come she read those she already had again and knew them now almost by heart.

Talking with Mother White, playing with Elmo, and occasional walks around the farm were almost her only consolation. She would have liked to listen to the radio more, but there was the inevitable war news which usually left her feeling worse. And Mother White discouraged it, for this very reason.

The only thing she looked forward to was Sunday services at Walnut Creek Church. Walnut Creek had become her only safe contact with the outside world. She would see her mom and dad and other members of the congregation she had been part of since childhood.

This week she was truly excited when Sunday came again and woke early, in a happy mood. As usual, she had prepared for it Saturday night, laying out her clothes and shampooing her hair and checking on any other little aspect of personal grooming that might need attention. And today she didn't bother to invite Mother White to go with her.

As always, she joined her mother and father in the church parking lot before they went in. The church looked to be unusually crowded as it took them a moment to find seating room. They were barely settled when the pastor took his place in the pulpit.

Annie had become intrigued by the Walnut Creek pastor, not so much by what he said as by his delivery. There was a consistent pattern to his preaching that made it even more interesting. At the beginning of his sermon he was the friendly neighbor, at times almost jovial. But once he was ready to preach, the Reverend Ernie Maxwell became an earnest messenger for God, stately in physical appearance and demeanor. He spoke with a powerful voice that demanded attention and left no doubt that he believed in his calling and would never rest until every soul was set for eternity in heaven.

The call to salvation always came at the end of his sermon. Leading up to that, he preached the gospel as it applied to any number of ordinary human activities. Today he had chosen to talk about war. Speaking from no visible notes, he quoted Scripture as if it were his first language.

"God tells us in the Book of Matthew, 'ye shall hear of wars and rumors of wars. See that ye be not troubled, for all these things must come to pass, but the end is not yet.' *Be not troubled*, brothers and sisters in Christ. Why? Because God still is in charge! In the second chapter of Isiah, God tells us he shall 'judge among the nations, and shall rebuke many people, and they shall beat their swords into plowshares and their spears into pruninghooks.'

"And isn't that a glorious promise, brothers and sisters? Imagine a world without the weapons of war! And God says 'nation shall not lift up sword against nation, neither shall they learn war any more.' These are God's words, folks, not mine. And we can't see into the future and know when God's promise comes to pass but we know it will."

Like a shepherd tending his flock, Pastor Maxwell led his listeners down the path he wanted them to follow. Annie could see they hung on every word. This was what they had come for. Her attention was split between the preacher and the people in his congregation.

"They may say we ought to be concerned about every human on the face of the earth," the pastor continued. "And at some general level I suppose we are. But that's not how it works when it comes to war, brothers and sisters. We find it too hard to accept God's call to forgive our enemies. We find it too hard to be concerned about whole nations of people we don't know. We find it too hard to worry about war's effects on those people, those people we don't think of as friends and neighbors but rather as strangers in a foreign land."

Annie regretted she could not see the faces of those around her. She could read in their postures the depth of their fascination with what they heard. And now their minister made it personal. Annie found herself becoming a serious listener, too.

"I stand and look in your faces, brothers and sisters, and I know you are generous and caring people. I know you would not turn a hungry person away from your door or deny the injured workman the care he needs. I know you worry about your aged neighbor and the child you see wandering the streets like a homeless stray."

The pastor paused and lowered his gaze. He took a deep breath and stroked his chin, as if thinking what he might say next. His congregation was deadly quiet, waiting. When he spoke again it was in a softer voice.

"So how do we view this terrible war going on this very minute across Europe and the Pacific Ocean? Yes, we hate the deaths and suffering. We abhor the destruction caused by the bombs dropped on London and the shelling of quiet French villages. The losses come in numbers almost too big for us to comprehend. Who can imagine the final count for the whole world we live in by the time the fighting finally ends?

"But there is one number we *want to hear*, brothers and sisters in Christ. It's a number we want to be low and a number we pray not to hear for much longer. And you know what that number is, brothers and sisters. It is the number of American casualties. These are the men—just boys, many of them—these are the ones we care about. These are our friends and neighbors, our families."

The congregation was completely on board with Pastor Maxwell now. He had served Walnut Creek Church for more than 15 years. He knew them and they knew him. He always made them feel that his sermons fit them, not only as a whole but also individually. *He is talking to me.*

His words struck Annie in a way difficult for her to comprehend. She wanted—she *needed*—to compartmentalize what he was saying. Casualty counts applied to the entire American armed force, while friends and neighbors and family referred to individuals, including Gil. She didn't realize she played this mental game to keep from making a connection in her own mind. Pastor Maxwell gave her an excuse for a quick mental leap forward, though, and saved her from the inevitable emotional stress rooted in any combination of "Gil" and "casualty" spoken in one breath.

"You all know that Gilbert Bennett, a member of our church family, is with the Army in Europe," the pastor said. "It brightens my morning to see among us the smiling face of Miss Annie, in waiting to be Gilbert's bride. I know she will excuse me if I take the liberty of inviting everyone to visit with her and send your best wishes to Gilbert."

Her mother whispered to Annie, "Show them it's okay. Wave or something."

Her father added his own advice: "Stand up, Annie."

Annie was embarrassed by the attention, but thrilled by the acknowledgement of Gil and his service. She stood for a moment and waved her hand. Pastor Maxwell applauded, bringing a round of cheering. Two people in the pew behind her stood and then, almost as if in a coordinated move, the entire congregation was on its feet giving her a standing ovation.

"This is all for you, sweetheart," her father said, raising his voice just enough to be heard.

"No, I don't think so. I hope it's for Gil."

When the service ended, everyone came around and paid their respects. Most of them had known both her and Gil since childhood. Annie knew their well wishes were sincere. Accepting all their greetings and allowing for at least a bit of small talk kept her at the back of the church for a long while. She would have liked to stay and talk with her parents longer, but she also was eager to get home and tell Mother White about what had gone on at the church. She promised her father a visit soon.

"We miss you, Annie," her mother said as she hugged her only daughter one more time. "But I know what you are doing is good for both you and Mother White. Give her our love and we'll see you again real soon."

Annie walked around the back of her father's pickup and eased herself into Mother White's old Dodge. It took a few minutes to work her way out of the church parking lot, as everyone was leaving at the same time. When she got on the road, she had an urge to drive fast, eager as she was to tell Mother White about her morning. Hills and curves discouraged speed, though, and anyway it was such a short drive she would be there in no time.

Mother White was waiting eagerly for any news Annie might bring. Although she no longer felt comfortable sitting through church services, she missed seeing friends and catching up on things at Walnut Creek. She was delighted by Annie's report.

"Gil is such a sweet boy," she said. "I know everybody in the church misses and worries about him."

Annie agreed. "And I was thinking when Pastor Maxwell was talking about the war how many others there are like him, who have to leave their sweethearts and wives and families for who knows how long and face such danger that so many of them won't come back. It's just not fair, Grandmama."

Elmo had been sitting in a corner grooming and pretending he hadn't noticed Annie's return. She was supposed to pay attention to him first. He got anxious when that didn't happen and finally gave up his pride and went to her. He rubbed around her ankles until she reached down and picked him up and pulled him up to her face and rubbed noses. "You big baby," she teased, "I'll bet Gil would love to have you on his lap right now."

Annie's comment led Mother White to tell a story from her own thick catalog of memories. Annie loved it when this happened. Her grandmother always had a story or two in answer to Annie's questions, but they always seemed to be more interesting when they were spontaneous.

"Your grandfather had a big collie dog he hated to leave more than anything when he went off to his war. You probably wouldn't know but they called it the 'Great War' back then. Anyway, I think he missed that dog more than he missed me, but then the dog already was family and I wasn't. The dog missed him too. Wouldn't hardly eat for a few months after he left, got down to nothing but skin and bone."

"So what happened? Did they get him to eat again?"

Mother White laughed that glorious laugh Annie loved. It sounded as if it came from deep within and Annie's mother had always said it must be truly heart-felt and it really was an emotion after all.

"I used to refuse to tell this because it kind of hurt his feelings," she said, "but it started eating after I began to come around his house more and that dog came to love me as much as it loved him. I guess you could say it turned out to be right fickle."

Annie always hoped to hear more stories about when her grandfather was in the Army, but Mother White usually had other things she wanted to talk about. Just now, she kept asking more questions about people at Walnut Creek. Did Annie see so and so there, was Mr. Olander walking better after his two knee surgeries, had the preacher put on as much weight as she had heard, and so on. These were things she really was interested to know and Annie wondered again why she didn't just go back to Walnut Creek services and keep up with everything on her own.

Most of her questions, Annie couldn't answer as specifically as her grandmother apparently would have liked. In one instance she didn't know the woman Mother White asked about and relative to all of the questions after Pastor Maxwell started preaching about war she hadn't been all that much aware of things she normally might have noticed.

"I guess I was so caught up in the big honor to Gil I barely knew anything else was going on," she said.

Mother White asked to be excused about mid-afternoon as she often did so she could take a nap. Annie rarely followed her lead, but today she felt like she needed more sleep, too. They both went to bed and slept until it was almost supper time. When Annie woke she knew she had been dreaming about Gil, but she couldn't remember exactly what she dreamed.

Her grandmother had made one of Annie's favorite casseroles and she ate more than usual, to Mother White's delight. They enjoyed listening to the radio on Sunday nights because there were entertaining programs and no war news. And after the long naps they were able to stay up late. When they felt ready for bed and started for their rooms, Mother White walked over and embraced Annie and wished her good night.

As Annie opened her bedroom door, her grandmother called from down the hall, "Thank you honey for brightening my days. I'm so happy to have you here."

Annie felt very much rewarded.

7

GIL LAY AWAKE for much of the night thinking about home and Annie. The old farmhouse had a leaking roof and several broken windowpanes, leaving it damp and drafty and hardly appealing as a potential long-term habitat, but it was his unit headquarters. This realization gave him a sense of belonging.

Yes, he was a U. S. Army sergeant and he had been assigned to a reconnaissance platoon with a commanding officer who believed strongly in the importance of their mission. This was his new home and for the first time since he'd been sworn in to military service he felt a measure of stability. He found it impossible not to compare now with then, here with there.

From what he could tell, other members of the platoon were sleeping soundly. There were no lights in the house and on this night there would be no moonlight. The blackness was total. No one stirred until morning light came with the dawn.

Captain Daniels, who had slept in a narrow hallway that separated the two downstairs rooms, moved around quietly as if he didn't want to disturb any of the men. He offered morning greetings to those who were getting up, then climbed the stairs to check on those who had slept on the second floor. Gil listened for some kind of morning hustle, but there was none. There would be no reveille for the 2nd Platoon. Henry and Jeff were sitting up now, but had not made any effort to get on their feet. Everyone had slept fully clothed.

"Rise and shine, Three Bees," Gil called out just loud enough, he thought, for the two men closest to him to hear.

"Who are you, Bennett, the captain of the guard?" His response came from someone at the far side of the room. Harris, he thought, but maybe Harrison. He was still learning to associate the names with the faces.

Henry pulled himself up from the mattress on the floor and was leaning against the wall when Captain Daniels came back down the stairs. The captain stopped beside Gil.

"Okay, I'm still learning," he said. "It's a pathetic commander who doesn't know his men. Let me see if I can get this right. You are Bennett?" He posed this more as a question than a statement of fact, indicating he was uncertain.

"Yes, sir, Captain. Private—sorry, Sergeant Gil Bennett."

The captain turned to Jeff and Henry in succession and went through the same identity check. He got both names right and obviously was pleased with himself.

"Well, help get everybody up while I put on the coffee pot," he said, not directing his words at anyone in particular. "We've got work to do."

The captain turned and went through the door to the farmhouse kitchen. He apparently had learned earlier that the old cast iron kitchen range burned wood, because he had it stuffed with kindling that he set ablaze and, good to his word, quickly had a large pot of boiling water ready for making coffee.

As the men lined up with canteen cups at the ready, Captain Daniels dumped a carton of ground coffee into a strainer and poured boiling water through it into each of their cups. Gil burned his mouth trying to drink it too soon. The aluminum mess kit cup was not a container made for fast cooling.

"We've got dry biscuits and powered eggs coming up," the

captain announced after filling the last cup. "The Army's going to take good care of you men."

"Oh, yeah," somebody mumbled, "that's why we don't get any of that fatty old sausage or bacon."

Even though it wasn't appetizing, the platoon lingered over breakfast. The captain was liberal with the coffee pot and Gil soon found himself on his third cup. He knew Henry was, too. But standing around the kitchen drinking coffee was safe. What was to come next? They would find out soon enough, and they really were eager to know. Based on what they had heard so far they assumed they were operating in dangerous territory.

After another hour of small talk, Captain Daniels called them to order. Not in any kind of rigid formation but alerted that they needed to pay attention. They were about to learn exactly what kind of action 2nd Platoon could look forward to. Their first actual U. S. Army duty began now.

"Okay, men, we have some requests for intelligence we need to fill," Captain Daniels began. "As you probably assumed, we don't just freelance it on our own. There are American units of all kind out there that find themselves in dangerous situations where a little bit of intelligence from us could make all the difference. And like I said before, that difference is measured in terms of lives saved. I mean good guy lives, of course. American lives.

"You may be interested to know, we are currently in the U. S. Third Army sector. That means you're working for General Patton. You don't want to make Uncle Georgie unhappy. I can tell you, though, that Patton is demanding but he is by far the best damned general out there. He makes the best use of intel and that's why his forces suffer the fewest casualties. Now, before we break up into small teams, do you have any questions?"

Gil had a lot of questions, but he wasn't going to ask them. He wasn't sure they were appropriate at this point. None was directly related to what the captain had said, but they were old concerns he still hadn't felt to be fully resolved. The captain had said the whole platoon would seldom if ever be working together, and if not who would be in command? The captain couldn't be in two places at once. Everyone else was a sergeant with the exact same time in grade so none had authority over any other. He was not going to ask now, though, because the formal session was breaking up.

A platoon member Gil believed was O'Dell apparently had a question, too. The captain noticed and said he waited to hear it.

"Sir, you said we're in the Third Army area. Third Army's been at the front of the Allied advance pretty much the whole time, as I've heard it. So does that mean we are close to the front?"

"You're O'Dell. Am I right?" The captain waited for verification before saying more. O'Dell nodded his head.

"Okay, then. Here's the deal on that. The best I can tell you is probably yes. But the front is not a static line, as I'm sure you know. We are not in trench warfare anymore. The front is an area, at best a broad and wavering line. Given that, we probably are close. But I don't expect us to see any combat. You will see plenty of German troops, but they won't see you. That pretty much sums up what we're all about."

There was one more item on the captain's agenda. While the men waited, he pulled out one of the supply boxes from the stack and took off the top. "Gentlemen," he said, "I want you to see your new outfits. As long as the platoon is here, you will not wear the uniform of the United States Army. Your magnificent new wardrobe will come from these boxes."

He pulled out a pair of overalls and a plaid shirt and held them up for display. They would go about their assigned duties dressed as Frenchmen—farmers, mechanics, cooks or bakers, pedants in general, whatever clothes they happened to get from one of the boxes.

After a few minutes more of clothing discussion, the captain divided the platoon into four teams of three men each. He said they could forget their individual rifle squad roles if they expected to be scouting or packing a BAR. Now, everyone was a rifleman.

"And by the way," he added quickly, "I hope you are not in love with that heavy M1 rifle. When you go armed it will be with carbines."

The Three Bees stuck together and huddled in a corner of the living room. Captain Daniels got to them quickly. He had a mission for them, starting now.

"We've got an infantry battalion up north a ways that the regimental commander is worried about," he told them. "He thinks they are in danger of being surrounded and wants to pull them out. They need to know where the heaviest concentrations of enemy troops are so they can fight their way out against the least opposition."

Gil raised what was to him an obvious question. "Couldn't they get that faster by aerial recon? I mean, one plane could cover the area for miles around them in an hour."

"You may be good at this, Bennett," the captain responded. "That's exactly what an intelligence officer would do. But the weather has been too foul for air recon for the last week or more, and that's plenty of time for massive troop movements. They've got some preliminary stuff, but nothing dependable. They need eyes on the ground."

The captain sketched out a quick action plan and an hour later, after digging through the unit map file and finding the most detailed map of the sector they had to operate in, they were on the road. Henry was the driver and would stay with the Jeep. Gil and Jeff would be dropped off at specified points from which they would make their way to designated sites where they should be able to spot enemy troop movement. Then Henry would pick them up at a specified time at the same place he had dropped them off. Henry had a carbine in the Jeep, but neither of the other two was armed.

"Old Captain Daniels really knows how to pick his men," Henry said, as he turned the Jeep east on the road in front of the dilapidated farmhouse that now was their base. "He figured out real fast that a pair of country boys like you guys were perfect for this little adventure. Hell's bells, you two probably lived in the woods half your life down there in the hillbilly country you come from."

Jeff had a ready response. "Yeah, you're exactly right, Sergeant. He probably knows that any guy who grew up in Philadelphia has stole a car or two, so you definitely are the man to hide the Jeep in the woods and sleep while me and Gil are out there doing the hard stuff."

It had taken Gil a while to get used to the good-natured mental jostling that went on between Jeff and Henry. He had been offended by some of the things Henry said early on. But Jeff had recognized from the outset that Henry wasn't serious and played along and Gil had come to enjoy their pretended insults. He felt as if this was something he'd missed growing up, lacking brothers or male cousins, or even friends he spent much time with. He tried to play the game with his two teammates but seldom was fast enough to come up with something both appropriate and witty.

He wanted to get his bit in, though. "The captain just knows the Three Bees are the best of his lot," he said. "We're likely to get the toughest assignments all the way to Berlin. Don't you think?"

"Count on it, brother," Henry said.

Not one of them would have admitted it, but all their efforts at humor this time were somewhat forced. They were scared. They had no clue what might lie ahead. They were at the front, even if not in the shooting. They might be in enemy-held territory now, and if not they would be soon. Their mission was to get inside it and see as much as they could without the Germans being aware of their presence. As the captain had pointed out, working as individuals and small teams was the only way such a mission was possible.

As the captain had put it, "I think it's pretty clear you're not going to march an infantry company in there and expect it to avoid detection. No way you can hide an infantry company behind a tree."

Henry drove too fast for the poor road they were on and hit a dip that caused the Jeep to bounce so hard Gil was nearly thrown out. He almost yelled, but caught himself just in time. Quiet was the order of the day. The sound of a motor vehicle wouldn't be anything unusual to a German sentry, but an impulsive yell might. He took his best alternative and slapped Henry on the back.

"Hey, I'm sorry, man," Henry said over his shoulder. "I forget I'm not driving my Porsche."

He had said this once before, and hearing it again left Gil and Jeff wondering if he really did own an expensive foreign automobile or whether this was in jest. He might actually be from a wealthy Philadelphia family. They hadn't learned much about Henry's background and Gil remembered how he'd often heard his dad say someone must be as "rich as a Philadelphia lawyer."

Henry slowed the Jeep to a crawl and shifted into low gear as they approached a steep hill. If he had checked the miles right, they were almost to the point where Gil was to be dropped off. Jeff was to go a couple of miles farther. The forest had become so dense it was almost dark although there was a bright sun. Paradoxically, the darkness made their mission seem more sinister at the same time it gave them more cover.

Gil wasn't certain of the connection, but his consideration of the danger he felt he was in led to thoughts of Annie and an intense longing to look into her eyes once again. His life might not be worth much, and he was ready to sacrifice it for his country if need be, but he had someone to go home to.

Henry stopped and turned the Jeep engine off. Gil took a few minutes to study the map one more time and get a compass bearing to the high ridge he was supposed to go to. It would be a three-mile walk through the dense woods. He could see the concern in both his teammates' eyes. Jeff reached out awkwardly as if to shake hands then put a hand on Gil's shoulder instead.

"See you in a bit, man," Jeff said.

"I'll be right here in four hours to give you a ride home," Henry told him. "You be careful out there."

"Hey, I'll buy you both a stein of good German beer when we get to Berlin. Jeff, go do what you do best. You know, that's whatever you're supposed to do."

Jeff gave him a mock salute and Gil turned and walked into the woods. He heard the Jeep start and move on down the road. He was somewhat tentative at first, as if feeling his way, but soon got into full stride and only looked ahead in the direction mandated by his compass. The forest was eerily quiet.

Thank you, whoever invented the compass. He thought about how he had walked in the woods so often, but always knew where he was going. In this forest the trees were so thick it would be hard to have any sense of direction. The trees in Soloman's Woods were thick, too, but didn't form a closed canopy overhead the way they did here.

He reached the high bluff he was looking for sooner than he expected. After a long trek up a steep slope, he was suddenly at a cliff that would present a sheer drop-off if he'd planned to go any farther. He guessed it was at least fifty feet down to a river below. There was no apparent current, and he wondered which way the river ran.

He saw at once that the forest was much less dense across the river and beyond. He quickly found a place where he could sit with his back to a tree and be virtually invisible from all directions except from the top of the cliff at his feet.

He raised the binoculars—the only thing he carried except his compass and a canteen of water—and focused on the flatland below. At the same instant he heard it, he saw what he took to be a troop-carrier truck moving parallel to the river some two hundred yards distant. Given the angle he couldn't see the ground and tell if there was a road, but the vehicle was moving at moderate speed. Then he saw the markings. It clearly was German.

By the time Gil had finished calculating with his compass the direction the truck was traveling, there was a second vehicle. This one looked like a staff car. And then there was another truck and not long after that, three more. Yes, he was watching an organized movement of enemy troops. This mission was paying off big time.

Gil no longer feared for his own safety. His worry about being discovered was replaced by a feeling of great satisfaction. Not only was he doing his duty, but his orders had put him in a position to provide critical intel to benefit Allied forces. He couldn't wait to report back to Captain Daniels so his input could be forwarded to some higher headquarters and distributed to any number of units that might benefit.

Not only did he feel good about being in a reconnaissance platoon, but he felt like an important member of a U. S. Army team fighting for his country. His father would be thrilled to know what was happening, and he would love to tell Annie.

When it came time for him to get back to his pick-up point, he was in such high spirits he became careless walking through the woods. He started to whistle. *Shut up, you damned fool!* He suddenly realized what a risk he was taking and thought about all the warnings there might be enemy sentries anywhere in the region his team was operating in. *Man, it's your duty to make it back and report!* Otherwise, he thought, his day's success was for nothing.

He moved cautiously, sometimes pausing to hide behind a tree, and soon came to the road where Henry stood by the Jeep nervously waiting. The man and the vehicle were a sight he was most happy to see.

Henry welcomed him with a wide smile. "Man, I'm glad to see you," he said, struggling to keep his voice low. "This has been the longest day of my life. Jump in and let's go look for Jeff. That struck me as a pretty hairy place I had to leave him."

It took only a few minutes to drive the two miles to the pre-arranged site where Jeff was supposed to be. Gil could tell that Henry was nervous. When they reached the site Jeff was not there.

8

HENRY'S FEAR WAS palpable, something unusual for him. He shut off the Jeep engine and looked at Gil with an expression that marked his determination. Orders be damned, he was not going to leave. Gil jumped out onto the edge of the road and Henry climbed out on the opposite side. They both walked to the front of the Jeep without saying anything.

Unlike the area Gil had gone into, Jeff's orders had taken him in the opposite direction from the road, down a sparsely wooded slope thick with briars and a low-growing bush Gil didn't recognize. His would have been a much more difficult walk than Gil's easy hike through the forest. And also more dangerous if there were enemy troops in the area because standing and walking he would have been easily seen.

"What do you think?" Gil asked Henry. "We have to wait, right?"

"My orders as driver are not to wait."

"But—my God, Henry. We can't just go off and leave him! He wouldn't leave one of us."

Henry could no longer contain his emotional stress. He threw up his hands and looked as if he was about to burst out in a rage. Instead, he began to cry. "Come on, man," he pleaded. "We're the Three Bees, man. But I have orders, Gil. There's gotta be a reason for that. What if I disobey orders and get us all killed? I don't want to, but we *have to go*, man. Come on."

Gil said nothing more but turned and climbed into the Jeep. Henry got behind the wheel and started the engine and almost frantically began to turn the vehicle around on the narrow road. This led them to face the direction Jeff should have come from and Gil saw something move, a few hundred yards down the slope. It was Jeff, standing and wildly waving his arms.

"There he is, Henry! He's coming."

Jeff covered the intervening distance as fast as he could make it, trying hard to run through the brambles. He tripped and fell twice. When he reached them he looked like he had deliberately tried to camouflage himself with all sorts of underbrush.

Henry and Gil ran forward to meet him and he collapsed as they met. They helped him to his feet and more or less dragged him to the Jeep. As soon as they got him in, Henry rushed to get the vehicle on the road, headed toward their unit headquarters in the old farmhouse.

"You two are the ugliest angels I'd ever hope to see," Jeff told them, spitting out his words between gasps for air. His face was purple from exertion and his chest heaved. But on his face was the widest smile they probably ever would see.

"Man, you had us scared," Gil said. "Don't you know if you're late at the rendezvous point you could get left? What the hell happened?"

Henry was quick to voice his support for what Gil had said. "He's exactly right. My driver's orders were not to wait if you weren't there. I guess you could take that as the captain's confidence in you, like if you weren't there it would mean something had happened to you so you couldn't make it. Get my point?"

Jeff had caught his breath a bit, but still looked pained from his exertion. He was eager to respond, a modest level of excitement in his voice.

"Yeah, Henry, I get it," he exclaimed. "And I damned well would have been there on time."

"But you weren't."

"I didn't finish. I would have been there except I got stuck in quicksand. I swear it took me nearly half an hour to get out of it and get on solid ground. I tried to run the rest of the way back to where I was supposed to be but couldn't keep it up."

Gil slapped him on the shoulder. The only thing that mattered now, he told Jeff, was that everything worked out. The Three Bees still had their sting.

Captain Daniels was eager to get their reports when they got back to platoon headquarters. Jeff had maintained surveillance at his assigned position for the duration called for and had seen nothing. He was in relatively open country, he told the captain, and would have seen and heard any enemy activity for some distance. There simply was nothing to see or hear. The captain thanked him for doing his duty well and turned to Gil.

"I hope you have a different story," he said.

Gil promptly affirmed his supposition. He gave a detailed account of what he had seen and stressed that the enemy troop movement still was going on when he left his position. Captain Daniels quickly plotted on a field map the direction of the movement Gil had calculated. The three team members could hardly have missed his confidence in his interpretation of the situation Gil's report offered nor his satisfaction in their performance.

"This tells me exactly what Colonel Beasley needs to know before he orders the movement of his battalion," the captain said. "We know where the enemy is and we know where the enemy isn't—at least in significant numbers. Chances are you just saved a great many American casualties, and like they say, that's what we're here for."

The Three Bees were little short of euphoric as they went to the kitchen and got food and drinks. Field rations available were hardly appetizing but very much appreciated by the three hungry troops. Anyway, it wasn't the prospects for getting something to eat that led to their high spirits. It was the successful conclusion of their first intel assignment. They had completed their mission and brought back information the captain assured them could save the lives of American soldiers. They felt like heroes.

With few places to sit in the old farmhouse, they decided to go out to the rickety back porch. Not only was it a matter of comfort, but they also needed to stay clear of the living room area where Captain Daniels was taking reports from the two other teams. There would be time later to hear from the other men about their first days in action; for now, the Three Bees wanted only to talk among themselves. It was something like having played the big game and won and this was the locker room talk after the game was over.

After an ample allowance for self-congratulatory give and take, the discussion turned serious. There was no denying that the pick-up operation at the end was close to disastrous. Even after playing loose with the driver's orders not to wait, they had been within minutes of abandoning one of their own. This was something that very well might happen again, and this was something they had to talk about. Without saying so, they all knew they wanted to present a united front in any discussion with Captain Daniels.

"Okay, so I'm not a military genius," Gil said. "In fact, I'm still the greenest greenhorn. I get it that we all have to be on the same wavelength and all that, but it's never going to work for me that we have to leave one of our team behind. I'm willing to talk to the captain about it, but what do you guys think? Am I missing something?"

Jeff was eager to respond. "Having just come that close to being the one left," he said, "it's probably too personal for me right now. I can't hardly just view it from the sidelines. Henry, how 'bout you? You were the one with the orders not to wait. Do you get it?"

"No way," Henry told him. "Gil knows how hard I was fighting that order. I'm not sure what I would have done if you hadn't popped up when you did. I was trying to make myself go by the book and take off, but that's not where my heart was. I was pretty close to parking that damned Jeep and taking off on foot to look for you."

It was clear from their discussion that they all agreed. If the driver's orders had been different, even with no specific directive on what to do if the man to be picked up wasn't there, they could have gone with what they had and taken their chances this wouldn't happen again. But direct, specific orders to leave a member of the team were too hard to take. They would take it up with the captain. And they wouldn't have long to wait.

Captain Daniels called a platoon meeting after the third chow. He was ready to review the first day's activities and get started on tomorrow. Besides the Three Bees, only one of the other two teams had been in the field. The captain had kept three men there to make benches and tables so the headquarters would be functional space. He would keep another team "at home" tomorrow to do more but hadn't picked it yet.

Gil nudged Henry. "If we were here all day we'd have a better chance of talking to the captain about our problem with orders," he whispered.

"So, what? You want to volunteer?"

Captain Daniels heard them. Among the several things he absolutely would not tolerate was any sort of disruption within the ranks when he was speaking. He stopped in mid-sentence and glared at Henry. The other men in the platoon looked too, wondering what the captain's problem might be.

"Sergeant Burnett," the captain snapped, "am I interrupting your conversation?"

"No, sir. Sorry, sir."

"Do you think it possible you might need to hear what I'm saying?"

"Yes, sir!"

The captain's demeanor lightened. "Well, I hope you will be paying more attention, then," he said, struggling not to smile at Henry. "We've got important work to do."

Gil felt guilty. If someone was to get a black mark, it should be him and not Henry. He made a mental note to apologize to Henry when they were free to talk.

Captain Daniels went on to give a quick outline of the next day's assignments. He reminded them that, as an intel unit, their job was to find out everything possible about the enemy. Where were the Germans? What were their strengths? Were there weaknesses the Allies might capitalize on? In the end he fell back on the old infantry adage, "Find 'em, fix 'em, and fight 'em."

"Men," the captain concluded, in the most serious tone of voice he could muster, "we're going to whip the Germans. We have to fight them and to do that we have to find them and fix them wherever they are. The first prong of that three-pronged spear is to find them. That's intelligence and intelligence is what we do. I've said before, and it bears repeating, you may never get the credit you deserve, but what you do today will save countless American lives in the days and weeks to come. You can tell your grandchildren that's what you did in the war."

Gil felt foolish later, but on impulse and without thinking he began to applaud. The rest of the platoon clapped, too. Captain Daniels obviously was momentarily flustered, facing a rare situation in which he was not sure what to do. He recovered quickly and held up his hands for quiet.

"Well, I don't believe that was proper military behavior," he said, smiling. "But, damn, you men are the greatest. I'm proud to be your commander. Now let's see if there's not some cold beer in the cooler and take the rest of this day off."

The Three Bees relaxed on one of the new benches and savored bottles of beer from the ample stock in the cooler where it was, mysteriously to them, regularly replenished. Jeff had seen a truck at the back of the house after dark the night before and said what looked like two Frenchmen were unloading something, but he couldn't see what it was. O'Dell said they were supplied by battalion, and that no doubt included the beer. Gil had assumed as much. Who else even would know they were there, much less have any responsibility to support them?

Henry thought he knew. "French resistance," he said. "They're probably just looking for ways they can help."

Captain Daniels, in what would prove to be his regular habit, moved easily from one team to another and talked with the men as if they were equals in rank. After sitting and chatting for a while with each of the other three teams, he approached the Three Bees and addressed Gil directly: "Sergeant Bennett, do I remember correctly that you are a farm boy?"

"Yes, sir, I am," Gil told him.

The captain pulled the end of another bench closer and sat. "The reason I ask is, I've found farm boys generally to be pretty handy with tools," he said. "Battalion is supposed to slip in tomorrow with another load of scrap lumber and I've got a few ideas what to do with it. If you can use a saw and hammer, I think I'll keep this team here to do some more construction tomorrow. Any problem with that?"

He watched all three men for their reactions, and they all indicated they had no problem with his proposal. He confirmed their assignment. After a few more minutes of meaningless conversation, he got up from the bench and retired to the over-sized kitchen storage room that had been arranged as his quarters.

They waited cautiously until he was inside and had the door closed before breaking into a round of self-congratulatory conversation.

"Hey, man, you called it!" Jeff said to Gil. "You can bet your sergeant's stripes we are going to spend a lot of time tomorrow just sitting around. There's got to be a good chance to talk to the captain about our problem with the 'don't wait' orders."

"Well, yeah," Gil answered. "That's exactly what I was hoping for."

Henry entered a word of caution. "When it comes up, be careful not to sound like you're being critical," he warned. "Remember, those are his orders. They come directly from him, not some higher headquarters."

"That's a good point," Gil said. "We sure don't want to risk offending him if there's personal pride involved."

Gil went to bed feeling good about things in general. The military lifestyle was not one he ever would choose, but given that he had no choice he had adapted to it pretty well. The 2nd Platoon intel unit would have to serve as interim family. He hoped to be in it until the end of the war. But thoughts of his real family back home and especially images of Annie in his mind's eye kept him awake long after his body had called for sleep. He repeated to himself mentally a line from her last letter: "Gil, darling, when I sleep I dream and when I dream I dream of you."

Morning came much too soon. He was dead to the world when Henry shouted in his ear and woke him. Other members of the platoon were up and putting on their varied civilian dress and three men already were sitting on a bench eating breakfast rations. The smell of fresh-brewed coffee flooded the makeshift barracks the old farmhouse had become. Gil was happy his team would not have a field assignment today.

"So, are we supposed to just sit around until the captain comes and tells us what to do?" he asked Jeff, who was pulling on his second boot. Jeff threw his hands out to his sides signaling that he didn't know but said nothing.

Captain Daniels came out of his room just a moment later and went straight to the coffee pot. Carrying his canteen cup filled with steaming brew carefully, he walked among the teams to tell them what was to come. He got to the Three Bees last. They just needed to hang loose, he told them, and after breakfast he would get the other three teams started on their intel assignments and then get back to them. So far, he added, the lumber hadn't got there from battalion, but he expected it at any time.

"Excuse me, sir," Jeff said, "but will they unload that in broad daylight? I thought we only got deliveries after dark."

"That is the way we'd like it, but things don't always work out the way we'd like them to. I think battalion has had to move forward a couple of times and that puts little units like us on the back burner. Now if you men will excuse me, I need to get the other teams in gear and ready to roll."

Henry went to the big coffee pot and refilled his canteen cup. Gil and Jeff sat idly and waited for something to happen. Jeff said he wished he had old Jake, his collie dog, and asked Gil if he had a dog waiting at home. Gil laughed and said no dog, but he had a beautiful girl waiting to be his wife. Jeff asked him to talk about her and Gil tried hard to describe Annie without getting emotional. They ended up speculating about what people at home were doing this very minute and homesickness was at a high level by the time Henry rejoined them.

"Took you a long time to get a cup of coffee," Gil told him.

"Don't let it get out, but I've been doing a little intel work close at hand."

"I hope you're joking," was Jeff's quick response.

He wasn't. Speaking very softly to avoid even the slightest chance of being overheard, Henry explained that he'd been moving around casually eavesdropping on Captain Daniels' orders to the other teams.

"I can tell you," he added, "they've got some hairy assignments today."

The captain rejoined the Three Bees moments later, as the rest of the platoon moved out. They sat facing him as he leaned forward toward them from another bench and waited for him to speak. When he did, he voiced an unusual note of uncertainty. He had received a message from battalion alerting him that the lumber had been sent and should have been delivered by now. He was both frustrated and worried.

"I'm guessing one of two possibilities delayed them," he said. "The one I worry about, of course, is enemy action. The one I'm hoping for, and think most likely, is they simply got lost and are still out there somewhere trying to find us. You know damned well the last thing those truckers want to do is call battalion and ask for directions!"

"Sir, couldn't they call you?" Jeff asked.

"Negative, Sergeant. Our contact info is highly secret to lessen the possibility of a German intercept. Battalion will go to any lengths to guard its little intel platoon against discovery. See how important we are!"

Gil was dying to ask about the "don't wait" orders. He was ready to do it as soon as the captain stopped talking. He didn't have to.

"Captain, since we don't have the lumber yet," Jeff said somewhat timidly, "could we maybe ask you some questions about our orders yesterday?"

"Of course. Ask me anything."

Jeff hesitated, clearly not sure how to begin. Henry jumped in to bail him out. "It was my driver's orders specifically that we were concerned about, sir," he said to Captain Daniels.

"Okay," the captain said, "I think I know where this is going. You don't want to abandon a teammate, right?"

"Yes, sir. And, well, I guess we wondered why we should," Henry said. "I mean, we'd rather go in and try to rescue him if he was in trouble. Wouldn't the Army say—"

Captain Daniels held up his hands. "Yes, Sergeant, the Army would say we won't leave a man behind. And we sure as hell try never to do it. But here's something I maybe should have put a little more emphasis on. The intelligence service is more demanding than any other. We have to do our work in secret, very often behind enemy lines. It's not by accident that we are a small group—just a single rifle squad, only a tiny bit of an infantry regiment. But if we were a bigger unit we'd be harder to hide.

"Let's look at it this way. In a big battle, you would likely have several infantry battalions involved. You are about to get your nuts crunched and lose four or five regiments. Your only way out is to hold one tentative defensive position—say maybe a river crossing, or something like that—and a single company can do that long enough to let everybody else get out alive. No commander wants to do it, but some colonel is going to have to give that glorious duty to one company even though he knows he's sacrificing them to the enemy. That's war, gentlemen."

The captain paused, as if to catch a second breath. Gil could see this wasn't easy for him. At the risk of making a big mistake, he interrupted. "Sir, would you like me to get you a cup of coffee or drink of water or something?"

The captain smiled. "Thank you for your consideration," he said. "But I think I can finish this up. I didn't mean for it to be a long lecture. But I recognize the hard place that driver's order puts you in and you deserve the best explanation I can give you. I had a course in Command General School where they drilled into us that the hardest part of command is to know you are putting men in extraordinary danger. But I think you see my point. In our tiny intel platoon, one man is that single infantry company that may have to be sacrificed. We have to trust every team member to do his job and since he probably is operating in enemy territory, if he doesn't get back in time we have to assume the worst. We can't sacrifice the other two team members any more than that colonel can sacrifice a couple of battalions.

"And finally, and this is most important, we have to be willing to risk it all to protect our larger operation from discovery. That individual soldier may pass for a Frenchman for a little while, even if he arouses the interest of the Germans, and if, God forbid, he loses his life he's not going to be seen as an American soldier where no American soldier is supposed to be. But if the Germans are led to the other two team members and a Jeep, all bets are off. The life of every man in the platoon is in the hands of every other man. It's a big load, but that's war. Have I made any sense of this at all?"

Gil answered quickly. "Captain, you not only made sense, but you made us proud. You make serving in this little intel platoon kind of a gallant service. That's my take, anyhow."

Jeff and Henry hurried to signal agreement, by way of motion if not by words. Jeff nodded his head vigorously and Henry offered a thumbs up.

"Well, men," the captain said, "before you get to feeling downright cocky, I have to tell you there would be stiff competition from your British brethren. I hear their men get behind enemy lines by parachuting from bombers, going out through the bomb bay doors with the bombs. 'Stout fellows,' they like to say."

Before anyone could say more, they were interrupted by noise from behind the house. It was the two trucks from battalion, bringing the lumber they had been waiting for. The Three Bees would have a busy day after all.

Captain Daniels directed the battalion drivers to move their trucks under what remained of the old machine shed behind the house, where the platoon's Jeeps were parked. Nothing under the roof would be visible from the air. Two of the Jeeps were out so there wouldn't be much room.

The drivers complained briefly that they weren't driving Army trucks, but old French farm trucks that wouldn't arouse suspicion if they were seen, so why did it matter? The captain had a quick explanation. It was not only the trucks themselves that must be hidden, but any significant activity around the old farmhouse that was supposed to be deserted.

"And does one of you have the bunk beds we're supposed to get?" he asked.

"We both do," a driver said. "No way we could get all of them on one truck."

As soon as the trucks were moved, the Three Bees went to work unloading them. One truck hauled mostly scrap lumber and three beds and the other's whole load was beds. It took the better part of an hour to get everything off and stuffed into the back of the shed, where it would be out of sight until dark.

After a generous statement of appreciation from the captain, the drivers left twenty minutes apart for their return to battalion. One of them had told Gil it was about a 60-mile trip, made longer by the necessity to take a route avoiding the heaviest concentration of German troops.

Captain Daniels wore a sheepish grin when the team got back inside the house.

"The bunks are my little surprise for you and the other men," he told them. "I couldn't see how this place ever could feel like home as long as you had to sleep on the floor." He couldn't have known that Jeff had just made that same point to Gil and Henry as they walked in from the shed.

9

WHEN THE NIGHTS began to get cold, the 2nd Platoon sergeants found themselves huddling around the old cast iron range in the kitchen more often, in no hurry to go to bed. Having bunks to sleep on instead of only mattresses on the floor made their nights more comfortable but added no warmth and blankets promised by battalion had not come yet. Captain Daniels had shown a rare flare of temper as he reported his dissatisfaction to the men.

"Hell yes," he told them, "I know they have to move battalion headquarters a lot and I know they have a lot to do and I don't question all the reasons they give me for the delay but I don't accept their reasons as excuses. Give me ten minutes in there to get hold of whoever dropped the ball and some supply sergeant is damned well going to lose some stripes!"

Gil saw this display as so out of character it was almost funny, but at the same time was glad not to be on the receiving end of his commanding officer's ire. Captain Ron Daniels was not one to make idle threats.

The men of 2nd Platoon were all very much aware of the captain's constant efforts to make their situation better. They had been handed heavy winter coats—civilian, of course—well before they needed them, and they gave the captain credit for all the small things like baskets of apples and pears that showed up in the kitchen. Platoon headquarters, given the condition the old farmhouse was in when they took it over, was probably as comfortable as anyone had a right to expect.

Captain Daniels himself made no bones about trying to make headquarters the best "home" he could. His rationale was simple. It was the 2nd Intel Platoon's duty to be in the field collecting information. Scarcely a day passed that at least one of his four teams was not in danger. It was his responsibility to give his teams such orders, and surely he had a parallel responsibility to take care of his men as well as possible when they were not in the field.

Even Henry, never one reluctant to criticize, rarely spoke of the captain in negative terms. Gil thought back to Henry's early comment that the captain was not one who thought he should be a four-star general. And by extension, Gil would say maybe it was unfortunate he wasn't.

Overarching all was the fact that this was the Army. The men in question were soldiers in war. It was not their comfort that was important to their country, it was their devotion to duty. And that duty was to be ready to sacrifice themselves if necessary to defend the American way of life. They existed in a world at war and, fortunately, this was a temporary universe and not their real world.

For Gil, Annie's letters were his contact with the real world. The 2nd Platoon was a fantasy land, living in secrecy, one dangerous mission after another, the same dozen men his only human contacts. His life might have been a scripted play acted out on the same stage every night for a different audience. Yes, they were a tiny but critical unit of the U. S. Army doing their duty as best they could and confident they were making a significant contribution, but for them the fighting was remote even when it was happening nearby.

Most important, he and the other men of the 2nd Platoon faced reminders every day that they were expendable. Merely cogs in a machine that could be replaced by another cog without notice. This is how they were trained and this was why they wore uniforms.

Gil and Jeff had discussed the matter of uniforms, and the significance of not wearing them now. Jeff had mixed feelings, one day happy he was not in uniform and the next day wishing he was.

"It's no big deal," he told Gil. "Everybody knows they put armies in uniforms to make sure individuals don't count. If individuals count, they might not be willing to die for the cause. An army of individuals would collapse like a stack of dominoes in battle. You know what I mean?"

"Yeah, I think so. And I think there's another thing. If you're in uniform and you are going into battle it's supposed to screw up your courage to see yourself as just one little fish in this sea of uniforms. You're not an easy target."

They talked about not wearing uniforms in their field assignments and agreed it was a good thing. Jeff repeated Gil's "little fish" analogy and said being out there all alone in a combat zone in uniform and not just one little fish would make you a whale.

"Talk about an easy target!"

Gil knew he was lucky to have Jeff and Henry to talk to and felt as close to them as he ever had to any other friend in his whole life. At the same time, he recognized that they almost never talked about real world things. They talked about their world at war.

Gil lay on his bunk and held Annie's letters, every one he had received, in order. They would be precious regardless of content because they had been held in Annie's hands but reading her words again let him pretend he was hearing her sweet voice.

And there was an added element he had only recently come to understand. Annie wrote about *home*. This was where he belonged, in the places where she was, doing the things she did, at her side. What at one time he had seen as visions from his past he recognized now as visions from his future. This war could not last forever and this is what he would be going home to.

He knew these words, but he read again:

Dearest Gil,

I wish you could have seen the July 4 celebration at the fairgrounds. I've been to several but none as great as this one. There had to be more than a dozen bands and flags flying everywhere. They had a bugler who played taps. That really got to me. Do you hear that every day?

I think it is at times like this that I miss you most. When I see something I wish you could see my heart aches that you are not there with me. But I can honestly say one good thing has come from this war. I will never take having you at my side for granted again. How spoiled I was when you were always here and we thought it would always be that way.

But it will be that way again, soon I hope. And what we thought then will be true. It will be forever.

Love and miss you so much. See you in my dreams.

Forever and ever,

Annie

My Darling Gil,

Mother White tells me you've only been gone for four months, but I swear it's been a year. The summer's gone and before you know it winter will be here. And I'll worry about you even more—are you someplace warm, do you have warm clothes, will you remember to wear your mittens if you have to be out?

My life is so empty without you, my sweet man, that summer, fall, or winter makes no difference. Mother White and I will sit and drink our coffee and talk all morning and she takes a nap in the afternoon and before you know it it's time for supper and then bedtime. Every day just like every other day and without you my days are long, long, long.

I go to Walnut Creek Church every Sunday. That's about the only time I see my parents. Pastor Maxwell and everybody always ask about you. I think Pastor Maxwell feels like a father to everyone in what he calls his flock.

Elmo misses you, too. I didn't realize until I moved in with Mother White how much time you had spent here. Every time I turn around I find something that you fixed when it was broken. I only thought of it this minute, but do you think we might live here in this old house with Mother White after we are married? You will be doing the farm, anyway. I don't have a lot of things to tell you so my letters are always short.

But someday soon we'll be together again and I'll probably talk so much you get tired of hearing me. Please remember to wear your mittens, and think of me every time you put them on. You know I will be thinking of you.

Love you more than words can tell,
Annie

Darling Gil,

Somebody at church said the Army always serves a big Thanksgiving dinner to all the troops, with turkey and all the usual fixings. I sure hope he knew what he was talking about. And if he did I sure hope they have it where you are. I hate to think you might be stuck in a hole somewhere and miss it.

With Thanksgiving just a week away now, it's still a big undecided question what we are going to do here. I know either Mother White and I will go to mom and dad's or they will come here. I hope they come here, because I'm not sure Mother White is up to all the work of doing Thanksgiving dinner.

Gilbert—I'm trying to get used to that because our first boy will be named Gilbert Junior—do you remember when we were in school and they used to have us coloring and cutting out turkeys and pumpkins and all that? And you colored your pumpkins green and turkeys orange or something just to irritate the teacher? You were bad!

I know, I'm always thinking about things in the past, but that's because you were here then. I should only think about the future because you will be here then, too. I have to admit I feel like I am going to be old and gray before we get there. Will you still love me when I'm old and gray, Gil? I know I'll still be loving you when they stick me in my grave and throw the dirt in on top of me.

You may not see them, but I'm putting two dozen extra kisses in this letter. I hope you like them as much as I do.

Love you now and forever,
Annie

He and Annie were together in his dreams during the night, walking in the woods on a beautiful spring morning. They listened to the chorus of songbirds and picked flowers and held hands as they walked and when they came to a shallow creek he picked her up and carried her across and they sat on a fallen log and he looked into her beautiful eyes. And in his dream world life was good.

He still was in that dream world when Jeff shook him awake. He felt like he had barely gone to sleep but it was time to get up. There probably was not enough coffee in the whole world to make him fully alert.

After breakfast, Captain Daniels called the platoon together for what he offered as a general update on the war. There had been little movement in the front lines over the last several weeks, he told them, but he believed this was going to change soon. And once there was any movement to speak of, changes were likely to come pretty fast.

He asked Gil to pull the largest scale map from the file, then spread it on the floor. With the platoon sergeants gathered in a circle, he took his broken flag staff pointer and aimed it at their location on the map.

"We are sitting here pretty much in the middle of a dozen or so scattered combat units about equally ours and theirs," he told them. "I'd say the Germans have at least six battalions of infantry and at least one artillery outfit spread around in this sector. We are about equal in combat-ready infantry but no artillery. The Germans' big guns are blasting the hell out of our guys but we haven't been able to find the artillery unit and pin it down. Our next intel challenge is to locate that artillery unit.

"Only thing I'd add is air power, and that's an element that's completely unpredictable. It depends on the weather and the whims of the top brass in London. And I've got a feeling they are looking toward Berlin, not our sector here in the middle of France."

The platoon sergeants had followed his comments carefully.

Gil had a question.

"What size artillery unit are we talking about, sir? If it's more than one battalion it would be hard to hide, wouldn't it?"

"Exactly. It has to be a small enough unit they can scatter it out in the forest and hide it. But they've got some big guns with long enough range they've really hurt at least three and to some extent four of our infantry battalions."

Henry had leaned over the map and was studying it closely. American forces would be moving generally to the east into this sector, he noted, making a sweeping motion with his hand. "And I don't see any real natural barriers for the next hundred miles or so. Maybe a little creek or two, but there's no river and nothing close to mountains. So we know the terrain and we can forecast the weather. This just leaves the enemy to study, right?"

Gil and Jeff exchanged glances, surprised and impressed by Henry's apparent understanding of the situation. They didn't remember learning anything in combat infantry training at Fort Jackson that would have let them state things so well. Henry seemed to have picked up something they missed.

"Well, you just summed it up the way they teach it," the captain said. "Know the terrain, know the weather, and know the enemy. And your summation was right on target. We can't know the enemy until we find that artillery unit. We have got to silence their big guns."

Captain Daniels' general information session quickly became a planning session for Gil's squad, which the captain chose to carry on the assignment to find the German guns. They would go tomorrow. The captain was not one to waste time once he knew what had to be done.

Gil was thinking how his father would be impressed by Captain Daniels. *He admires men who can make quick decisions.* He remembered his father saying many times the most common trait among Bennett men was being wishy washy. "Your

Grandpa Bennett couldn't do anything until he'd changed his mind on how to do it three or four times," he said. *Well, Dad, he wouldn't have lasted long in the 2nd Platoon. We have to have men like the captain.*

The captain laid out the most likely options for finding the enemy artillery, keeping in mind that it was mobile. He said it was possible that American units on the receiving end of its shelling would be able to calibrate the direction of incoming fire and find it through triangulation, but the right combination of things would have to fall in place for that to happen. He doubted this was likely.

The second and third options would involve the intel team, so this was what he wanted to talk about. One, they might get within the sound of the big guns and two, they might find artillery shells being delivered. It took a lot of ammunition to keep the guns firing at the rate they had been and this meant hauling it in from somewhere.

"Can you come up with any other reasonable possibilities?" the captain asked.

Jeff asked the question Gil was considering.

"What about the civilians? Aren't there any French still living out there? They would most likely be on our side, wouldn't they?"

"You mean why don't we just go ask around?" the captain answered. "That makes a lot of sense. But they won't talk. They are afraid. And even if they did, you'd get somebody who said the guns were there last week and they would have moved since then. A couple of other intel units have worked that angle real hard and got nothing."

The captain swept his flagstick pointer in a wide semicircle to the east of the 2nd Platoon headquarters' position on the map, which was marked with a vivid red X.

"They're in here somewhere," he said. "The Germans are

fighting like hell to keep us from consolidating into a cohesive front and advancing on the homeland but it's pretty clear they can't form a solid line of defense. They will try to keep us spread out like we are now and even a single artillery unit will help do that. We've got to knock out their big guns before we go very far."

"You sound like we're not making much progress," Henry said. "The Allies, I mean."

"We're not moving much. But that's going to change real soon. And once the first U. S. Army troops cross the Moselle River, the war is not in France anymore. It's on German soil. Old Adolph is going to have a lot of worried homefolks on his hands, watching us move on Berlin."

Gil felt as if the division by rank between Captain Daniels and the three sergeants had narrowed to little more than a required military protocol. The captain had been talking to them as equals and he felt at ease now to express himself.

"You think the war's going to last for a long time yet?" he asked.

"Let's just say I hope that pretty girl waiting for you—where, southern Illinois?—let's hope she cares enough to wait a long time."

The captain went on to lay out critical details of tomorrow's mission, but Gil hardly caught a word. The captain had implanted Annie in his mind and she was not to be dislodged. He rationalized that Henry and Jeff would be able to tell him what he needed to know in the field, as the operation was carried out.

The captain always rotated individual roles on the teams. Gil didn't realize until morning that he was the driver on this assignment. He wished now he had listened more closely last night instead of letting his mind wander through memories of Annie. His job would not be complicated, though. Captain Daniels had scribbled map coordinates on a slip of paper and all he had to do was get Henry and Jeff there. Gathering the intelligence information would be their responsibility.

The team wouldn't leave platoon headquarters until midmorning. He had to put a few gallons of gasoline in the Jeep, but there was nothing else to load. O'Dell's team looked nervous and he wondered what their assignment was. Anyway, there was time for leisurely breakfast rations and a second cup of coffee. Jeff and Henry were in no more hurry to get under way than he was.

Henry pointed out another difference on today's orders Gil hadn't noticed. Each of them was to be armed. They got carbines out of the rifle chest and picked up enough ammunition to meet their expected needs, which were minimal.

"Hey, too bad these pretty little air rifles don't come with bayonets," Henry quipped. "I promised Uncle Joe I'd stick one of those little stabbers in the guts of a Kraut soldier."

Gil saw an opening too good to pass up. "O'Dell says Philadelphia boys learn to knife-fight before they learn to tie their shoes," he told Henry. "Is it really that bad?"

"Yeah, well, O'Dell's so dumb he probably couldn't find his mama's teat," Henry answered. Gil listened for a response to this from O'Dell, who was only a short distance away sitting on a bench with his teammates Shelby and Jansen. If he heard, he didn't show it.

Captain Daniels had created an informal checking-out procedure for the platoon's teams leaving on field assignments. He wanted to make sure they understood the specific information they were to try and find and he wanted to wish them luck. He let them know he didn't expect a salute, and if they gave one he returned it with a simple wave of his hand. When the Three Bees were ready to go he reminded them to be sure they had their compasses.

"Pretty hard to navigate by the stars during daylight," he

said. "Be careful out there."

10

GIL HAD DRIVEN a Jeep only a few times before and still had a problem shifting gears. He fell back on Jeff's advice to double-clutch. After a couple of miles on the rutted road he got the hang of it. The Jeep was a snap after the old John Deere tractor. He soon learned its peculiarities he hadn't found before.

They soon ran out of road and he still had another twenty miles or so to navigate before reaching Henry's drop-off point. Jeff's was another five miles past that.

The landscape began to change, as thick forests gave way to rolling pastureland with only small groves of trees here and there. Trying to stay hidden was a daunting challenge. Gil tried to maintain a steady speed. There could be enemy units any-where now, and the extra noise of a revving up engine and mul-tiple gears shifting were far more likely to give them away than the little hum of the Jeep's small Willys engine not stressed.

"So what kind of outpost are you looking at?" Gil asked Henry. "I don't see a lot of hiding places out there."

Henry's destination was an old barn that sat in an open field and could be watched by the enemy from all directions. He said it was supposed to be dilapidated to the point of almost falling down but still had a hay loft where he would be well hidden and have a clear view that should make it a perfect observation point. Jeff, on the other hand, not only risked exposure getting to his post but also shouldn't expect to find an obvious hiding place. Gil wished he could just keep Jeff with him and even offered to, but Jeff wouldn't hear of it. He accepted Gil's reminder to calibrate his compass and was gone.

With both teammates on their own, Gil looked for a hiding place for the Jeep and found a dip in the land in an old apple orchard that offered a bank with a large brush pile below. He nuzzled the Jeep into the brush, pulled some branches over it, and crawled beneath it. This was where he would spend the next three hours, and he felt comfortably remote from the rest of the world. It might have been easy to forget that he was in a war, that he was in France, and that he was in a sector held by enemy forces.

But not for long. After some twenty minutes, he heard the distant rumble of moving vehicles and they were moving in his direction. He was struck by the realization that if something happened to him, Henry and Jeff would be stranded, too, with little chance of escape. For the first time since he had put on a U. S. Army uniform he felt responsible for the lives of others.

He crawled farther into the pile of brush, trying to wedge between some of the bigger branches apparently pruned recently from the apple trees. If a German soldier looked over the bank and saw the Jeep and felt obligated to destroy it Gil wanted to be as far away from the vehicle as he could manage. He pushed harder at the mangled apple tree limbs and managed to get a little past the center of the brush pile. A sharp stick had stabbed him on the side of his neck and he could feel the blood oozing from an open wound and beginning to run down inside his collar.

With the vehicles close now, he froze in place. There were voices just above him along the bank.

Wait! They were speaking French. Although he knew

neither language, he recognized the lisped accent that was not the guttural German. It still was possible they were not friendly, but whoever was up there it was not German troops. Gil felt a great sense of relief but still held his breath as the voices and the machines he now took to be tractors moved away. He may not have been in the danger he believed he was, but the depth of his emotion was a realistic response he hoped would help him be ready to face death on the battlefield if this should be his lot.

But he was not ready to surrender to such likelihood. Annie was waiting. He would go home again and, with her, raise a family and maybe one day he would be able to talk to his children about the sheer terror of war. And if they asked why he was in France to begin with, he would try to explain how America had joined the British to free France form its German conquerors and block Hitler's plan to rule much of the world. If they asked for more detail, he would be the one to surrender.

Gil watched his time carefully. He must be perfectly on schedule to pick up Henry and Jeff. Being the team driver gave him a better feeling for the urgency of keeping things on schedule. He hoped his teammates would have critical intel to report back to the captain.

But they didn't. Neither Jeff nor Henry had seen or heard anything they could associate with artillery. The team's day had been a complete waste of time and the Three Bees were disappointed.

Captain Daniels didn't see it that way. The fact that they found nothing cleared a substantial sector from further consideration, he said. There still were two large sectors they had to get into and one of them was substantially farther from platoon headquarters.

"Most likely looking at an overnight trip into it," the captain said.

Henry had a question. Since this whole operation was an

attempt merely to locate an artillery unit that was hitting the American forces hard, what would happen if they found it? Just knowing where it was didn't take care of the problem.

"I'd guess our infantry battalions are getting a little more pinned down every day," he said. "When you're getting incoming artillery you have to dig in. It's too risky to try to advance."

The captain said the quick answer was, he didn't know. But the only likelihood he could see was calling in an air strike. They could do that once they had pinpointed the guns' location. He went on to express his frustration that he rarely got follow-up information after he reported intel to battalion.

"We tell them what we know and move on," he said. "By the time they act on our intel, we've moved on to something else. I'm not talking about the big picture here, but the stuff we do for specific small operations."

"Yeah, like that battalion about to get surrounded," Jeff said. "You hear anything more about that, sir?"

The captain shook his head. "I've not heard from Colonel Beasley, but I'd guess that if he hasn't moved it he's close to the point where he's damned if he does and damned if he doesn't. From what he told me before if he didn't do something soon that battalion faced virtual extinction. A lot of American sons and brothers wouldn't be going home."

Gil imagined he could once again feel the fear that had gripped him when he thought he actually was about to face the enemy for the first time. It was hard to see how it could be any different being in an infantry battalion about to be overrun by an enemy force two or three times its size. And unlike the usual situation, these men knew exactly what they faced and there was nothing they could do about it.

"Sir," Gil said, "I don't pretend to know anywhere near enough to make the tough decisions you have to make, but I have an idea that I think might work. Nothing much different, really, but it could get results faster."

"I'm all ears, Sergeant. God knows I don't have all the answers."

"Okay, sir, I've been trying to add up two or three different things here. The weather's been good enough we must have had at least some air recon. They would have concentrated on finding those big guns and they didn't find them. I think that means, just like you said in the beginning, they are keeping them under the trees. This takes me to obvious point two. They have to be in an area of at least some dense forest. I know there's a lot of it, but there wasn't much where we were today. And, well, third, they have to be hauling in a lot of ammo and the only way they can hide that is to do it by night."

Henry pointed a finger at Gil. "Man, you have thought this out, haven't you!"

"Yes, he makes a lot of sense," Captain Daniels said. "Let's see if we can figure out what to do with his assessment of the situation."

Gil took this as approval for him to say more. "If I'm right, the first thing we have to do is get in there at night. They can't move things on a big scale without at least some light and trucks heavy enough to haul shells of that bore would make a lot of noise. I'll bet we'd hear them from a mile away."

The captain slapped a hand on the table. "I'm on board," he said. "When do we start?"

Gil looked at his teammates. "How about it, Three Bees? Ready to get back to work?"

"Right behind you, man," Jeff said.

Henry signaled with a thumbs up.

Difficult as it would have been to imagine an hour earlier, Gil and his team were going back into the field. The captain spent a few minutes studying the field map, circled a detailed region he wanted them to cover, and wrote down compass points defining a triangle that measured about 15 miles on the longest side. He handed this to Gil and said, "Good luck, men. Hope you come back with what we need."

They hurriedly loaded the Jeep with bottles of water, an extra flashlight, and their carbines with an extra clip each. They checked their compass settings and Jeff climbed into the driver's seat and the other two jumped in after him. They were on their way to the field again. This assignment had a different feel, as if they really were going to war and possibly about to meet the enemy head on.

The sector Captain Daniels had assigned them to this time was a little more than 25 miles farther away than the area they had been in before. Jeff drove for less than ten minutes on the road that ran in front of 2nd Platoon headquarters before exiting onto what may at one time have been a farm road but obviously hadn't been tended to for many years. It paralleled one of the ubiquitous hedgerows that separated the French farm tracts.

Driving without lights, Jeff had Henry and Gil walk in front with flashlights. This got them to the end of the old farm road, but they were well behind schedule. Jeff calculated they must make it to the planned observation area within an hour or else scrub the mission. Whatever they did there they still had to make it out while it was still dark, too.

A stretch of cultivated fields gave way to relatively clear pastureland and then they came to a thick forest. It was past midnight, but they had reached their goal in time.

The plan from here was for Gil and Henry each to walk a mile or so, one to the east and one to the west, and be alert for any sights or sounds that could reveal enemy activity. They carefully checked their compasses and promised Jeff they would be back within the two hours allotted. With Jeff on lookout in the center, they had eyes and ears on a substantial section of enemy territory in the region where the German guns were most likely to be.

Henry, never one to be shy about stating his opinion, had labeled their plan "promising" strictly on the basis of its "deceptive simplicity." Other than the risk of being captured or killed by the Germans, he declared, the action was very easy on them and carried good odds of being successful.

Gil felt pretty much the same but Jeff was far more skeptical. Captain Daniels had been clear that time was running out. Either they find a link to the enemy guns tonight or it might be too late to hold out much hope for the American infantry battalions to merge into a united front capable of advancing into the enemy-held territory any time soon. They not only were pinned down by the German artillery but were suffering heavy losses to the constant shelling by the enemy's big guns.

Gil set his compass position and started walking north. He wanted to get about another two miles into Grman territory. There was only a faint trace of moonlight. He resisted using his flashlight as long as he could, but after tripping over dead branches on the ground twice and one time taking a nasty fall he switched it on and cupped his hands around the lens to minimize the amount of light that would be visible.

He moved as quietly as he could and stopped often and stood unmoving for a few minutes and listened. After an hour he reached the site he had aimed for, a wide, steep-banked creek that without bridging would be a barrier to heavy trucks.

The Germans would need a road for trucks coming from either the east or the west and it likely would parallel this stream, on the other side. He arranged a comfortable place to sit and rested and listened. He calculated that with Jeff in the middle and Henry some distance beyond but both parallel to him they were covering a front as much as 15 miles wide.

The scent of lavender was overwhelming. There were no

night sounds like he expected—no bird calls, no animal noises of any kind. Back home he would be listening to a pair of owls talking back and forth from different treetops, a whippoorwill or two, and possibly, even at night, a chattering squirrel venting its frustration over an insufficient supply of hickory nuts. And certainly there would be croaking frogs along the creek. But the natural environment he had known had not suffered the ravages of war.

About a half hour later, just after he had given up hope of gaining any intel tonight, he heard it. Not far distant to the east and coming toward him was a convoy of heavy trucks. They came at a good rate of speed, meaning there was a road on the other side of the creek. He wanted to jump up and shout. In short order he counted eight trucks go past and then there was quiet again.

Gil was more careless as he hurried back to the Jeep. He used the flashlight more freely but slung the carbine over his shoulder so his hands were free to muffle the powerful beam. Speed was urgent now. Henry and Jeff would be there at almost the same time he arrived, and as fast as they could manage they would get back to platoon headquarters to report to Captain Daniels.

Henry was there and Jeff got there right after Gil. Their reports made the night's mission even more successful. Jeff, who had been to the east of Gil, not only had heard the convoy but in fact had seen glimpses of it through the trees no more than a hundred yards in front of him. He had seen enough to know they were heavy freight trucks, exactly the kind that would be hauling shells to the big guns. Henry had seen or heard nothing. This would give Captain Daniels the pattern he needed.

"Let's get out of here!" Gil urged. Henry jumped in the back of the Jeep and Jeff got behind the wheel. Gil unslung his carbine and was about to hand it to Henry when suddenly he was blinded by a powerful flashlight beam aimed directly at his face.

"Anhalten!"

The Three Bees scrambled for cover, Gil ducking behind the Jeep and the other two throwing themselves on the ground.

"Sie sin Amerikaner!"

Gil could see only an outline of the German sentry silhouetted in the dim light. He saw the muzzle flash of a rifle and heard bullets shatter the windshield of the Jeep. In desperation he pointed his carbine at the enemy soldier without any effort to shoulder the stock and squeezed the trigger. The impact of his bullets knocked the German backward and left him lying motionless on the ground.

Henry dashed to his side for a close look and yelled, "He's done for. Let's get moving."

Gil stood beside the Jeep, trembling, his carbine hanging from his hand loosely, barrel-down.

"Come on, man," Henry yelled. "Let's get moving. We've got the whole German army after us now."

Gil did not respond. Henry grabbed his arm and Jeff helped him get Gil into the passenger seat of the Jeep. Jeff started the engine and jerked the vehicle into motion so fast Gil was nearly thrown out. Jeff turned on the headlights and drove as fast as he could manage through the rugged and varied woods and open fields.

"Look back," Jeff told Henry. "They're probably going to be coming after us."

No trailing lights showed up, and in considerably less time than it had taken them to cover the distance in the opposite direction they were back at the old farmhouse. Captain Daniels got up as soon as he heard the Jeep in the driveway and was eager to get whatever reports they had. It took him no more than five mantes to craft a full intelligence report to be forwarded to battalion.

"You saved a lot of American soldiers tonight," he told them. "Our infantry battalions won't be pounded by those big guns much longer. And by the way, if I had had to guess without your work tonight, I would have guessed wrong. That's what intelligence is all about."

Gil was tired beyond description. He sprawled on his bunk without undressing, and Jeff and Henry did the same. Just getting boots off was all the exertion they wanted. Gil heard sounds of sleep from the other two almost at once. He wanted and needed sleep, too, but he was hit by a wave of emotion at a level he'd never felt before.

He had killed a man.

It was as if an image of that German soldier stood over him, and over and over he heard and saw the impact of his bullets destroy that human life. Who was that man? Was he young? Did he have a sweetheart like Annie waiting for him? Were there parents and favorite aunts counting the days till he came home?

There would be no answers to such questions. But these things didn't matter. *You took his life. You killed another human being.*

Gil had not slept when other men around him began getting up. He lay still in his bunk when Henry and Jeff got up and, not having undressed, made straight for the coffee pot. Most of the platoon had coffee and breakfast rations in hand by the time he finally forced himself to swing his legs over the side of his bunk and get feet on the floor. He was still sitting when Captain Daniels approached.

"Sergeant," the captain said, "can I see you in my office, please?"

Gil pulled himself up and followed the captain. He stumbled over someone's boots and nearly fell but caught himself and went forward to the captain's open door. He had not seen the inside of the captain's makeshift quarters before and would have been disappointed if he had expected anything elaborate, befitting a commanding officer. The furnishing consisted of a bunk and chair and two empty ammunition boxes stood on end to form a table that was loaded with a stack of folders and loose papers.

The captain asked him to close the door behind him, then motioned to the single chair and asked him to sit. Gil reacted almost mechanically. At another time he might have worried that he was in trouble, but his mind was still numb from events of the last several hours.

"Sergeant Bennett," the captain addressed him, "or if I may, Gil, your teammates just now told me what happened last night. Can we talk about it?"

"Not much to talk about. I killed another human being."

"But you know he was a German soldier? He would have killed all three of you."

"Yes, I know that," Gil answered. "But being a soldier didn't make him less human. I'm a soldier. If I'm killed I will have a sweetheart and family at home who will hurt for my loss. They're not going to say it's okay because I was a soldier. Do you understand what I'm trying to say, sir?"

Captain Daniels had been standing. Now he seated himself on his bunk. The two men's knees almost bumped in the narrow confines of the old farmhouse's supply closet that served as the captain's quarters.

"Gil, I would not want a man in my outfit who took killing easily. Not wanting to be in this war and not wanting to kill people is what makes us the good guys. But let's try to put this into proper perspective. You know you killed a German soldier. Where did this happen?"

"I don't know, sir. Out in the middle—"

The captain interrupted: "No, I mean in what country?"

"Well, France."

"So, you didn't kill this soldier in his homeland. It was in another country. He was an invader in the country we came to help protect. This is why wars happen, Gil. Ruthless dictators with grandiose visions of world domination try to take over other countries and end up having their own people taken down with them. Hitler is a showman who somehow took in the German citizens who should have seen through him. It could happen anywhere, I suppose. Maybe even in America someday. I hope not, but you never know."

Gil would have felt better from nothing more than the captain's concern. He had listened to his words, though, and accepted the captain's wisdom. Nothing could take away the indelible scar left by taking another's life, but the pain had been significantly mitigated by the captain's words.

"Sir, I get your point," he said. "All you say makes good sense to me. Thank you very much."

Captain Daniels stood, a clear signal their conversation had ended. He extended a hand as Gil stood too, but rather than shaking he just held Gil's hand in a firm grip. "Being a soldier in combat is a hard life, Sergeant," he said, speaking in little above a whisper. "We still have a ways to go and you may have to kill again. Remember this: If you do, it will be as the hero, not the villain."

He held the door open and Gil stepped out into the open kitchen area. Jeff and Henry were watching for him. They rushed over, the quizzical expressions on their faces speaking as loud as voices might have. Gil nodded and told them, "Good session with the captain. He's a wise man. He made me feel a lot better."

They all went to refill their canteen cups with hot coffee but the pot was empty and O'Dell was just putting grounds in for more. Given the size of the pot, they knew this would take a while. They took seats on one of the benches and waited, not only for more coffee but also to see what the new day would bring. Henry put a hand on Gil's arm.

"You doing okay, buddy?" he asked.

"Yeah, Henry," Gil told him. "I'm ready to do my duty, whatever comes."

11

CAPTAIN DANIELS ANNOUNCED to the men of the 2nd Platoon that there would be a mail pickup by battalion in a couple of days. He said there still was a limited supply of writing materials in the supply cabinet if anyone wanted to get some while they had plenty of time to write. Gil was the first to make that move. It seemed like a long time since he'd been able to mail a letter to Annie.

So much he wanted to say, and yet he was reluctant to begin. How could he pretend he was the same man, her promised husband, the man who would be the father of her children, the Gil to whom she had pledged her love and promised to wait no matter how long the war dragged on. He was not that same man. He had killed another human being.

As a practical matter, there was not a lot he could tell her about his day-to-day activities. He could recite memories from their time together and fill space with questions about her life with Mother White and had she seen his mom and dad and Aunt Gloria and was Elmo still fat and so on and these would not be phony questions but things he really would like to know. But he would not be communicating honestly. He would not be sharing his most intimate thoughts with the woman he loved.

How could he do this without revealing what he had done?

Although he had picked up writing materials planning to write to Annie immediately, he found his mental dilemma so discouraging he decided to put it aside and wait until he felt like he had a better notion of what he was going to say.

He smiled as he remembered the words of a third grade teacher who scolded him because he wanted to change something: "Now, Gilbert, you can't take back something you already wrote and handed in." He always had found it a mystery why little recollections like this popped up from thin air.

Gil had developed a coping skill sometime in his younger years that he'd often fallen back on at times like this and maybe it would help him now. It was simple. He would force himself to consider even harder questions related to the one that had him bogged down. A question about the relationship between ocean tides and the moon, for example, could grow into an immensely more complicated question like was there life on other planets? The effect, of course, was to make the one thought to be so hard to begin with seem easy in comparison.

He tried to use this now, but couldn't think of a way to frame his problem as a question. He realized it wouldn't work. His problem was not about difficult external facts but internal feelings, as different as daylight and dark. What a fool he was to even think he might have a quick solution!

After his talk with the captain, Gil had regained some balance in his self-analysis. There were clear cause and effect relationships that could hardly be missed. Most basic was that he shot the German because the German was trying to shoot him. At a more complex level, he did it because he was a soldier in the U. S. Army and the United States was at war with Germany, thus it was his duty to shoot the German soldier.

He could find some comfort in the fact he killed another man not by choice but out of necessity. He would try to lean on this and hope it lessened his unbearable feeling of guilt.

And once again he would lean most heavily on the always dependable crutch of Annie's letters. He had planned to read her most recent one again before trying a second time to write her, so he had a ready excuse for taking it in hand and burying himself in her words as if seeing them for the first time:

My Darling Gil,

Last night I wished on the Evening Star the way we used to. Do you remember? And I'll bet you can guess what I wished. Yes, I wished the war would end today and you would be coming home.

Have I told you I miss you? Can I tell you again? I miss you, I miss you, I miss you.

Even southern Illinois is not so beautiful in the winter time. I drove by Soloman's Woods yesterday and it was depressing seeing all the trees bare. I know how you love it, and you probably love it in the winter time, too. But I hate it when everything is brown and dead.

But guess what? I just now remembered what you taught me about life being continuous and so, instead of hating the winter I will look forward to the spring. And when the dogwood trees on the bluff bloom again I'll not think of it as new life but, like you taught me, the continuation of old life.

And dear sweet man, I think as long as you are gone I will be like those bare trees and feel like I might as well be dead. But then you will be here again and I'll spring back to life.

Please don't think I'm foolish, Gil. There are only so many ways I can try to say how much I love you. And only so many times. I love you. I love you. And have I ever told you I love you?

With more love than words can tell,
Annie

He folded the letter and put it in his pocket. He no doubt would read it again before he wrote to Annie later.

In the meantime, his team still did not have their new assignment. Gil joined Jeff and Henry and sat on one of the benches waiting for Captain Daniels. When the captain joined them, they could see he was unusually well satisfied with the way things were going. He greeted them with a wide smile, pulled up another bench, and sat down facing them.

"The 2nd Platoon is making a name for itself," he proclaimed. "Just heard from Colonel Beasley that he was able to move his battalion without a single casualty. He is very grateful."

Even though this took them back in time, the Three Bees nodded to each other with mutual satisfaction. As the captain liked to remind them, their action had saved the lives of American soldiers. This was ingrained in their thinking now as their measure of success and a powerful incentive for them to make every effort to succeed on every mission.

"I think we're about to see things move a lot faster," the captain told them. "Not sure what the Brits are doing up north, but Patton's to our south and I think he's ready to rumble. We are going to cross the Moselle River and walk on German soil before you know it."

Being careful not to sound as if his decision had anything to do with Gil's recent experience, the captain said he needed this team to "stay home" today and help plan some more fixes for the old farmhouse. With winter coming on and no heating system, they needed to do anything possible to keep out the cold.

"It worked so well to call on the farm boys last time I thought I should do it again," the captain told them.

Windows had been boarded up on the inside so they could have light at night that wouldn't be visible from the outside, so that most obvious first step already had been taken. About all they could add was to find cracks and crevices the cold could come through, and there were many of them. They had a coil of heavy rope from the shed out back they planned to cut up and use to stuff into these as insulation.

Henry was standing on a bench trying to reach a narrow crack along the top of the wall, where it joined the ceiling. He had to get down and move the bench, then stepped back up on it again.

"Up and down, up and down," he complained. "Kind of like life itself. You ever think how life's like a merry-go-round? You're up one minute and down the next and there's nothing you can do but ride."

"Sure I have. It's just that for me, sometimes it seems like there are a lot more downs than ups."

"How old you think this house it is?"

Before Gil could answer the bench Henry stood on suddenly tilted and Henry fell hard against the wall. Gil was afraid he was going to fall on the floor but Henry managed to steady himself just in time. He got both feet on the floor and sat on the bench he'd been standing on, leaning forward with his elbows on his knees.

"Are you okay, Henry?"

"Yeah, but I came damned close to breaking an arm or something. I guess if I had, everybody would have said it was on purpose."

"A ticket home injury?"

"That's what they'd say."

Gil sat down beside him, ready for a short break. "Henry," he said, "you never seem to be really upset about anything—always calm, like everything is under control. But a while ago you said life's a merry-go-round, full of ups and downs. What's your secret, man? How do you do it?"

Henry unwittingly paid him a great tribute: He took his query seriously.

"You know, I don't have a simple answer for that," he said. "I can tell you it wasn't always that way. I used to get tied up in knots over things I couldn't do anything about. My mother and I spent a lot of time together when I was a teenager and I kind of learned from her to roll with the punches. My attitude used to be pretty much, 'Fuck 'em all,' but that's throwing out the good with the bad. I just tried to reverse that, you know, and try to stay positive. It sounds like being selfish, but it's putting myself first. I try to find what's good for me and move on."

Gil had listened intently. Henry had given him a lot to think about. Was there any reason for him not to live the same way? Aunt Gloria always had encouraged him to be more expressive. "Jump up and holler!" she'd say. Or, "Nothing wrong with crying if you feel like it." He had liked Aunt Gloria so much he'd probably worried too much about her opinion, but ironically didn't seem to have been much affected by it. He still was a quiet man, but even though he didn't express them outwardly he had come to feel his emotions more intently and this had become a problem.

He was ready to confront it head on. *I'm not going to be like that anymore. I'm going to be like Henry!* He made himself repeat the vow mentally ten times. As his dad always said, come hell or high water he was going to keep it.

The Three Bees finished doing everything they could to block cold air leaks in the old farmhouse early in the afternoon. Captain Daniels seemed contented with what they had done and told them to just hang loose till chow time. The two other teams had been on daylight assignments and were coming in now with reports. Jeff and Henry wanted to listen to these. Gil sat on his bunk and began again to write a letter to Annie.

This became the first test of his self-determined new philosophy. Tell her! He had killed a German soldier. Try to remember how Captain Daniels had explained it. He was a soldier and soldiers had no choice but to kill the enemy.

But, no! He was trying to justify what he had done. He didn't have to. *Tell her you have killed! The Gil Bennett she remembers was not a killer. She will understand you will not be the same man when you return. That's all there is to it.* He would write a candid letter to his dearest Annie, the woman he loved who waited for him at home. Some things never changed. Love was forever.

He began to write:

My dearest, sweetest Annie,

I'm so glad we have a mail pick-up coming soon and I can write you. It seems forever since I did. I think of you all the time, even in the field. You are a danger to me there, my love, because I need to pay full attention to the war. But I like thinking of you better. When I lie in my bunk, especially, I think of you and often pretend you are here. I'll let you imagine the rest.

I'm not allowed to say anything about where we are and what we are doing. We are censored, as you know. Well, I don't think the enemy could learn anything from my letters even if I sent them copies because I never know anything. I am a soldier in the U. S. Army and I just follow orders. I suppose the same could be said for the German soldier I killed the other night. Like they say, that's war.

They don't let me write much. I'm doing fine. I hope you are, too. Give my love to Mother White, my mom and dad and Aunt Gloria if you see them, and scruff Elmo for me.

Love you forever,
Gil

He dropped the letter in a box Captain Daniels had set out for that purpose and rejoined Henry and Jeff with their third-meal field rations. He usually wasn't hungry, but tonight he was starving. Even the meal of some unidentifiable dried seafood tasted good. It simply was too small and there would be no second servings.

12

HOW CAPTAIN DANIELS managed to do it during the night without anyone hearing him would be a mystery to the sergeants of the 2nd Platoon for the rest of their lives. It shouldn't have been possible. But he did, and when they woke on Christmas morning they were like little kids who thought they really had seen Santa Claus.

Standing in the middle of the living room conference space was the most beautiful Christmas tree they could have asked for. Under the tree were a dozen gift boxes, identical in red wrapping paper with white bows. The tree was a skinny little fresh-cut pine decorated with crumpled paper ball, but it meant someone had thought of them and cared enough to offer this most important symbol of the holiday. Gil was speechless. Jeff looked like he was about to cry,

Henry, as usual, was confident he could explain it. "French resistance friends," he said. There was no element of surprise in his voice.

"But Captain Daniels—"

"Well, sure, the captain had to invite them."

Captain Daniels soon would explain that, yes, the platoon was the recipient of a Christmas visit by friends in an organized French resistance group and, yes, he had help arranging it. He had kept this connection top secret until now, but was comfortable there was no risk and wanted to give them credit.

"These French men and women have risked their lives at times to help us," the captain said. "And I can admit to you now that some of the things I've told you came from battalion came from them. I have thanked them for you, so let's enjoy what we have."

The captain's confession came after the 2nd Platoon sergeants had found they were recipients not only of the Christmas tree and gifts, but also a full Christmas dinner, centered by a baked turkey. All this had been slipped into the kitchen during the night.

The captain picked up the wrapped gifts and tossed them, one by one, to the sergeants. Each box contained a pair of hand knit mittens. Gil tried his on and found they fit well and were delicately crafted from soft yellow wool yarn. His first thought was how Annie would admire them.

All formalities ended at this point and the twelve platoon sergeants tore into their Christmas dinner. They found it easily the equivalent of what they might have expected of a traditional Christmas dinner at home, and in some regards better. As Henry noted, this dinner had been prepared by people who could be chefs at the best restaurants in Paris. Jeff's answer to that was, maybe they were.

Somewhat reluctantly, Captain Daniels called the platoon to order when it was clear everyone had finished eating. The men quickly became quiet and waited to hear what he had to say. Surely they would get this day off!

"Merry Christmas, men," the captain said. "Don't worry, I'm not going to start handing out team assignments. Intel we need to gather will still be there tomorrow. For this day I want you all to forget the war and relax and enjoy the holiday. Does that sound good?"

The chorus was loud and clear. "Yes, sir!"

"And merry Christmas to you, sir," someone called out.

"Thank you for that. Now, I thought one way to be sure we all got thoroughly into the Christmas spirit was to have a little program like you used to have in school. Remember?"

"Yes, sir!"

The captain's pleasure in trying to brighten their day was obvious in his smile. Seeing that he was pleased made the men feel good. They had come to admire and respect their commanding officer and, beyond that, felt he was a friend. In Henry's words, they would follow this man's lead "to hell and back."

Gil had a peculiar mix of feelings. It was Christmas and he longed for Annie and the folks at home. At the same time, what the captain had done and the happy response he saw in the other men of the platoon gave him a sense of togetherness that made here and now a pleasure, too. And intertwined with these was a complex element of nostalgia that called up images from so many Christmases past—childhood days, school programs, services at Walnut Creek Church, exchanging gifts with Annie, all those instances of joy that had left their mark in his collected memories.

"You doing good this morning, Gil?" Jeff asked. "You look a bit sad or something."

"I'm fine. Just thinking about some times in years gone by. Christmas makes us do that, I think."

Captain Daniels raised a hand to signal he wanted their attention. "Before we go any further," he said, "I want to make sure none of you is of Jewish or other background that you don't celebrate Christmas. We don't want to impose. Anyone?"

Getting no response, he went on, "Very well, then. I happen to know a few secrets some of you have shared with me and I'm going to take advantage of one of them right now. Sergeant Allison used to be a choir leader, he told me. And I'm going to ask him if he will lead us all in singing 'Silent Night.' Would you, sergeant?"

Allison stood, showing both surprise and pride.

"It would be my pleasure, sir," he said. "I'll bet you all know it, so let's sing like we feel it."

Gil could see that every man in the platoon sang, evidently knowing the words. Their version may not have been of church choir quality, but it was delivered with unassailable sincerity. He noticed that Henry, probably the last person he would have expected to feel the words deeply, actually showed some emotion as he sang.

When they finished singing, the room was quiet. Yes, they might have been in church.

Captain Daniels took the floor again. He thanked Allison and complimented him on his performance. "Gentlemen," he said then, "as much as a celebration of Christmas, I'd like for this to be a celebration of our brotherhood. We are, as William Shakespeare said, 'a band of brothers.' More than a dozen individuals—thirteen, counting me—we are a unit, the 2nd Intel Platoon. Each of us is a cog in the mechanism that makes us run. All important, all equal, and yes, all expendable. Do I make myself clear?"

"Yes, sir!"

"Thank you, gentlemen. Now, while this marvelous celebration of Christmas has all in pretty much the same mood, I believe, I'd like every cog in the mechanism I mentioned to be seen and heard. If everybody's willing, I'd like for each one of you to tell us something of your personal Christmas memories. That work for everyone?"

"Yes, sir!"

"Sergeant Allison, since you already are warmed up, would you like to go first?"

Allison stood. He took a moment before he started to speak,

pacing deliberately to the front of the room with head down, his chin almost touching his chest.

"I'm sure we all have lots of Christmas memories," he began, "and I've tried to call up one that was special for some reason. I think I have it. See, I'm from Minnesota. Way up practically in the North Woods. We have a lot of Indians in Minnesota, mostly Chippewa around us. I was one of only three non-Indians who rode my bus to high school.

"One of my best Christmas memories is the time my Indian friend, Jackie—he had a different Indian name but I never could remember what it was—anyway, Jackie spent Christmas eve with me and my family and stayed overnight. We always had a big tree and lots of presents and all that, and I think that was new to him. But my mom, knowing he was going to be there, had put together a package for him. I don't remember what was in it. Something that was to be mine, some candy.

"Anyway, they apparently didn't do Christmas at Jackie's house and he was just overwhelmed. He broke down and cried, and hugged us all, especially my mom. And one good thing that came from it, my dad, who had always been a little bit prejudiced against the Indians, had a complete change of heart. So that was my best Christmas story."

Sergeant Shaw stood, ready to tell his story. He started with a laugh. "My choice was easy," he said, "and it's a short one. My best Christmas memory was when my little sister was born on Christmas day. I was an only child then, I think eight years old. I was excited to have a sister, and she's never disappointed me. We've always been close, and I miss her a lot."

He sat down and Henry stood. "Some of you know I'm from Philadelphia," he said. "And maybe a couple of you know that Philadelphia is just across the river from New Jersey. Well, it's not a great story, but when I was little I heard my dad and mom talk about New Jersey a lot and thought it really must be a special kind of place. My dad worked with and was good friends with a guy from Jersey and I think I was about five years old when we went to New Jersey for Christmas eve.

"Well, guess what? I was really disappointed. New Jersey wasn't any different from Philly. So, I learned a lesson. Don't judge something till you've been there and done that. That's saved me a lot of disappointments in life. Know what I mean?"

Henry sat down, leaving several men with puzzled looks on their faces. Gil nudged Jeff with his elbow, his way of saying "that's Henry."

Sergeants Sampson, Elliott, and Shelby made simple statements about Christmases that were favorites because they got a certain gift: Sampson a dog, Elliott a bicycle, and Shelby a hunting rifle. Sergeant Harris said his favorite Christmas was one on which his father got home after a long international business trip.

Gil was not eager to make a presentation, but since he had to do it he wanted to get it over with. Jeff kept urging him to go next and finally he did. He began with a warning that his was not very exciting compared to some they had just heard. "Some of you know that I'm engaged to be married to a beautiful girl named Annie," he said. "Well, Henry says if she's old enough to be married I should call her a woman instead of a girl. Anyway, I have known Annie for a long time. We were kids together in school and all that. I knew that whatever I came up with for this would involve Annie.

"So, after considering a couple of different ones, I think my favorite Christmas was five years ago. We were just teenagers then, hard as that is to believe. But we were just teenagers and when we drew names for a gift exchange in our Sunday School class I got her name. I got her a gold chain necklace, the nicest one I could afford, and when I gave it to her I just kind of blurted out, 'I love you, Annie.' Technically, this did not happen on

Christmas day, but it's my favorite."

Henry gave him a thumbs up as he sat down and Jeff nodded approval. Gil hoped Jeff would follow him, but Sergeant Harrison stood. His story was about a Christmas in Ohio when he was about ten years old and the family was snowed in by a severe blizzard. Instead of the stressful time it might have been, Christmas day was one of remarkable closeness. "It was kind of like we were the only people on the face of the earth," he concluded, "and that was okay because we had each other."

O'Dell and Jensen stood at the same time. They looked at each other and laughed, each motioning for the other to go first. Jensen finally did and told about a Christmas when his grandmother was on her death bed and his last talk with her. It was a sad occasion but he made it into a happy story. O'Dell said his story was nothing special, and told about a year he and his brother had been fighting and made up on Christmas day.

When O'Dell finished, Jeff was the only one left to speak. He got up slowly, as if reluctant to tell his story. Gil and Henry said things to encourage him. Gil knew that Jeff, like him, was on the shy side. He also knew Jeff was an effective story-teller when he chose to be.

"Okay," Jeff began, "we've heard where several guys are from today and I'm always interested in that. I've always wanted to travel, but on my own, not on Army orders. But, hey, I might never have made it to France, you know. And we might even get to see Paris someday. So, anyway, I'm a farm boy from Indiana and that suits me just fine.

"I didn't have to put a lot of thought into my favorite Christmas. It was the one my mother came home on Christmas Eve after being in the hospital a week or so and having heart surgery. We had been afraid she might not make it."

Jeff paused and didn't speak for a moment. Gil could see he was becoming emotional.

"I may have misunderstood," Jeff began again. "If we were supposed to talk about our happiest Christmas, this wasn't it. I thought it was our most memorable Christmas. Well, I guess this one was happy for a day or so. But the end of my story is my mom passed away a week later. I was just fifteen. It was hard."

All the other platoon members were silent as Jeff went back to his bench and sat down. Gil put an arm around his shoulders and told him, "Man, I didn't know. I'm sorry."

Captain Daniels was somber when he stood to speak again. "I'm sorry for your loss, Sergeant Bartlet. But thank you for sharing that with us. We are all as one here, and that means sharing our grief as well as our happy moments. So, I guess we're finished with the formalities. Let me just wish you Merry Christmas one more time and let's get to the leftovers in the kitchen and enjoy the rest of the day. Tomorrow we go back to work!"

Late in the afternoon, Gil sat at the end of a table by himself and wrote:

Dearest Annie,

Well, the Army actually gave us Christmas day off. We had a nice one and we all enjoyed it. Tomorrow it will be back to work.

I'm thinking about being home for Christmas and next year I know I will be. And we'll be married and 'home' will be our own place. If you will let me, I'll even help with housework!

Wherever we live, Annie, I want us to have lots of flowers and a vegetable garden. Gosh, right now I'd give my left thumb for a big ripe tomato. And I must have a dogwood tree. When the dogwoods bloom it is the surest sign of spring and renewal. And I'd like hollyhocks, pink ones. I know you love hollyhocks.

Henry makes fun of me whenever I mention things

like this. He thinks anybody who is not from the city like he is has to be a 'hick,' whatever that really means. He's not nasty about it, though. Henry really is a very nice guy.

If there is a single good thing about being drafted into the Army it is having a chance to know people like him. I most likely would have gone my whole life without knowing anybody from Philadelphia.

Well, it's about bed time. I hope you had a Merry Christmas. I hope I dream about next year, when we will spend it together. My love to all, but especially to you, Miss Annie.

Forever and ever,
Gil

13

SINCE GIL HAD been on the move, Annie hadn't had a letter in ages. She found herself at loose ends. It seemed like Gil had been gone forever and now that he was in France and probably in a combat zone his letters had become few and far between.

Her daily conversations with her grandmother no longer kept Annie's spirits up. Mother White lived in the past; Annie looked to the future. She ached for something interesting to do.

They were clearing the breakfast dishes when she had a thought. "Grandmama, why don't we go to Paducah and see a movie or something?" She spoke on impulse but surely it was a reasonable request. She was surprised by Mother White's response.

"My goodness, Annie! How do you come up with such wild ideas?"

"Why do you call that a wild idea?" Annie didn't care that her irritation showed. "That's what people do. We live holed up here like we're not even a part of the real world."

Mother White slammed a saucer down angrily. When she spoke, it was in a tone of voice Annie had not heard before. "Well, missy, being holed up here was good enough for your grandfather and me for fifty years and for your mother, too, when she was growing up. But I guess we wasn't part of the real world you live in."

Annie was at a loss for words. She had no idea why her question was offensive. She wanted no quarrel with her grandmother, but at the same time she was irritated that her simple suggestion had led to such an unreasonable outburst. She put her plate in the sink and went to her room.

She closed the door and lay on her bed. *I should have stayed and talked out our differences. Now I've just made it harder.* But then she thought, no, Mother White was the one being unreasonable. Let her make the first move to smooth things over.

She got up and pulled aside the curtains to let more light come in through the window and took Gil's letters from a drawer in the nightstand. Then she lay down again and started to read the letters once more, even though she had read them so many times already she almost knew them by heart. She found more comfort in reading them aloud for some reason. She took one of the most recent letters from the thin stack and began to read.

Gil wrote about something he remembered from Fort Jackson and about Army training. When it came to where he was now and what he was doing, it seemed there really was nothing he could tell her. He tried to make it sound as if everything was routine Army life and she wondered what he might have told her if he could have. And then the passage she had read over and over:

"I can't see to write after lights out so I must hurry and finish now. I want you so much, my sweet Annie. I will hold you in my arms in my dreams and I hope you dream of me, too. I long for the day when this war is over and we lie together in the flesh and not just our dreams."

This was the most passion Gil ever had expressed. She read his words again and imagined his dreams were real and she lay in his arms and they made love and they were the only two people in the world and the night was theirs alone and Gil's passion was alive and physical and she wanted it never to end. The words—Gil's words—had ignited her own passion and she longed for her lover, to have him here and now.

There was a light tapping on her door.

"Annie, honey, can I come in?" her grandmother called softly.

Annie put Gil's letters back in the drawer and opened her door. Mother White's remorse was apparent, and she opened her arms wide as an invitation to embrace. Annie's response was to accept the invitation. As they came together in a strong hug, Mother White said the things Annie wanted to hear.

"I'm sorry, Annie," she said. "I don't know why I was a crochety old woman all at once. Maybe you just reminded me of all the things I've missed. I live in the past because that's all I have but you have your whole life ahead. I want that life to be better than mine. I want you to get out and have some fun, okay?"

"You're so good to me, Grandmama. I'm lucky to have what I have."

They went to the kitchen and sat at the table and had more coffee. They talked about Gil and how different things would be when he got home. Mother White said she wanted Annie to go to Paducah and see a movie and have supper in a nice restaurant or do any of the other fun things she assumed someone could do there. She went to a cabinet drawer and took something out and brought it back to the table. It was the key to the old Dodge.

"I want you to take my car," she told Annie, "and drive it like it was your own. Go to Paducah or anyplace you like and find some young people who do things you like. Find places you want to take Gil when he comes home and let him see you didn't just set around with your old grandma and cry in your coffee while he was gone."

She dropped the key on the table and went to a closet and

got her purse. When she came back she had a $10 bill, which she extended to Annie. "Take this," she said, "and get out and enjoy life while you're young."

Annie tried to refuse both the key and the money, but Mother White insisted she take them and Annie gave in. This was what she wanted, after all.

Two days later, wearing her prettiest dress, she was on her way to Paducah. She was both excited and a bit nervous. She had never been to Paducah and was uncertain what to expect. Gil had always said in this situation you just have to take the plunge and see what you're diving into. But Gil wasn't here; she was on her own.

Even had she been prepared for Paducah, nothing could have readied her for the Brookport Bridge crossing the Ohio River into Kentucky. As she approached the steep bridge access she looked ahead to the massive steel framework that towered high above the narrow bridge floor and was so intimidated that had it been possible she might have turned back. She didn't have that choice, of course, but she did slow Mother White's old Dodge to a crawl and tried to steer down the center line as far from the edges as possible.

Annie didn't know she had to pay until she came to the toll booth and an attendant asked for fifteen cents. All she had was the $10 bill, which she held out to the elderly man in the booth.

"Is that all you got, lady?" he asked rather rudely. "Ain't you even got a one?"

His tone made her feel like she had done something wrong. She apologized and said that was all the money she had.

"Well, I ain't got a lot of change," he said, and handed the bill back to her. "You can go on across for free this time, but next time at least have a quarter or something."

She drove ahead, still wondering what she was getting blamed for. That small worry soon was replaced by a more serious concern. She was just across the bridge and back on level ground when something in the car's steering seemed to go crazy. The steering wheel was almost wrenched from her hands and the vehicle veered off onto the shoulder of the highway and was headed toward a steep drop down a high embankment when she managed to stop.

She sat with her face in her hands wondering what to do when the car coming behind her pulled off the road in front of her and stopped. The driver got out and walked back beside her door. She rolled down the window.

"Looks like you got a little trouble, ma'am. Anything I can do to help?"

"I don't know," she told him, barely able to hold back her tears. "I don't know what happened."

"Well, I don't know if it blowed out or what, but what happened is you got a flat on that right front wheel. Pulled you right off the road."

Annie got out and walked around to the front of her car and was dismayed by what she saw. The tire on the right front wheel not only was flat, but looked to be coming apart. Following the directions of the friendly driver who had stopped to help, she opened the Dodge's trunk to look for a jack and spare tire. There was neither.

"Well, ma'am, it looks like you're kinda between a rock and a hard place." As Annie struggled for a response, he went on. "I know somebody down in Paducah who can help you out. Come on and get in and I'll take you down there."

When they were back on the highway, he told her they were going to Howard's Garage and Tire Shop, that was run by a young mechanic who could do about anything an automobile needed to have done.

"They say he's got some kind of physical handicap that kept him out of the war," he said, "but I don't know what it is. He's a fine-looking young man, strong as a bull, and seems like he's got a heart of gold. Ain't no doubt in my mind he'll get you back on the road."

Despite her doubts, Annie was grateful to the stranger for giving her at least a ray of hope. She did her best to express her gratitude but he shrugged off her words and said he had only done what anybody would have done and he was glad he could help. When they reached their destination, he went in ahead of her and got Howard's assurance he would take care of Annie, then wished her luck and went on his way. Annie held her breath as she waited.

She had concentrated on Howard the mechanic, but her focus quickly shifted to Howard the man. He probably was Gil's age and he was strikingly good looking. He greeted her with a warm smile, introduced himself, and assured her he would get her back on the road. She told him her name was Annie and he said that was a pretty name and did she live in Paducah and when she said no he said he thought not because if he had seen her around he certainly would have noticed.

"We've just got one problem that may slow things up a little bit, Annie," he said. He seemed to make conversation as easily as if they were old friends. "As I'm sure you know as well as anybody, the war's caused a lot of shortages. One thing we can't get is tires. The man that brought you said you're driving a Dodge and I can pretty likely guess what size shoes it wears, but I won't be sure till I see it. I keep every used tire I can get my hands on and if we're lucky I'll have something that fits."

Annie tried to tell him how grateful she was, and when she spoke he seemed to give her the same strict attention he would give the governor of Kentucky. And when he looked her straight in the eyes she felt a deep blush creeping up her neck and flushing her cheeks.

"Tell you what," Howard said, "you are the most important

customer I have right now. I'm going to close the shop and grab a jack and let's load up in my old truck and go check things out. Sound to you like the way to go, Miss Annie?"

The truck was behind the garage. He loaded whatever tools he needed and drove it around to the front. When Annie came out he locked the shop door behind her and opened the passenger side truck door and offered a hand to help her in. Once again she felt herself blush.

Shortly after the Brookport Bridge came into sight, they reached her car sitting on the opposite shoulder headed toward them. It was right on the edge of the highway fill and tilted slightly to the right and Howard said it looked like a frog about to jump. With a couple of quick stops and reversals, he turned the truck around on the highway and parked on the shoulder in front of the old Dodge. Annie was fascinated by the quick skill with which he took off the wheel and put a block under the car, threw the wheel in the back of the truck, and was ready to head back to the shop.

"May just be your lucky day," he said as he climbed into the driver's seat beside her. "Pretty sure I've got a good tire that will fit."

He did have, and in a matter of minutes he had it mounted on the Dodge wheel and was ready to go back and put it on. Annie had worried all along that she didn't have enough money to pay for all this but had been embarrassed to ask. Now she had to.

"Well," Howard said, "tell you what. I have to get five dollars for the tire, but the labor is on the house. I kind of feel like it was my pleasure to get to meet and help a pretty lady like you and I hope the next time you make it to Paducah you will stop by the shop and let me take you to lunch or something."

Annie could feel that she was blushing again. It was embarrassing, but there was something in Howard's authentic politeness that she found charming and, yes, attractive. She fumbled with her purse to get the $10 bill. He went to his cash register to get change and she remembered the bridge toll and, embarrassed again, asked if it would be any trouble for him to give her some small change.

"Ma'am," he answered with mock seriousness, "as a Paducah businessman it is my duty to serve your interests in any way I can. If you'd like your change in nickels and dimes I'll go to the bank and fetch you nickels and dimes."

Annie had to laugh and she could tell he was pleased that she did. He rewarded her with his brightest smile.

An hour later he had the new tire on her car and when she said she was going home rather than drive on to Paducah as originally planned he turned her car around on the highway. They lingered, neither of them really wanting to say goodbye. Annie extended her hand and he took it, raised it to his lips and kissed it.

"I want to see you again, Annie," he said, then walked to his truck and drove away.

Before Annie started, she took a dime and a nickel from her purse. She would not be made to feel guilty again for not having the right toll! She already knew she was going to have problem enough with guilty feelings about her attraction to Howard.

14

AFTER THE THIRD chow Captain Daniels called for a formal assembly of the platoon so he could bring the troops up to date on
a number of things. Foremost among these was the status of the
war itself. Let there be no doubt the Americans were winning,
he told them, and Germany was on its last legs. Hitler's desperate winter counteroffensive out of the Ardennes, although it had
been costly to American forces and no doubt extended the war
and slowed the Allies, had been successfully blocked by Patton's
Third Army and now Patton was moving like a freight train toward Germany. At a high cost, American bombers already were
laying waste to the German heartland.

"As always, the good news is tempered by the fact that a lot
of your brothers in arms have given their lives," the captain said.
"The Germans are good soldiers and a tough enemy. It's been a
tough slog freeing France but pretty soon we're going to be
fighting to take Berlin."

More directly to the point, changes at the front were beginning to affect the nature of the 2nd Platoon's work. They no
longer were remote from the combat zone and from now on
they might be involved directly in attacks on specified targets in
enemy-held territory.

"You never know," he said, "you might have to use some of

those things you learned in basic training at Fort Jackson."

This brought a laugh from the platoon sergeants.

"Sir, I hope you're not talking about using the bayonet," one of them called out. "I had as much bayonet fighting as I'd ever want. Pretty sure I could get along without ever seeing one again." This brought a good laugh from the other platoon members as well as from Captain Daniels.

"Hey, that just means you should be good at it," the captain told him. "How 'bout it? Anybody remember the *spirit* of the bayonet?"

"KILL!" they all yelled in unison. Then they laughed and clapped and the captain joined them.

"Well, I'm inclined to think that bayonet fighting has pretty much gone the way of the horse cavalry," the captain said. "And it may be true that nothing's certain, but I don't see any of you gentlemen charging an enemy line on a galloping horse thrusting a Patton saber."

The rest of the gathering was spent on small administrative matters that didn't seem to Gil to affect the men much, but obviously added to their commander's workload. For the first time since they had set up shop, no team had a night assignment. They all sat around nursing bottles of beer until time to hit their bunks.

Gil went to bed feeling almost no tension. He had bought into Henry's "system" and was determined to take things one day at a time, do his duty for his country, write Annie as much truth as he could get away with, and not spend sleepless nights worrying about things he could not change. Minutes later he was sound asleep. He slept through the night and when he woke in the morning did not even remember dreams of Annie. His emotional state was in his own hands and mental determination gave him the power to control it. The old Gilbert Bennett no longer existed.

His confidence would be tested soon enough. Captain Daniels' prophecy already had come true. For the first time, 2nd Platoon—Gil's team, anyway—would be directly involved in action against the enemy. The captain laid out his table-sized field map and pointed out a landmark some 25 miles to their northwest.

"In my opinion we've been way too long getting to this one," he said, "but I think I know why. It's an easy strategic bombing target and somebody higher up figured they could get that. Well, Flying Fortresses with big bomb loads coming out of England have bigger targets to get to and this one is nowhere close to making the list. Battalion says it's our baby, and the sooner, the better."

Captain Daniels went on to explain that the Germans, after capturing the little French village here, had converted the village's two water system storage tanks to use for gasoline storage. This had given them a superb location right in the middle of one of their toughest combat zones and made it a lot easier to maintain a vital fleet of vehicles, including at least a couple of tank battalions. These probably were 3,000-gallon tanks and they were mounted on steel legs raising them about twenty feet off the ground. Easy targets for a soldier packing any kind of small explosive. But it was somewhat more complicated due to the tanks' location.

"It's hard to see on a map this scale," the captain said, "but there is a narrow river here, in a deep gorge. And guess what? The tanks are at the top of the bank on opposite sides of the river."

This would be a challenging assignment, but he was confident the 2nd Platoon, and this team in particular, was up to the job. He was ready to lay out the details. They would destroy the tanks tonight.

Once again, Henry would be the driver on this mission. Gil and Jeff would carry small and easily rigged TNT explosive charges that had ample power to blow up the gasoline storage tanks and leave raging fires impossible for the Germans to extinguish. Given the topography, they would have to separate three miles above the village to be on opposite side of the river when they got to it. They would have no communications equipment, which complicated the need to blow both tanks at the same time.

Jeff offered a possible fix for this, wondering if they couldn't keep running signals by flashlight. The captain was receptive.

"I'm fully confident you two trail mates can manage that one," he said. "The village is on the west side of the river. There is hardly anything but woods on the east side. Intel reports indicate the Germans don't bother to post guards at the tanks, a ridiculous and costly mistake on their part, eh?"

All three sergeants were about to react to his mention of intelligence reports. The captain had a ready answer.

"Yes, gentlemen, I hate to break it to you, but we are not the only ducks on the intelligence pond. You wouldn't know, but 3rd Platoon overlaps our sector from time to time. I just hope they are as good as we are. Any questions on the big picture?"

Given no response, he turned to a few specific details he needed to cover. First was the explosives. Did they have any explosives training at Fort Jackson? They had, but not enough. He showed them the small TNT cannisters they would carry, said they merely needed to attach one to the top of a leg right under the tank, and demonstrated the timing devices they would set to delay the charges until they had plenty of time to get down and get some distance away before it blew.

"Sir, how much time should we put on there?" Gil asked.

"I'd recommend 15 minutes," the captain said. "Just be sure you are on the same page on this one. We don't want the tanks to go up a half hour apart."

Henry had waited patiently for any discussion of his role as driver. Captain Daniels had saved this for last.

"I hate to bring it up again," he said, "but sergeant it is essential that you follow those driver's orders to the letter. Certainly, I don't want to lose either of these good men and I don't think there's much danger of that. But I don't have to tell you this is a dangerous mission smack into the heart of German territory. Something could happen. I've plotted the distances and times and double checked them and there's nothing built in that should jeopardize the schedule. If one of the men is not there when he's supposed to be, *you will leave him!* Have I made myself clear?"

The Three Bees all acknowledged the captain's order. They were ready to get things together and be ready to load the Jeep as soon as it was dark and launch a mission that surely would have immense benefits for the Allied forces—if they were able to pull it off.

In his mind, Gil began to compile a litany of factors this one involved that gave it the potential to be a very tough assignment. First was the mission goal itself. This time, there would be no silent slipping in and slipping out; they had to blow up two large tanks of gasoline, which would hardly go unnoticed. The second worrisome factor was distance. There would be many miles to cover in enemy territory, including the getaway after blowing up the tanks. How fast could the Germans get forces out looking for the saboteurs? Next, he wished he knew more about the structures they targeted. He would have to climb twenty feet up one of the legs the tank was mounted on. Captain Daniels had shown concern about this one, too. He said his only information was a brief intel report calling the leg "climbable." He would rather it said there was a ladder. Gil's final issue was the topography. Especially on the village side of the river, how much of a factor might the deep river gorge be? It clearly limited both access and escape routes.

But what the hell? It was not like these were things for him to consider before casting a vote. The vote already had been taken at some higher level. The mission was on.

Henry eased the Jeep up to the backdoor and the other two men climbed in. There was just enough added to the cargo this time to make them crowded. Once Gil and Jeff were settled in their seats, Henry turned sideways in his, facing them. "Guys," he said, "I want to set a marker on this right now, and then it won't be mentioned again. You heard the captain's orders on the pickup schedule. He didn't cut me any slack. So, here's the bottom line. If you're not there, I *will* wait, but no more than ten minutes. So that's it. Let's get moving."

Gil thought the day had been hot, but if it had the heat went down with the sun. He wasn't dressed as heavily as he needed to be for the chilly night air and riding in the open Jeep made it a good deal worse. He had been careless in not preparing for this, but admitting this to himself now did not bring a second chance. He was happy when Henry finally said they were almost to their drop off point. They had been in open country most of the way, driving narrow country roads much of the time and frequently crossing farm fields. Now the area seemed to be mostly forested.

Henry parked the Jeep in what Gil thought surely was the darkest spot on the European continent. He hurried to get out of the Jeep and flap his folded arms to try and warm up. Henry and Jeff were pulling things out of the vehicle and laying aside those for Gil. Henry said he was supposed to check and see that they had everything, then snickered. "So neither one of you has mentioned it, but you don't know which side of the river you're working. Right?"

"I don't guess it makes any difference," Jeff replied.

"Well, the captain gave me instructions on how to handle that. Simple as black and white and he has it written out. Even stuck in a quarter, because the decision is made by a coin flip. So, heads Gil takes the west side of the river and tails Jeff does. That's the village side. Got it?"

They agreed and Henry flipped the quarter so it would land right at their feet. A quick check by flashlight and Gil had the duty of getting a TNT charge on the German gasoline tank on the village side of the river. Now he and Jeff had to coordinate their movement with flashlight signals as they made their way three miles down the river to their objectives. It was easy walking on Gil's side, following a narrow, rutted dirt road that ran close to the high riverbank. Jeff evidently didn't have it so easy; Gil had to stop often and wait for him to catch up. Coordinating their advance with flashlight signals proved harder than they had expected, too. The opposing riverbanks were not always parallel in height and there was a lot of underbrush that light might not penetrate on Jeff's side.

At one point, watching for Jeff's light through the trees somehow reminded Gil of Soloman's Woods. How he would love to be there, where he had found such contentment through the years. instead of here in enemy territory somewhere in France! *But, hey, man! You finally have a chance to do something to help shorten the war and make it home again.* That thought gave him such an instant charge of excitement he pumped a fist in the air like he had an audience.

Gil had concentrated only on getting to the village three miles downstream, without worrying about what he faced once he got there. While they expected Jeff's cover to last all the way to his target, Gil might very well find himself on lighted village streets. At least it was the middle of the night so there should not be many people out. And even if there were, his dress as a French laborer should get him by if he didn't have to talk.

It took longer than expected to get to the village, partly because of Jeff's slow going and partly because it was probably a half mile farther than expected. This discrepancy probably was due to misinformation in the original data the assignment was drawn from but could have been Henry's fault if he made an error in locating the drop-off site. Regardless, the late arrival gave them less time to get in, blow the Germans' fuel tanks, and get out. Gil waited at the edge of the village for one last signal from Jeff and having received it, walked ahead. He needn't have worried; the streets were dark and totally deserted.

He was within sight of the elevated tank on the riverbank in minutes. Once again, there was no reason for one of his greatest worries. The tank sat in the open, with no fence or any other kind of barrier around it and no guard post. Gil still found this hard to believe. He slipped carefully from one dark area to another until he reached the steel structure. Once again, good fortune was his lot; one leg had a ladder leading to the bottom of the tank. And across the ravine, he saw a quick flash of light from Jeff.

He unpacked the TNT charge, scrambled up the ladder, set the explosive's timer for 15 minutes, and all but slid back to the ground. He hoped desperately he could get back to the woods before the explosions rocked the village. When he had retraced his route back to the pickup point, Henry would be the most welcome sight of his life.

Heading back through the village, Gil kept to the darkest sides of the streets and walked as fast as he could. He was near the center of the village when the ponderous explosion of the tank across the river followed seconds later by the nearer one lit up the night sky and brought a forceful blast of rushing wind that caused trees to bend and windows to shatter.

He was fighting to stay on his feet when he was hit in the back of the head by blowing debris and momentarily stunned. He tried to get to a utility pole to hold onto and stumbled over a curb and went down. One leg was bent beneath his body and pain shot through it at a level he'd never felt before. Surely it was broken.

In what seemed to him to be little more than seconds, people were pouring into the streets and running about wildly. They all had heard and felt the explosions, but no one knew yet what and where they were.

Except the German soldiers. They were filling the streets and they seemed to have realized immediately that their critically important gasoline storage tanks had been destroyed by a saboteur and the saboteur had not had time to get far. He might be in the throng of people around them in the streets.

Gil hadn't seen it and as far as he knew it had not been mentioned in the intelligence reports drawn on for this assignment, but there clearly was a German military unit stationed in the village. This many troops had to be coming out of a barracks. He couldn't see the markings of rank but a few were barking orders and pointing while the others looked to be rounding up the French civilians like herding cattle. A woman on the street corner was screaming and trying to pull away from two soldiers who held her. An officer struck her across the face with his riding crop. A man broke out of the group and tried to run toward a side street but was struck down and dragged onto the sidewalk by two of the uniformed Germans

A squad of soldiers was moving up the street toward Gil, shouting instructions to the civilians moving as a small human wave before them. He tried to stand but fell back again and realized he had little hope of escape.

15

ANNIE DIDN'T EXPECT visiting her parents in the house where she had spent more than twenty years of her life to feel strange, but it did. It seemed like she should be the one inside, welcoming visitors at the front door. As she and Mother White got out of the car and walked the short gravel path to the front door it was almost as if she were viewing this scene in a mirror, looking in when she should be looking out.

She recalled very few times when her mother was not the one to welcome afternoon visitors and her father always had greeted those who came at night. But her world was spinning backward now and it was her father who suddenly appeared in the open door and stood waiting for them. He pulled Annie into a strong embrace and barely acknowledged Mother White with a nod. They went into the living room, where Annie's mother stood waiting, her face marked by an expression of modest concern. This was unusual to the extent it concerned Annie, in turn.

"Are you okay, Mama?" she asked. "You look like you're worried about something. Cows in the corn?"

The added inquiry was a family tradition, handed down by at least two generations. They all assumed that at some time in the past cattle getting into cornfields had been a real problem. It had been several years since there had been any livestock on the farm.

"Oh, no, it's nothing," her mother told her. "You go on with your father so Mother White and I can visit."

Her father stood waiting beside the doorway to the kitchen, like they had a prearranged commitment to go out that way. Annie felt like the easiest route for her was to just go along. Maybe she had missed something.

"I've got something to show you," her father said. "Come on. It's out back."

Annie followed him around the old smoke house, which hadn't been used for years and leaned precipitously front to back. "That's about to fall down, Daddy," she told him. He didn't say anything but made a point of showing he wasn't worried by a wave of the hand. He wasn't using his cane and walked so fast she was having a hard time keeping up. She started to complain but didn't want to be waved off again.

He was several steps ahead of her by the time they got to the weeping willow tree beside the small pond, and the bench he had made just for her when she was eight years old. He casually seated himself and motioned for her to come sit beside him.

"What is it you wanted to show me?"

"Oh, I ain't got nothing to show," he said, looking somewhat sheepish. "That was just a, what do you call it? A ruse? It was just to get you out where Mother White couldn't hear. Your mama doesn't want her to know yet."

Annie's curiosity was about to be overtaken by her irritation. "Know what, Daddy? What's the big secret, anyway?"

Instead of giving her the straight answer she wanted and thought she deserved he got up from the bench and, with his hands clasped behind his back, walked to the bank of the pond. He stood, silently, staring over the water as if contemplating the great issues of civilization.

"Daddy, what the hell is going on?"

He came back and sat beside her again.

"I'm going to tell you more than your mama wanted to let

out yet," he said solemnly. "We was just going to tell you we're selling the farm, but I'm going with the whole load. Annie, your mama and me are splittin' up."

Annie was stunned. She couldn't believe what she had just heard. And yet there was no denying it, given the source. Her mother and father, after more than thirty years together, were going their separate ways.

"Why, Daddy?" was all she could think to say.

"Well, girl, I guess it's hard to understand from where you are. It's took me and her a long time to get our heads around it, and even now I don't know if I can tell you in a way that makes much sense. It just seems like we have changed so we're not the same people anymore and don't want the same things. Your mama has decided she wants to live in the city—Evansville or Paducah or maybe even Nashville or Memphis. And, well, I just ain't cut out for that."

Annie still was trying to find words to give voice to her feelings. Her family roots were deep and, she'd always thought, stable. And now this anchor was failing and she felt like she was being set adrift.

Her father did what he'd always done. He walked away. Annie knew she would talk with him later about all this, but it was painful for him and he couldn't find the courage to face it yet. He walked on toward the meadow and she turned and went back to the house.

She wanted to talk to her mother but had to remember that her mother wouldn't know that she knew. Her father had been out front with more than her mother was ready to reveal. She found her mother in the kitchen talking with Mother White about what kind of cucumbers made the best dill pickles. She had nothing to contribute.

Later in the day, after she and Mother White had been home for some two hours, Annie was going insane with frustration over not being able to talk with anyone about her parents. Her father's revelation had been devastating and she knew there was a great deal more to it that she wanted and probably needed to know. Had Mother White picked up even a hint about what was going on? Annie decided to try and find out.

"I'm not very hungry for supper, Grandmama," she said. "I think I need a cup of coffee, though. Would you like some?"

She checked the pot and found there was plenty of coffee for at least two cups. Without waiting for Mother White's response she poured a cup for each of them and carried one to her grandmother sitting at the table.

"Mama seemed a little low today," she said as she pulled out a chair for herself. "Didn't you think so?"

The response was exactly what she expected. "No, I didn't notice anything unusual."

Annie tried every ploy she could think of to try to get anything she could out of Mother White: what did they talk about, did Mama talk about Daddy, didn't she think Mama looked kind of tired? If there were any crevices to be wedged into none of them surfaced.

The coffee was all they wanted. They skipped supper and tried to find some good music on the radio but had no luck. Mother White gave up easily and switched off the set. Annie had figured out a good while ago that her hasty action grew out of her fear of bad news from the war. She didn't mind because she worried about the same thing.

Most people seemed to think the war in Europe was going as well as they could hope. Paris had been liberated and Walter Cronkite of the United Press offered regular reports on advances by the Allied armies. Families of American soldiers were very much aware that reports on the war in general were not what mattered, though. Reports of individual casualties were their real concern. Armies won or lost, soldiers lived or died.

Annie had managed to delude herself that Gil was not in danger. Had she examined her own logic, though, she would have recognized the over-emphasis on his supposed location well behind the front lines and marked it as a self-serving rationalization. There was no safe zone and, anyway, troops on both sides were constantly on the move.

She would not admit to herself that in recent weeks much of her concern for Gil had been replaced by concern for herself and the nagging question of whether she possibly could have fallen in love too easily and too fast. She loathed herself for even accepting this as a thought in her head but she could not make it go away.

She remembered Gil saying once that if Mother Nature burdened us with many weaknesses, she also dangled before us an almost infinite array of defense mechanisms. She told him he was awfully smart and he said he had learned this in an anthropology class. But it was comforting to remember this now, and she decided to play Mother Nature's game. She would take advantage of Gil's teaching and move beyond her own stale thinking. She would ask her mother directly what was going on.

Annie slept well that night.

As soon as they had finished doing the breakfast dishes and put things in their proper places the next morning, she told her grandmother she had some errands to run and would be gone for a couple of hours. Before Mother White had a chance to ask questions, she snatched the key to the old Dodge from its drawer and was gone.

She drove fast, like she was on an urgent mission, straight to the place she used to live. She wasted no time on formalities like knocking, but pushed open the front door and charged in, unexpected and unannounced. The living room was empty. Her mother sat at the kitchen table, alone, drinking something that had odors of both coffee and alcohol.

"Annie!"

"Yes, Mama. The Prodigal daughter has returned."

Her mother stood and pulled out a chair. Annie slid into it and leaned her elbows on the table, opposite her mother. She accepted the proffered cup of hot chocolate, quite conscious of the fact it would be different from whatever her mother was drinking.

"Well, I'm glad to see you so early, but surprised you're back so soon," her mother said, her smile authenticating her words.

Annie went straight to the point.

"Daddy told me you two are splitting up," she said flatly. "I'm your daughter, Mama. Don't I deserve to know why?"

Her mother clearly was taken by surprise. She didn't know the word had got out and she was not prepared to deal with Annie's question. But her daughter's straightforward inquiry deserved an answer, and in any case it was not one she could ignore forever.

"I didn't expect that, Annie," she said. "I didn't know you knew. But, yes, you deserve to know. I'm not sure I can adequately explain it, but I will try."

"That's all I ask. And thank you for being open about this. I know it probably isn't easy."

Her mother took a long draught from her mug, then set it down easily on the table. It seemed as if she was in no hurry to speak. "You know," she said finally, "a month ago I probably could not have even come close to describing how I feel. And it's not like I've practiced or anything like that. But I wanted to make sure I was doing the right thing and I went over everything in my mind, over and over. And I know what I'm doing is right."

Annie felt closer to her mother at this moment than she ever had before. They were not communicating now as mother and daughter, but as two adult women ready to lay open their very souls to one another. She was swept by a wave of gratitude.

"Mama, I don't want you to tell me anything you don't want to," she said softly. "But please know that whatever you say will become a part of me just as it is a part of you. Let our spirits entwine so we can walk this long road together. I love you, Mama."

"Oh, my goodness, honey! You said that so beautifully! I don't think I can match it. But let's just say honest openness is more important than eloquence, and I'll do my best. It just seems like, I don't know, like life has been passing me by and I am running out of time to catch up. Does that make any sense?"

"Yes, of course it does. Tell me more about how you feel."

Her mother showed a touch of ambivalence, like she wanted to tell all but at the same time keep her deepest secrets. For now, she chose to tell.

"It's just like I'm living in the dark," she told Annie. "It's like I know there's a great, bright world out there but I'm not allowed to see it. I want more than just listening to Bob Hope on the radio. I want to see the Grand Ole Opry, Annie, and I want to see a movie. And I don't want to whine about all the things I've missed, but I have never danced. Oh, I could go on and on. Your father is a good man, Annie. He's a sweet man. And I'll always be grateful that between us we created you. But there has to be more to life . . ."

Her mother broke down and began to weep. She dropped her face on her hands spread flat on the table and sobbed softly. Annie rushed around the table and pulled out the chair next to her and slid in beside her. She clasped her mother in a soft embrace and the two swayed slightly as if to music. But the music that counted was from the beating of two hearts.

Two days later, Annie set out on a new search of her own. Her visit with her mother had melded her doubts and uncertainties with her hidden desires and her determination. She could not make Gil a good wife if she wandered through the darkness for thirty years like her mother had and then betrayed him by loosening their ties in her search for a brighter world.

She dug through the pots and pans in the lower part of the kitchen cabinet until she found what she was looking for. She held out a metal colander with one handle partially detached to Mother White and reminded her that she had mentioned getting the loose handled soldered.

"I know a man who can do it," she said. "His name is Howard and he has a shop in Paducah."

16

GIL KNEW HE couldn't stand without support and crawled to the utility pole just behind him and pulled himself up, pain shooting through his leg. He intended to run and try to find a place to hide but he barely could stand on the painful leg. Running was out of the question. He heard footsteps coming behind him.

"*Monsieur, venez!*"

He turned to find a man hurrying toward him, hands outstretched. The man saw that he couldn't walk and rushed to him and got an arm around his shoulders and virtually dragged him through a narrow gate and to the side of a house. While Gil leaned against a railing, he lifted a cellar door and, without speaking, helped him down steep steps into a semi-finished basement.

"*Nous serons en sécurité ici.*"

Gil felt like he was about to faint from the pain in his leg. His benefactor motioned for him to take a seat in a pastel green chair against the wall and went back to pull the cellar door shut and put something in the bolt so it could not be opened from the outside. He walked back to Gil with a big smile and extended his hand.

"I don't know how I can ever thank you enough," Gil said. "I would have been taken by the soldiers for sure."

"Ahh, American."

"Yes."

He wanted to say more, to introduce himself as Sergeant Gilbert Bennett, United States Army, but this was too much of a risk. He assumed from his behavior the Frenchman was pro-American and anti-German but he couldn't be sure. For that matter, he wasn't sure, even, that the man was French.

"Very sorry. English is not my best language."

Gil started to reply with a clever statement about his total lack of French when a pain like an electric shock shot up his leg and caused him to gasp. He didn't feel bone grating on bone as he might in a fracture, but if he had been standing the pain would have brought him to his knees. He lay back in the chair with his hands over his face and took a deep breath.

"You are injured, no?" the Frenchman said.

"I think it's broken."

Without saying anything more, the Frenchman hurried up the steps to the floor above and disappeared. Gil had no time to be curious; his combination of pain, physical exhaustion, and lack of sleep took over his body and mercifully he went out like a light. His mind was completely numb, as if he were unconscious. He would be this way for a full eight hours.

The two figures standing over him were nothing more than blurred images when he first started to wake. He looked about, trying to recognize where he was. The whole room was out of focus. As his vision cleared, though, he saw nothing that looked even remotely familiar. He was in a strange place and didn't remember how he got there.

"Ahh, on dirait qu'il est réveillé."

"Oui, il dort depuis longtemps."

Gil remembered the Frenchman when he saw his face. Standing beside him was a young woman he had not seen before. Both offered smiles of satisfaction as they knew he could see them.

"You have been sleeping well," the man said. "Is there less pain?"

Until he heard the question, Gil had not remembered the terrible pain he'd been in earlier. Whatever had changed, he was grateful for it. He told the Frenchman yes, there was less pain, and raised up on his elbows, almost in a sitting position. The woman stepped to him and put her palm on his forehead. The cool softness of her hand was in itself soothing.

"My daughter," the man said. "She has some nurse classes."

The young woman extended a hand. "Janelle," she said. "Hello, American."

He extended a hand to Janelle. "Hi. I'm Gil."

"Janelle will take good care for you," the Frenchman said. "Me, I have to go to the bakery. It is, as you say, my profession. The Germans go everywhere searching. But you will be safe here."

While he wouldn't have said he was optimistic, Gil felt hopeful for the first time since he saw the German soldiers on the street. He remembered now the storage tank explosions and the havoc that followed. *Jeff! Oh my God, I hope he got away!* He briefly envisioned the 2nd Platoon Headquarters and Captain Daniels hearing the report on the success of his team's mission. Yes, they had destroyed the tanks and, yes, the Germans got the message that they were vulnerable.

But he hadn't been there to make his report. What were the chances of him ever getting back? Once he didn't make the pickup rendezvous and Henry had to leave him, his teammates probably thought he'd been captured or maybe killed by enemy troops. Captain Daniels would have no reason to think otherwise. He would be replaced and no one would miss him at the 2nd Platoon.

Gil soon lost all awareness of the passing of time. Janelle brought him pain killers and sedatives and strong and delicious wines and there were periods when he hardly knew when one day ended and another began. He was as likely to sleep during the day as the night, and many nights he lay awake for hours at a time with no conscious train of thought.

When reality finally began to catch up with him, he tried to count back in his mind, separating days by events, but they all ran together and he had no other reference points. He still had some pain in his leg, but he no longer believed it to be broken. Janelle had manipulated it in various ways and found no evidence of a fracture. After that she had massaged it and regularly applied some kind of liniment, either of which seemed to leave him pain-free for several hours. She also had massaged the stressed muscles of his shoulders and upper back and he'd come to look forward to the feel of her hands on his bare skin.

Her father brought him up to date on things going on in the village every night when he got home from the bakery. It seemed that general excitement over the sabotage of the storage tanks had worn off some, although that act had brought significant lasting changes. Now that they were gone, the German troop garrison in the village had been reduced at least by half. But an even more important difference, the baker believed, was the hope and optimism the act had brought to the French townspeople. They recognized now that the Germans were not an indestructible fighting machine that would take over and rule France forever.

Gil tried to learn more about Janelle, but she was embarrassed by her complete lack of English and he hated forcing that on her. He did find out she had studied a year in Paris and came home to be with her father after her mother died of encephalitis when that disease swept Europe after the Spanish flu epidemic. She was remarkably competent at expressing herself in simple terms and a few words of English she preferred to write rather than try to say. Gil admired her courage and determination, but most of all was grateful for her medical knowledge. He was getting well under her care.

And his questions about the man who rescued him were about to be answered. Every day, the baker came to talk as soon as he was home from work. Today he had a clear agenda. He said it was time they both reveal their secrets.

"I think you are United States Army," he began, going bluntly into the subject. "And I think you might be our hero."

He paused, and waited a moment to see if Gil might respond. Gil was tempted to tell him the truth, but realized there still was much he didn't know about his situation and opted to be cautious. It also looked to him like the Frenchman didn't expect an outright admission.

"I can tell. You see, I am a soldier, too," the baker went on. "I fought in the first war and I have tried to be a part of the French resistance movement in last years. But there is little need here since we are too remote and I could not go to Paris."

Gil did not say anything, but felt he could trust this man. It was the baker who saved him, of course, by pulling him in off the street almost within sight of the approaching German troops. And most significantly, if the baker had ulterior motives of any kind they undoubtedly would have come out by now.

He responded physically, offering his new friend a serious hand salute.

The baker's intense facial expression barely changed, but there was the slightest hint of a smile. "Yes, we know and understand now," he said, returning Gil's salute. "We need no more talk about this."

For Gil, this had to be one of the proudest moments of his life. And one in which he was most grateful. They needed no more talk about the war, but he must offer his thanks.

"Please know I will always be most grateful," he said. "To you and Janelle. You have saved my life."

"Yes," the baker said, "and now is the time to go. The German garrison's replacements come tomorrow. They will be much too busy to worry about poor Frenchmen on the streets. In the morning a man will come for you, on a motorcycle. He is one of us. You can trust him."

"I don't know what to say," Gil began, "but please—"

The baker interrupted. "There is nothing to say. Except by the way, the man who picks you up knows where to take you home. See, we have our ways, too. Your little 2nd Platoon is not so secret as you think."

Gil might have been speechless, but there was one more obligation. "I'm guessing I won't see you again, sir. But I will always remember. And Janelle—"

"I can tell you the truth. I fear Janelle has feeling for you. There are so few young men these days. I don't want this to go more deep. You will have time to say goodbye to her as you leave. Good night now, my American friend. Sleep well your last night under my roof. God speed."

He turned quickly and hurried up the stairs, switching the lights off as he went. Gil lay in the dark and wondered, was it a danger he would wake and find this all was a dream. But he fell asleep quickly.

Sometime in the middle of the night he was awakened. Someone tugged at his blanket, pulling it aside. It was Janelle. There was enough light he saw when she dropped the robe from her shoulders she stood completely naked. Without speaking, she slipped into his bed. He would not have sought what she came for, but he didn't have to. Her soft woman's body gained for her all she ever might have desired.

It was barely after sunrise when he was awakened again. Janelle was gone and a young man in typical French workman's clothes was shaking him gently.

"Come, we must hurry," he said.

Moments later Gil sat astride the passenger section of the long saddle on a small German motorcycle as the young Frenchman eased it out of the small yard surrounding the baker's house, onto the street. He looked back. Janelle stood in a second-story window, waving a hand. Gil waved back just as the tall board fence blocked his view.

A little more than two hours later, the Frenchman skillfully jerked his cycle into parking position on its stand and Gil climbed off. They were at the back door of the old farmhouse that secretly hid the 2nd Platoon headquarters. He waited until Gil had tried the door and opened it, then was back on the cycle in virtually a single move. He tossed a casual salute to Gil as he turned back toward the road in front of the house and was gone. Gil had never heard his name.

When he first stepped inside, 2nd Platoon headquarters was so quiet Gil initially feared it was deserted. But when he walked into the middle room he found Captain Daniels and three sergeants huddled over a map spread across a wide area of floor too intent on what they saw even to hear him enter. Gil could not have described his own emotions at that moment. He might have been just home from a voyage around the world, he was so thrilled to see these familiar faces.

"Excuse me, sir," he announced himself.

Captain Daniels looked up. His face revealed more than surprise. He was shocked, as if seeing a ghost. As he would explain later, this was how Gil's unexpected arrival struck him. He had assumed Gil to either have been captured or killed by the Germans. He was marked in the captain's daybook as MIA—missing in action.

The captain's usual self-control appeared to desert him as he rushed to Gil with open arms and embraced him like a mother finding a lost child. "My Lord, man," he said, "we thought you were gone! Welcome home, Gil. Welcome home!"

The three sergeants, Elliot, Sampson, and Shaw, followed the captain's lead and shook Gil's hand vigorously and repeated words of welcome. If he had ever doubted, he understood now that he was a member of a *team.* The 2nd Intel Platoon was more than merely a sum of all its parts. Its parts mattered.

"And, hey, you guys must have done a hell of a job on those German storage tanks," Sampson said. "Your teammates didn't have much to say about it after thinking they'd lost you, but the captain says there was a big impact on the Germans."

"That's exactly right," Captain Daniels said. "Battalion got air photos of practically every German piece on wheels abandoned in bunches. Looks like they didn't have any other gasoline supply storage in the whole sector."

Gil had been so caught up in his own personal circumstances that he'd thought little about the mission. Now it was the most important thing he wanted to hear about. The captain's report was the most rewarding message he could imagine. He, Sergeant Gilbert Bennett, a quiet farm boy from southern Illinois, had carried out a mission that could seriously affect the direction of the war and help the Allied advance. His father would be awfully proud.

The captain had more to say. "I can tell you, Sergeant, the success of your mission made such a dent in the German's strength that it has the big guys up top changing their expectations and when they make changes, you know. It almost always brings changes all the way down the line. This time is no exception.

"As of yesterday, 2nd Platoon has an entirely new mission. We will still be going behind the enemy lines, but not quietly, to gather intelligence. Third Army is moving up from the south at a pace that could put American troops on German soil before they know what hit them. We are going to help clear the way."

17

ANNIE HOPED TO find both solace and inspiration at Walnut Creek Church, otherwise she probably wouldn't attend services today. Solace should come with the occasion. The inspiration she needed might be harder to come by. But Pastor Maxwell and church members had so honored Gil that she still felt indebted and surely they would approach her today and ask about him. Or maybe the pastor would mention him again in the morning sermon.

She needed to hear Gil's name, many times over, as if this would validate his existence and fill the blank space left in her memories by his long absence. She was not overly confident this would make much difference, but it was the best possibility she had come up with and she needed to try. It had been ages since there had been a letter from Gil and when Mother White talked about him it was mundane things like how he might manage the farm different from Uncle Ray or how she was sure Elmo missed him.

Nothing seemed to bring Gil's image back to her mind's eye and nothing left her lying in bed at night aching for his touch. Mother White loved to say absence makes the heart grow fonder, but Annie was beginning to fear absence could make the heart forget.

She still was thrilled by Gil's letters—when they came. She had read them all so many times she probably could recite them by heart. She had held them to her breast knowing his fingers had once grasped these very sheets of paper. But the newness of a letter inevitably wore off and there was little else that made her long for his presence the way she used to. She would have felt guilty about this in any case, but she felt horribly so when she came to realize she was thinking of Howard more often than Gil. The trip to Paducah hung over her head as a tiny sample of life as it could be, jerked away before it became real. Might she have fallen in love with Gil simply because he was virtually the only young man she knew?

This time, Mother White had decided she wanted to go to church with Annie. She readily admitted this wasn't for the religious experience; she didn't miss that.

"But, you know, I never dreamed I'd miss my friends so," she told Annie. "I don't think it's right to attend church for social reasons, but I'm afraid that's what it come down to. If God chooses to strike me down for it, well, so be it."

Annie supposed it was all her talk about the tributes to Gil that led to her grandmother's decision. In any number of instances when she had mentioned a specific name, Mother White had responded with a comment like, "Oh, is she looking well?" Or, "My goodness, I haven't seen her for years." For Annie, the positive side of this was the assurance that many of those old friends still were there when she felt sure many others were gone.

When they arrived at Walnut Creek, the parking lot was no more than half filled. Annie remarked that the crowd today was going to be a great deal smaller than normal and wondered aloud if there was any particular reason.

"Maybe they heard I was coming," Mother White replied. Had there been any question, her laugh told Annie she was joking. It would have been unusual had this not been so; Mother White saw the positive side of things.

"Actually, Grandmama, from all the stories I've heard you tell about you and all your church friends, it wouldn't surprise me if your return doubled the attendance. Pastor Maxwell would be very proud, thinking it was his sermons."

She tried to remember the last time she had seen her mother and her grandmother together and decided it was last Thanksgiving. It struck her as odd that her mother had not visited Mother White since she moved in there. This was a big change. As she remembered, her mother used to visit Mother White at least once a week and sometimes more often than that.

They were just getting out of the car when she saw the familiar pickup coming. Her father parked in a row directly behind them and she and her grandmother stood and waited. Her mother was out of the truck in an instant and rushed to them. And it wasn't Annie she seemed most eager to see. It was Mother White. The two of them hugged and talked at the same time and from all appearances could have been old friends coming together for the first time in years.

Annie stood aside and waited for her father. He walked slowly and she saw immediately there was something new. He walked with a cane and obviously leaned on it rather heavily.

"What happened, Daddy? How come the walking stick?"

He waited till he was closer before he responded, and when he did speak there was a touch of irritation in his tone. "Nothing happened. I'm just getting old. Got bad knees, you know." She wished she hadn't made a point of the cane. He may have been walking with one for a long time now and she would not have known.

She walked beside her mother as they went inside and her father and Mother White followed closely behind. As had been the case from the first time she ever attended services at Walnut

Creek, Pastor Maxwell waited just inside the door greeting people as they entered. His countenance, always happy, virtually lit with joy when he saw Mother White. He reached forward with both hands and grasped hers and told her how delighted he was to see her.

"I have to tell you, Sister White, there is a little spot in a back row that has seemed darker with your absence," he told her. "It was always my great pleasure to look over the worshipers and see your smiling face."

Annie might have realized then that it would be Mother White who would get extra attention from the pulpit today and not Gil. She didn't, though, and waited impatiently for Pastor Maxwell to mention Gil's name. He didn't, not now and not once through the entire sermon. And neither did any of the church members who greeted her before and after services. She sat between her mother and grandmother and could tell that Mother White enjoyed the attention engendered by the minister's acknowledgment of her presence and glowing tribute to her past loyalty and contributions to Walnut Creek.

Annie was not in a good mood when services ended. She had foolishly hoped for something that realistically was not likely to happen. Given that failure, she was determined to get some satisfaction on another front. When they got to the car and pickup in the parking lot, she almost rudely demanded of her mother an explanation for why she had not visited her and Mother White, especially since she used to visit very often. She stated the question in a tone that was almost accusatory.

"It's very simple, Annie," her mother explained. "I worried that after you moved in my visits might be seen as checking up on you two. I didn't want Mama to get the idea I might be looking over her shoulder and I didn't want you to think I was worried your grandmother wouldn't take good care of you. I know it was silly of me, but you may understand when you become a mother, yourself. Was that so bad of me?"

Annie was left with conflicting feelings. She decided to just let it ride, or at the very least wait till later and give it more thought. To merely accept it and move on was not her style.

Mother White had overheard some of the conversation. "I do understand," she said. "Nobody is going to fault you for being concerned about our feelings. And I think you can make it up to us really easy. Just come visit us soon."

Annie's father had avoided getting into the conversation. He'd scratched the back of his hand on a newly trimmed hedge that surrounded the parking lot and was dabbing at the trickle of blood with a white handkerchief. Annie reached for his hand to take a look at the injury but he waved her off.

"Nothing to it," he declared. "Barely a scratch."

"Just be sure and put something on it when you get home, Daddy. Even a little scratch like that can get infected."

Her father stepped closer and put an arm around her shoulders. "See, I miss having Annie there to take care of me. When are you going to make that visit you promised?"

"Well, hey, how about tomorrow?"

Her mother and Mother White turned to them to show they were ready to go. Annie's father opened the pickup door for her mother. "Annie's coming to visit us tomorrow," he told her, a ring of excitement in his voice.

Mother White had walked around her car and was getting in. There were no more words as the two pairs got settled in their vehicles and drove out of the Walnut Creek parking lot and turned toward home. Annie sensed that her grandmother was happy with the church visit.

In her usual manner, Mother White said little on the way home. Once they were there and inside, though, she talked almost endlessly about various friends she had seen and talked with for the first time in years. Annie listened patiently, voicing agreement when it was appropriate.

"Well, listen to me," Mother White said, as if suddenly aware of the extent to which she had dominated the conversation. "I just can't seem to hush. I'm sure you have something interesting to tell."

Annie said she really didn't, but asked about the visit she had promised her mother. "I'm going in the early afternoon for a couple of hours," she said. "Would you like to go with me?" Without the slightest hesitation, Mother White said she would.

Not long after supper, Mother White said all the day's excitement had worn her out. She got ready for bed early.

Annie stayed up and listened to the radio. She tried to find one of the broadcast network dramas that would hold her attention, but after several minutes of futile search she gave up. These were not broadcast on Sunday night. She caught the end of the NBC Symphony Concert and tried listening to Jack Benny for a short while. His jokes struck her as kind of stale and not really funny. The Edgar Bergen and Charlie McCarthy show was no better. She switched off the radio and, still not ready for bed, went on the porch and sat in the swing.

There was a pale-shining moon just above the horizon. Was it rising or setting? How was one to know? She and Gil had loved walking in the moonlight and would choose this over almost any other activity. Much of the joy no doubt came from the simple matter of discovery. If there were sources predicting the moon's behavior they didn't know them. They only knew there was moonlight when they discovered it for themselves.

Was this moon visible now over France? Could she and Gil be watching the same moon at the same time? This probably wasn't possible, given that they were continents apart. But she knew it was visible over Paducah.

18

GIL'S REUNION WITH Henry and Jeff was heartfelt all around. If there ever had been any doubt that the Three Bees had melded into a cohesive threesome whose mutual concern for one another ran much deeper than mere function as a team, it had been erased by the traumatic separation. Gil's worry didn't compare with theirs, of course, because he had known he was still alive and expected to be reunited. This had not been true for Henry and Jeff. They had given him up for dead or captured. They did not expect ever to see him again.

But now they were a team again, when except for their personal feelings it probably didn't matter. Captain Daniels had indicated that, for the first time, the 2nd Intel Platoon would be acting as a unit and not as four separate teams. For all practical purposes, they would function again like they were an infantry company rifle squad. Henry wanted to celebrate.

"We're going to see some real *action*, man!" he said to the other two with probably the greatest enthusiasm they had observed since Fort Jackson. "Hey, Adolph, bring 'em on! The Three Bees won't be hiding in the bushes this time."

Neither Jeff nor Gil shared Henry's enthusiasm for their new role. The captain had made no bones about it: they soon could be involved in the shooting. They knew very well that actual combat with a powerful enemy and the surreptitious collecting of intelligence information, even in the same war, were vastly different games.

Jeff pointed a finger at Henry. "Remember, this man's favorite activity at Fort Jackson was the rifle range," he said to Gil. "He didn't mind getting up early for that."

"Yes, I remember," Gil answered. "You would have thought he was looking at a day at the beach. But maybe we ought to remind him that at Fort Jackson we were shooting at targets that didn't shoot back."

As indicated by their conversation, they thought they had a good grasp of the mission to come. But when Captain Daniels called the platoon to order to lay it out in detail they found it to be a much greater challenge than they would have guessed. They still would be going behind German lines but this time they would not be hiding. They would be heavily armed and they would have to fight their way to their objective.

The captain had managed to get the map mounted on a jury-rigged tripod, where it was much more visible. Although it was of a scale too small for the men to see details, it was adequate for showing larger sectors. Using his pointer, he started at the approximate location of the platoon headquarters where they were and traced a line to the small French town of Neuveville, some eighty miles to the northwest on the Moselle River.

"This," he said, "is our objective."

The men strained to see. There didn't look to be a prominent site where he placed the pointer. He told them why.

"Neuveville is too small to rate a big mark on the map," he said. "And the town itself is not important. What *is* important is the Moselle River bridge there."

He went on to explain that the Germans controlled the little town and, more important, the bridge. This was the only bridge on a long stretch of the Moselle. The Allies would need it when the invasion of Germany began.

"They know its potential value to us as well as we do," Captain Daniels said. "They know U. S. Third Army forces are getting close. And they know, even if they wouldn't admit it, that sooner or later they will have to retreat. Once they cross the Moselle they will blow the bridge. We have intel that it already is wired and ready to blow. And this is where you come in, gentlemen."

The captain had the platoon sergeants' rapt attention. There was dead silence in the room while they waited for him to tell them more. He would not leave them disappointed.

"Battalion got orders from higher up to get a fighting force into Neuveville and unwire the bridge, so to speak, and protect it for our use. And guess what battalion said! Battalion said, 'Oh, yeah. We've got the perfect outfit for that job. Let's arm the 2nd Intel Platoon and send them in!' So you're victims of your own success, gentlemen! I'm sure you appreciate the honor."

The captain got a good laugh for his attempt at humor. The sergeants knew he only wanted to lighten the subject a bit; he had just given them ample notice that they faced a dangerous assignment. Now he was ready to open the floor to discussion.

"We'll be kicking off in two days. Any questions?"

Henry was the first to respond. "Sir, what kind of arming are we talking about? We are going to need more than our carbines for this one."

"I have that same question, Sergeant. And I don't have an answer yet. Battalion has barely had time to get into the details, but they know what they're doing up there. We will find out tomorrow."

Sergeant Elliott, who almost never spoke up during platoon formations, asked the question Gil would have.

"Captain, since we got to get there first, how thick are the Krauts? Between here and there, I mean. What kind of forces will we have to fight our way through?"

Gil could tell the captain was pleased to have Elliott speak up for a change and he was, too. It was an important question and now he wouldn't have to ask it. He had no doubt every sergeant in the platoon was eager to hear what the captain had to say. It was almost like everyone froze waiting for the commander's response.

Captain Daniels pulled the map up a little higher on the tripod. With his pointer he outlined an egg-shaped sector between their present location and Neuveville.

"We know that, on the whole, this sector has a strong enemy force," he told them. "We know the locations of their major infantry units and these will be easy enough to avoid. But there are pockets of smaller units, most of them moving, all over. You could run into a single infantry company, or even a battalion, anywhere. That's what you will be prepared to deal with."

The formation lasted another two hours. The captain answered every question he could, offering as much detail as he had, and candidly admitted when he didn't know the answer. In most instances he believed he would know tomorrow, the eleventh hour for battalion planners. Everything had to be in place soon if they were to kick off the operation in two days.

When the sergeants finally ran out of questions, the captain had two important announcements, both related to their rapidly changing situation. First, given that they soon would be on the move, there would be a mail pick-up and possibly a mail delivery tomorrow. And second, it was time to say goodbye to this beloved little home away from home. This platoon headquarters would cease to exist as soon as they were gone and the old farmhouse would be left empty again.

"I know you will be leaving a piece of your heart here," he said with mock seriousness. "If you feel you must take something to remember it by please feel free to cut a shaving off a windowsill. But please don't degrade it by carving your initials or writing 'Kilroy was here.' You men have too much class for that."

As the group broke up in a round of hearty laughter, the captain thought of one more thing: "Everyone get back in uniform," he called out loudly. "You will be seen as soldiers in the U. S. Army again, and no longer as French peasants."

"Can we take our favorite outfits?" Allison yelled. This was greeted by a chorus of negative epithets.

As the general chaos died down, Gil sat on his bunk to write a letter to Annie. He hoped desperately there would be a mail delivery tomorrow as well as a pick-up. He could barely remember his last letter from Annie, or from anyone else at home. He began to write:

My dearest Annie.

They say we may have a mail call tomorrow. I sure hope so and I hope I get a letter from you. It seems like months since I have had one.

He stopped writing and bowed his head. After what he had done, writing Annie was almost as difficult as speaking to her face-to-face would have been. What he had found so difficult to say before was nothing now. Yes, killing a German soldier was an act of brutality so inhumane he found it hard to accept as his own, but his night with Janelle was a wanton act of betrayal of Annie and his guilt was compounded by the fact he had felt little remorse.

Circumstances under which he had acted as he did were vastly different. Killing an enemy soldier was an obligation in war, his duty to his country. The night with Janelle was unfettered pleasure. No, he didn't initiate it or plan it, but once the temptation lay at his side he had been more than a willing accomplice. He had committed his whole being to Annie and now he had broken that commitment so easily. How could he pretend he was the same man who had exchanged passionate goodbyes that night in Evansville as he waited to board a train to Atlanta and then South Carolina and Fort Jackson for an absence manifestly the duration of the war?

He still hadn't written more when Shaw stopped to see if he might take Gil's letter along with his own letter to his wife and deposit them in the pick-up box. He made the excuse that he still was not quite finished and said he would take it himself later. But he did need to get it done, and as soon as Shaw went on he began writing again:

> We are about to go on a special mission that they say could help end the war faster if we are successful. I can't tell you any more about it, of course, but wish us luck. We are a tough fighting force that stands more than ready to represent the U. S. Army in any meeting with the Germans.
>
> I love you so much Annie. I wish I held you in my arms this very minute.

He stopped writing again and read what he had written. He sat for a moment, then tore the letter into tiny scraps and threw it in the trash.

19

THE SOLDIERS OF the 2nd Platoon, B Troop, 4th Infantry Recon Squadron, sergeants all, were restless that night. There were too many uncertainties lying before them. They had little time to get ready, but then not knowing exactly what they were getting ready for probably left that worry null and void. What kind of armaments were coming from battalion tomorrow? What kind of enemy force would they have to contend with? Did battalion hastily arrange a mail pick-up simply to give them a last chance to say goodbye?

Their fears were not irrational fears of the unknown. Rather, they were quite rational fears of what they knew all too well. Not only were they about to face the real shooting war, but they were about to be thrown into it like animals to be led to slaughter. For Allison and Shelby, who had lost cousins in the Normandy invasion, there was an added reflection on what the loss of their lives might mean to relatives back home.

And there were loved ones waiting at home for all of them, of course. Shaw and Harris were married and all the sergeants still had living parents. They were young men and several had one or more grandparents as well as uncles, aunts, and nieces and nephews and cousins. All the armies in the war and all the civilian populations combined might be a mass totaling millions of people, but the mass was made up of individuals like the men of the 2nd Platoon.

Gil was spared the other men's darkest anxieties. He had thought it out carefully and made a decision. The inevitable live firefight was an opportunity he would not fail to take advantage of. Whether by German bullet or his own, he would be left on the battle site as food for the vultures. The decision left him peace that let him slip into a deep sleep in a matter of only a few minutes.

The sleep was peaceful, too, rich in ancient John Deere tractors, the solitude of Soloman's Woods, walks in the moonlight with Annie, games in the schoolyard, praise from his father for some task well done, and the spring renewal marked by the blooming of the dogwood trees. His dreams placed him in a beautiful southern Illinois world where people were gentle and considerate and cared for each other and life was good—until it wasn't.

Gil's desperate pleas for mercy, little short of screams in the black of night, woke Jeff first. Before Jeff could wake him Henry was up, too, and Sampson and Elliott were awake just enough to think something terrible was happening but they couldn't tell what. It took a sharp slap to the face by Henry, and then another, to make him fully aware of himself and the small spot he occupied on God's green earth.

"Are you okay, man?" Henry demanded. "Look at me! Look me in the face, Gil!"

Gil tried to respond forcefully, in a manner that made him look to be in control. "I'm good, Henry. Guess I was having a nightmare. Sorry I woke you and everybody up. Was I that loud?"

"Naw, I've heard more noise from drunks at the bar. Let's get you back to sleep before the captain hears us."

It was too late for that. As Gil had heard his dad say a million times, "That train's already left the station." Captain Daniels walked up almost in time to hear what Henry said.

"Bennett, we need to talk," the captain commanded. "Come to my office right now."

He turned and went back to his room and Gil followed.

Once they were inside and the captain had closed the door, there were no formalities. Even when the captain told Gil to sit and motioned toward the single chair, it sounded much more like a formal order than a friendly invitation. Gil was a soldier from the enlisted ranks and the captain was his commanding officer.

"Bennett, I want you to be candid with me. Have you ever had or are you now having mental issues?"

"No, sir."

"I don't think you are one who would lie to me but to be clear, if I ever found out you did I'd have you hanged by your thumbs."

"Yes, sir."

The captain appeared to have relaxed some, but Gil knew they weren't finished.

"How is everything at home?"

Gil told him there were no problems.

Captain Daniels had a bemused expression as he seemed to study Gil's face. "Correct me if I'm wrong, but I believe you have a girl waiting back in, where is it?"

"Southern Illinois, sir."

"Oh, yes, I remember. So is everything all right with her? And how about the rest of the family?"

Gil was more relaxed now, having been able to answer the captain's questions without putting himself in jeopardy. He told his commander there were no problems in these personal relationships.

"Well, then," Captain Daniels said, "let's assume you were

just having nightmares. But I want to be sure you understand, the platoon is about to start on a pretty dangerous mission. Every man's life will be in the hands of every other man. No room for losing it out there. If there is even the slightest chance you might fall apart under pressure we need to know it now."

"I understand, sir. I'm ready to do my part."

Regardless of the disturbance Gil's crying out had caused, it was time for the platoon to be up and ready to go. They were about to get their first real taste of being fully visible in an active combat zone.

A major change in how the platoon would operate now was apparent immediately. While the men went about filling their canteen cups with hot coffee and grabbing up breakfast rations, there suddenly came a rumble of vehicles behind the old farmhouse. The promised battalion armaments had arrived. They were impressive.

Gil and his fellow troops left cups and rations sitting on benches and hurried out. Captain Daniels was ahead of them, eager to see what battalion had put together and see if his men were prepared to use what they got. These were not gunnery sergeants, after all. They all were surprised and well satisfied with what they saw.

An artillery trained lieutenant had led the battalion convoy and was there to make sure the intel platoon sergeants could handle the weapons battalion offered. The sun had barely cleared the horizon and the semi-darkness was cool when they all got out of the farmhouse to see what they had. Before them sat four Jeeps fitted with .50 caliber mounted machine guns and an M8 Greyhound light armored car with a 37-millimeter canon. A dozen carbines and ammunition for all the weapons filled the cargo space in the Jeeps. The platoon of only a dozen men was to be equipped as an awesome fighting force. They might have been designated an armored cavalry unit about to be shot like an arrow into the heart of Germany.

It was the M8 that got their attention. Jeeps were highly functional little motor cars that would be seen in numbers anywhere there was an Army unit and as familiar as corporal's stripes. The M8 was an impressive mixture of tank, gun carrier, Jeep, and whatever else might have been familiar to the designer. It was manifestly a killing machine but it also had an aura of comfortable and reliable wheeled transportation that would get them to hell and back.

Captain Daniels probably was the one most impressed, given that he immediately recognized the firepower arrayed before them. The men of his platoon soon would learn.

"Think this will do it, captain?" the lieutenant asked. "I'll be glad to let battalion know what you think."

"You can let battalion know that I can see they know this mission is a lot more dangerous than they've led me to believe. We wouldn't need this much firepower unless they knew we would run into a lot of Germans. I don't want to exaggerate, but it damn near looks like a suicide mission."

"Well, you know you can back—"

"Save your insults, Lieutenant," Captain Daniels barked. "If you mean cowardice, say it to my face."

The lieutenant held up a hand, as if signaling the captain to stop. "I'm sorry, sir," he said. "I didn't mean that, but that is what I implied. I was way out of line. I have to confess, though, I was thinking something of the same thing. About your mission, I mean."

"Forget it. We follow orders. But, yeah, I'd rather not have to lead this platoon of fine young men into what almost could be a death trap, you know?"

The lieutenant looked down, as if studying the ground. He pushed around a couple of rocks with the toe of a boot for a moment before looking up. "Captain," he said, speaking in a low voice, "I've never held command. I want to someday. But what you face here is a heavy load. I admire your courage and dedication and I salute you, sir."

He snapped to attention and delivered a smart salute. Captain Daniels returned it with what was little more than a wave of his hand.

"Forget it," he said. "We've got work to do. Think you and your guys can teach my guys what they need to know about these fancy guns?"

"Captain, that's what we are here for. Call 'em out!"

Gil walked between Henry and Jeff as they moved up into the tight circle needed for everyone to have a good view of the weapons demonstration. They would watch first and then get hands-on instruction.

"Jeff, I have a question for you," Henry said, speaking just above a whisper. "You ever have an inside dog? And how about you, Gil?"

"Never did," Jeff said.

"Me neither," Gil added. "Why?"

"Cause I got a theorem that ought to be in the books. If you got an inside dog you get messes on the carpet that your mama has to clean up. But they leave spots, and years later somebody says what made that spot and your mama says, 'Oh, that was Jeff's dog.' Compare that with us now. Let's say one of us gets a Kraut bullet through the heart. What happens? Our body lies there in a bunch of weeds until the buzzards finish it or it rots. I guess it would leave a spot, but not for long. Nobody is going to say years later, 'What made that spot?' So my theorem, see, is that dogs that live in the house are more likely to make their mark on history than dumb U. S. Army sergeants who give their lives for France."

"Damn, Henry, you're not even funny," Jeff said. But he laughed.

The lieutenant from battalion and his drivers were ready to do a formal do-and-tell show to get the 2nd Platoon sergeants ready to use the guns on a moment's notice. Not only would they get instructions, but each of them would have a stint of firing the mounted machine guns and the M8 cannon.

At the end of the gunnery session, Captain Daniels had one last demand to make of his troops. First, though, he called for a salute to the lieutenant from battalion and his men for their contribution. "Without their great work here today," he proclaimed, "we'd be setting out on our mission as little more than targets. But that's not true now."

Then, to his men, "We have plenty of firepower at our fingertips, gentlemen. That is absolutely essential if we are to carry out our mission. And while I don't want anyone to get trigger happy, even more I don't want anyone to be slow. If you have enemy troops in your gunsights blow them to hell where they belong. This is war, gentlemen. If we do our job we are going to leave dead Germans scattered all over the place. That's all I have to say."

Had there been any doubt in their minds, the men of the 2nd Platoon would end the day fully aware that they were soon to take on the enemy head-to-head. It wasn't something they looked forward to, but they were U. S. Army soldiers and they would do their duty. No letting up. They would drive as hard as they were able and be prepared to fight to the last breath.

20

ANNIE WENT TO great lengths to rationalize what she was about to do. She knew it was wrong, but her mother's story on top of her own growing doubts let her claim in her own mind she owed it to Gil to know she would be a loving and faithful wife before she vowed a lifetime commitment. Her physical attraction to Howard, she insisted to herself, surely was coincidental.

She tried to hold back the building excitement as she paid the toll and drove across the Brookport Bridge and entered Paducah. Even though she had made a point of remembering and mentally rehearsing the way to Howard's shop, she made a wrong turn somewhere and had to backtrack for a few blocks to get her bearings.

And then she saw it. The overhanging sign marking Howard's Garage and Tire Shop. She carelessly parked at an awkward angle that took up at least two of the four spaces available and picked up Mother White's steel colander from the passenger seat. She sat for a moment to get herself together, took a deep breath, and got out of the car and went in.

There was no one inside but the sound of the opening and closing door brought a vocal invitation from the back, the open spaced garage section.

"I'm in the garage. Come on back."

There was no mistaking Howard's husky voice.

Annie put the colander on a counter and pushed open the door leading to the back. There sat an old Chevrolet coupe and Howard lay beneath it on his back on a mechanic's crawler. His feet and ankles were visible and Annie saw something that took her breath away. One ankle was a steel joint, an artificial leg wearing an ordinary shoe and disappearing under the jeans.

Howard scooted out on the wheeled crawler, a pair of wrenches lying across his chest. His face lit with a bright smile when he saw Annie.

"Well hello again!" he exclaimed. "I'm glad to see you made it back to Paducah."

He maneuvered the crawler around to the front of the car, put aside the wrenches, and awkwardly used the front bumper and grille to pull himself up to a standing position. His eyes never left Annie's face as he pulled down and straightened the legs of his jeans and brushed off any dirt that might have fallen from the underside of the old coupe.

"As you may have seen," he said, "part of me is not flesh and bone. But I'm really lucky they fitted me so well I get around without even a limp. I guess most people don't even know I have it."

He dealt with the issue so easily Annie was able to conceal her surprise and respond in kind. "I never would have guessed," she said. "How did you lose it?"

"Farm accident when I was eighteen. I carelessly rolled a tractor down a creek bank and was rewarded by a crushed leg and ankle. They took it off just below the knee. But I'll bet you didn't drive all the way to Paducah to hear about my ugly physical limitations. What can I do for you today, Miss Annie?"

He remembered her name! Artificial leg or not, Howard was the charming man she remembered and his attraction was not diminished. She wanted—she *needed*—to be close to this man.

They went to the front of the shop and she showed him Mother White's colander and asked if he could fix the loose handle. He could. A simple act of soldering and he could do it now. No more than fifteen or twenty minutes, he said, if she wanted to wait.

They went to the back again and she stood close as he locked the utensil in a bench vice and quickly soldered the handle back in place. She admired the skill he demonstrated, even in this small task. He made every move count, wasting not a single motion as he worked step by step to repair the colander. She knew he had learned much of what he needed to know through experience, but surely it all began with a natural talent for working with his hands. She felt like she was watching the hands of an artist.

When he finished, he held the utensil up for her inspection. The repair was flawless. They went back to the front and Annie opened her purse to pay him. He held up a hand to signal refusal.

"I won't take money for that little job," he said, "but I will ask you to have lunch with me. Have I got a deal?"

She accepted his invitation without hesitation. She put Mother White's colander in the car and let him drive the shop truck for their lunch date because, "I know my way around Paducah and you don't." Her desire grew with every block.

Howard said it still was a bit early for lunch and asked if she might like to go down to the riverfront for a while and watch for tugs and steamboats. This would be something Annie had never done before and fit well into her search for new experiences. She said she would love to although in truth she doubted there would be much excitement in watching boats on the Ohio River.

The riverfront had a virtual carnival atmosphere. They got to Howard's favorite spot just as a large, multi-decked steamboat docked and began to disembark passengers. Loud music was playing somewhere and there was something of a continuous celebration as those waiting on the shore spied the friends and loved ones they were waiting for coming down the gangplank.

To her complete surprise, Annie found the riverfront atmosphere intoxicating. She would happily spend as much time here as Howard wished. They stayed for an hour before he said it was time for lunch and they went to a small boutique restaurant and took a two-person booth in a corner. Food was of no importance to Annie. She ordered whatever Howard suggested and hoped service would be slow. She would like to sit and face this man forever.

"Tell me all about yourself, Annie," Howard said. "I believe you said you live with your grandmother?"

"Yes. That is her colander you repaired."

"You wear a ring. There is a man in your life?"

"Yes." She suddenly felt like she was on slippery ground. To talk about Gil would be to defeat the whole reason she was here. Yet, how could she deny her promise to marry a man who had been away for so long now he could be a stranger? Would knowing the truth make her less attractive to Howard?

"He is a fortunate man," Howard said. "Who is he?"

"His name is Gil Bennett and he's in the Army. It seems like he's been gone forever. I know he remembers me, but I seldom even get a letter. And I'm very lonely, Howard."

Their food arrived and the young waitress slowly and very carefully placed everything in proper order on their table. Annie noticed her faint blush when Howard asked her name and was she a local girl and how long had she worked here? *He's only being nice! He's not interested in you!* But it occurred to her that if he came here often he might like to see more of this pretty young woman. She wanted him to be aggressive, but please let her be his first target.

"So this Gilbert Bennett," Howard began, picking up where

he had left off, "I assume is overseas, then. Do you think he's in danger?"

"He's somewhere in France. That's all I know."

Howard looked directly into her eyes, but she could not see this stemming from interest in her. Just now he was more interested in Gil. She soon learned why. He looked away, gazing out the window for a moment as if lost in thought.

"I should be there," he said. "Millions of young American men risking their lives for our country and I sit here living the good life with one of their sweethearts because I was so stupid I drove a tractor off a creek bank! Sometimes I despise myself, Annie."

His despair was visible in his eyes. She wanted to make it better, to comfort him and convince him he had done no wrong. The strong, desirable man she had come to Paducah to see suddenly had become the needy one. This didn't matter to Annie; she wanted him no less.

Howard's dramatic change in mood signaled it was time for them to go. There still was food on both their plates and drinks only half consumed, but they slid out of the booth, he left a generous tip on the table and paid the cashier, and they were on the street walking toward the truck with its modest door signs for Howard's Garage and Tire Shop.

Howard offered no hand to help her in, but crawled in on the driver's side as if he were alone. They rode a few blocks in silence before he suddenly braked sharply and pulled to the curb. Annie couldn't imagine why. He never looked at her but when he spoke it was to address her directly.

"I want you to come home with me. Will you?"

"Yes."

Annie's desire for this man was beyond control. She wanted him to take her in his strong arms, throw her on his bed, and ravish her to complete exhaustion. This was not from love, as it should be with Gil. It was from lust, pure and simple. It was what she had come for.

Howard's second floor apartment was a single room. It had a barely serviceable kitchen in one corner and an adjacent bathroom. Its one prominent feature was his bed, dominating the room with its fluffy blue spread and an array of pillows. There was a single chair, to which he motioned. She sat, unsure what to expect. Her search for new adventure had brought her to an unfamiliar playing field.

Howard dropped onto the side of the bed, ripped open his belt and the front of his jeans, then stood and let them fall to the floor.

"Look at me, Annie," he demanded. "Watch how the non-human part of me can be separated like kitchen garbage and thrown in the trash. See what a pathetic cripple I am in the true flesh."

He sat back on the bed again and unstrapped his artificial leg and threw it across the room. What was left was a pointed stub extending no more than ten inches or so below his knee. He deliberately highlighted this by waving it in circles as he sat.

Annie's desires evaporated like an ice cube dropped on the sidewalk in the hot noonday sun. Howard was not a masculine idol but a whimpering child. She loved him now, but she did not ache for his touch. She got up from the chair and hurried to him, sat beside him and put an arm around his shoulders and pulled him to her.

"Dear, sweet Howard," she said softly, "it's not two good legs that make you a person, it's the warmth and caring and gentleness of your mind and spirit. You are a wonderful man and I love you dearly."

"You think my father cared I was hurt? My mother did." Annie started to answer but he hadn't finished. "My mother cried every time she had to help me with my leg. My father didn't care.

Not about me. He was just mad that I broke his damned tractor. Couldn't stand to look at me anymore and told me to move to Nashville or Paducah or somewhere."

Howard leaned his head on her shoulder and cried, his gentle sobs those of a child. After sitting this way for a few minutes, they lay back on the bed and she stretched an arm across his body and in no time at all they were asleep.

It was late afternoon when Annie woke. Howard still was sleeping soundly. It took a moment for her to get her thoughts together and remember what had happened. She wanted to comfort Howard more, but she needed to get back to her car and start home. She should have been on her way some time ago. She shook Howard gently and urged him awake, letting him know she had to go.

When Howard woke, his first words were, "I'm sorry."

"You have nothing to apologize for," Annie told him. "Thank you for sharing feelings with me. Looks like you and I are pretty much like the rest of the human race, trying to hold things in that we need to let out. Absolutely amazing what a little fresh air can do for that load of bricks we've been carrying."

"You're funny, Annie. And I'm so embarrassed after what I did, I'd like to just crawl under the covers and hide, you know?"

She pulled his hand up to her face and kissed it. "Nonsense. I'm honored you shared your feelings with me, Howard. You've tried to stick a knife in your own back, and might have, but I pulled it out a while ago and threw it away. And I'd really love to stay and play a little longer, but I've got a long drive home."

"Oh, Annie! I'm sorry."

She playfully punched him on the shoulder with a clenched fist. "There's that word again. Now get your pants on and get me to the shop!"

Twenty minutes later, they were there. Annie was about to leave. Their collective outlook on life had brightened immensely now that they had talked about what had come and gone between them and they fit together comfortably, with no secrets. Except that Annie still had not revealed hers.

She got behind the wheel of the old Dodge and asked Howard to get in the other side and sit beside her. He did, obviously a little puzzled. Was there still something serious?

Annie took his hand and swiveled in the seat so she faced him.

"You have given me the courage to try to be as open and honest as you are," she began. "You can call it false pretenses, I guess, but I didn't come to Paducah to get the handle on that whatever it is fixed. I came to get you to go to bed with me. I can't explain it, really, but I've been lonely for so long and you are such an attractive man. And I may even regret later that it didn't happen. But it would be the wrong thing for me now. I love Gil so dearly and I know he'll be home soon. So are we good with this?"

Howard was about to laugh. "Your body language spelled it out all the way," he said. "I'd hate for word to get out among the guys that I might have had that chance and missed it because of my own stupid behavior. But, Annie, I'm glad it didn't happen. You would have had regrets and always identified them with me. I don't want that. I want us to be dear friends and when Gilbert gets home please bring him down and I'll take him fishing."

He crawled out and Annie left for home. The warm feeling she had for Howard was far more pleasing than the hot feeling that had brought her. She felt no stress as she drove home and felt good about having got Mother Whites's utensil so expertly repaired.

When Sunday came, Annie and Mother White were nearly late for services at Walnut Creek Church. They barely had time to get inside and slip into the pew beside Annie's mother. Pastor Maxwell was beginning to speak, but Annie whispered to her mother, "Mama, I want talk with you some more, okay?"

Pastor Maxwell opened with his usual "real life" story, just as his listeners expected.

"I was down in Arkansas last week," the pastor began, "and had a couple of days with a rather rowdy collection of what I'm going to call, without being judgmental in any way, 'hillbilly preachers.' They told a lot of good stories, but I guess the one I liked best came from a local pastor who said he'd performed a wedding ceremony recently and before that had been called on by both parties for counseling.

"Turned out both the man and the woman had the same concern. Their new mate was a regular church goer, but had something of a loose reputation. They wanted Scripture to cite as a foundation to encourage, let's say, monogamy. He said it didn't take him long to come up with just the right passage for the woman, and he suggested she cite First John 2:16: 'The lust of the flesh, and the lust of the eyes, and the pride of life is not of thee, Father, but is of the world.'

"But he said it took him a little longer with the man, since he wanted something plainly aimed at a woman. He came up with it, though, and told him he could copy 2nd Timothy 8 and paste it on the bathroom mirror: 'The husbandman that laboreth must be first partaker of the fruit.'

"And so, well, I guess you can see why I'm always glad to get back to Walnut Creek."

The congregation laughed and a few actually applauded. Annie wanted to shrink until she completely disappeared.

21

FOR THE FIRST time since basic training at Fort Jackson, Gil and his platoon mates fell out for reveille at 5 a.m. dressed in full combat gear, including the steel helmet. The Jeeps and M8 had been fueled to the brim and their weapons loaded and ready to fire. Henry had even made a show of cleaning the windshield of the Jeep he was going to drive. To a man, they had come to sense that the five vehicles from battalion were more important than they were. This hurt a bit, but was easily understood. The platoon could lose every man except one and still reach its target. Without a vehicle, no way.

They had topographic maps now, too, brought with everything from battalion. There were areas that would not offer easy advance, even if they didn't encounter heavy concentrations of enemy troops. Captain Daniels pointed one out to Sergeant Jensen, who was driving his lead Jeep, and said it looked to be almost as rugged as any they might encounter if they were fighting jungle warfare.

"It's not like we had a choice, Jensen," the captain said. "Our orders are to take a direct route, fight our way through any enemy we encounter, and be on that bridge in no more than three days."

"Yes. sir," Sergeant Jensen answered. "And maybe the 'any

enemies' we have to fight through includes that swamp."

Sergeant Elliott, who would be the gunner on the captain's Jeep, laughed heartily and said fighting a swamp instead of Germans with weapons would suite him very well but he doubted they would be so lucky. "But my first choice would be neither one," he added.

With everything loaded, the captain, standing in his Jeep, gave a forward motion and the 2nd Platoon set out on what more than one man considered a virtual suicide mission. Gil was in the back of Henry's Jeep, manning the machine gun. Jeff drove the third Jeep, with Harris as gunner. O'Dell and Shaw were in the fourth Jeep and Allison drove the M8 with Sampson, Shelby, and Harrison manning the guns. Battalion had succeeded in making a twelve-man infantry company rifle squad, an intel platoon of late, into a formidable armored force. And they would have the advantage of surprise.

Only one short stretch of the route Captain Daniels had sketched out had a map-worthy road. The rest of the estimated eighty miles would be through woods and open fields where the topography was relatively flat but also included two high ridges with steep cliffs on at least one side. The captain, whose sense of humor tended to come out more often when he was under pressure, quipped to Jenson that battalion obviously had failed to include the essential mountain climbing gear that surely was on the list.

"But like some poet wrote," he said, "ours is not to reason why, ours is but to do or die."

The captain's words, though intended to be facetious, actually defined their mission. There was nothing in their orders allowing for any shortfall. They were to prevent the Germans from destroying the Moselle River bridge so it would be there for American forces to use to invade the German homeland. And Captain Ron Daniels considered it his duty to lead these men to accomplish that mission or die trying.

As the small armored convoy moved away from the old farmhouse headquarters for the last time, Henry pumped a fist in the air and yelled an epithet Gil didn't catch. They might have the advantage of surprise but they did not have quiet on their side. The Jeeps alone would have announced their coming, but the M8 roared like an enraged beast. Its noise drowned out any attempt the gunners and drivers made to communicate. Gil wanted to emulate Henry's spirited farewell and pumped his arms in the air, holding his carbine, but didn't say anything.

Captain Daniels had emphasized more than once that, no matter the opposition, this mission must be accomplished in no more than three days. This simply reflected the speed of the Allied advance. Patton's Third Army was likely to reach the Moselle in two weeks at the latest. The Germans, in retreat, were not likely to wait till the last minute to blow the bridge at Neuveville. The 2nd Platoon goal was to get there in time to keep this from happening.

"The alternative," read a tongue-in-cheek written advisory from battalion, "is to ask General Patton to slow down. We got no volunteers for that mission."

Gil tried to stand up full height in the back of the Jeep, bracing himself with both hands on the machine gun mount. He had refined his plan for self-destruction, seriously committed to not being a negative force affecting the platoon's mission. Unless he was killed in action earlier, he would do what he had to do after the Moselle River bridge at Neuveville was secure. But standing tall so as to be an easy target for a sniper might get the job done with few complications.

He soon found standing nearly impossible with the bumpy ride and swaying of the Jeep. He would be worn out physically from the exertion required. Determination was one thing. but foolish stubbornness was something else. The last thing he wanted to do was sabotage his own mission.

"Just keep that up, Gilbert. You ain't hurtin' nobody but yourself." He could almost hear his father's voice, and those words he had heard many times when he was little. Yes, he always had been a bit "hard headed" as Aunt Gloria would say.

The platoon had run into nothing more challenging than a shallow creek crossing by early afternoon, when Captain Daniels called for a rest stop in a small woods that offered lots of cover. Everyone was ready for a stand down that gave them time to grab a field ration lunch and make their toilets in the underbrush.

Henry couldn't miss such a golden opportunity to hassle his Three Bees compatriots. Jeff and Gil should be right at home, he suggested, because "I know this is the way you hillbillies have always done it." Neither of them found him funny, and neither responded. Henry was just being Henry.

The captain allowed them a good ninety-minute respite. He spent most of that time studying maps, including one of the city of Neuveville. Once they hit town they needed to know a direct route to the bridge. He saw that the only numbered route into the city entered from the south and went straight through town the eight blocks to the bridge. A direct route, yes, but one easily defended by German forces.

"Our intelligence says most if not all the French residents are allies," he told Jensen. "Once we hit town we can hope to get help from the locals to get us to the bridge."

Jensen nodded. "You better believe they don't want to see that bridge go down. But anyway, Captain, we got to get there first."

Jensen's qualifying comment might have been prophecy. Twenty minutes later the 2nd Platon's midget armored squadron drove head-first into a German unit, probably an infantry rifle company on the move, taking a respite in a shallow, willow-encircled draw beside a farm pond. There was no posted guard to alert them and the platoon gunners opened fire and brought down most of them before they could get to their rifles.

Captain Daniels told Jensen to gun his Jeep straight ahead and get as far away from the scene as they could as fast as they could. The element of surprise was no longer theirs; word of their presence would be spreading like lightning through the enemy forces and 2nd Platoon was now a moving target.

Gil remained standing, clinging to the machine gun mount. He had fired as many rounds as his gun would permit and seen many of the Germans fall. He was not the only gunner, of course, but there was little doubt he was responsible for a share of the enemy casualties. He felt no remorse. Henry was happy to acknowledge his action. "Fantastic shooting," he yelled back over his shoulder as he gunned their Jeep to keep up with the captain's lead vehicle.

The captain had marked a route to a densely wooded section where he wanted to settle the platoon for the night, after ruling out any attempt at night movement. They couldn't make enough distance without lights to make the effort worthwhile. It was after sundown by the time they reached the site, with little time left before complete darkness.

They all knew the drill. The captain had been careful to cover this kind of detail before they got the arms from battalion. The vehicles would draw up bumper to bumper. There would be no lights and no conversation. Every man was responsible for his own rations. They would eat now, then sleep, either in their vehicle or on the ground. Nothing would move until daylight. They would have one-hour guard shifts, with a guard always on duty and alert for even the slightest sights or sounds that might signal enemy presence. Jensen would be the first guard, then in succession each guard would pick and arouse his replacement. They would not be surprised the way that German unit had been and so would be spared the consequences.

Gil knew sleep would be elusive. Although he was deathly tired, he was mentally wired after the day-long tension and dramatic contact with the enemy. He wanted to sleep, and would try. Tomorrow probably would be even more hectic than today had been and he needed to be ready. He felt around in his bag and found the canvas raincoat, which he pulled out and threw on the ground to lie on. As he crawled down from the Jeep, Henry whispered that he was going to sleep in the vehicle and wished him good night.

He was wrong about sleep. It came almost at once. His weary body won in competition with his wired brain. And he was in deep sleep two hours later when Henry woke him for guard duty.

"Nothing happening, man," Henry whispered. "Just keep your head up and your eyes open for an hour and then grab a replacement."

Gil waited for Henry to climb into the Jeep, then pulled himself up to a standing position. "Where am I supposed to be?" he whispered to Henry.

"It doesn't matter. Wherever you want."

He had forgotten whether he was supposed to carry his carbine, and decided not to. If there were orders to do so he would remember. It was so dark he almost had to feel his way around the front and to the other side of the captain's lead Jeep. He did feel his way from there, keeping a hand on the vehicles back to the rear of the M8 armored car.

No brilliant idea about what to do from here came to him so he sat on the ground and leaned back against the M8. It was almost fun, like playing schoolyard games again, now that he had no worries about his own life. He would do anything he could to protect the captain and other men in the platoon, but his mortal existence soon would run its course.

Gil put in his time on guard duty and roused Harrison as his replacement. He barely had got back to sleep when it was time to be up and start a new day.

The men of the 2nd Intel Platoon would have paid generously for Captain Daniels' big coffee pot, but didn't have that option. As the sun rose and the world grew brighter they had whatever amount of cold water was left in their canteens to wash down their field ration breakfast of a dry biscuit and tablespoonful of grape jelly. And they had to get this done fast. The captain was checking the roll, silent, making ready to issue the order to load up and get moving again.

By his best calculations, Captain Daniels told Jensen, they were just over a third of the way to Neuveville. He wanted to make better distance today. They were on schedule to complete their mission in the time allotted but there was little margin for error. The site he had marked for tonight's bivouac was about 35 miles away but the topography was favorable.

Within minutes, the midget armored convoy was on the move. Gil and the other gunners were at their stations. "This baby feels just like my Porsche!" Henry yelled. "Hang on, man. I'm gonna show you some Philly driving."

The captain's hope to make better distance looked reasonable for the first couple of hours. They traveled over mostly flat land, skirting farm fields and taking advantage of any cover available. Gil thought of the fencerows that bordered parts of the Bennett farm and was glad they weren't in any way comparable to the thick hedgerows common in France. The thought brought a twinge of sadness; he would never set foot on the Bennett farm again.

His reverie was interrupted by the sound of machinegun fire and bullets ricochetting off the M8 armored car at the back of the platoon convoy. Then there was a burst from the M8 cannon and he saw the target, a small band of German infantrymen about two hundred yards off to the left partially hidden by low-growing shrubbery. As fast as he could, he swung his machine gun to that direction and opened fire. The other Jeep gunners did the same and before they had time even to think about taking cover the enemy troops were obliterated.

As soon as the shooting stopped Captain Daniels stood and, looking back, called to ask if anyone had been hit. After a responding chorus of, "No, sir," he pumped a fist in the air and yelled, "Good shooting!" then thrust his carbine over the windshield in a mock "charge" gesture. The men behind him knew that, although the gesture was deliberately exaggerated, the demand was an order meant to be obeyed.

"Like shooting fish in a barrel, eh?" Henry called over his shoulder to Gil. "Dumb sons of bitches shouldn't have given themselves away. This is a powerful Kraut killing outfit!"

Gil offered no response.

Captain Daniels went back to his topographic map and altered his planned route slightly to take more advantage of natural screens like woods and ridges. There weren't many he hadn't found before, but now that the Germans knew they were coming the convoy needed every advantage available. "I think we can assume the joy ride is over," he told Jansen.

Unfortunately, the first change the captain made turned out not to be a good one. The price of a modest amount of concealment proved to be too high. With the captain's Jeep still leading the way, the convoy almost plunged into an area of swamp that was a total surprise. The lead Jeep was deeply mired and Henry's was stuck before either driver knew what was happening.

It took two cables connected to both the other Jeeps to pull them out, and for the captain's it looked briefly as if the power of the M8 also might have to be added. Except for Jensen, none of the drivers or gunners had been aware the cables were on the backs of their vehicles, and they were grateful to an anonymous soul at battalion who had anticipated their need.

Henry told Gil they should put the M8 at the front of the column as the captain's lead vehicle. Gil said he wasn't sure the captain could stand in the armored car and make his dramatic carbine-thrusting "Advance" signal. He had too much respect for Captain Daniels ever to make fun of him, but that particular action had begun to take on the characteristics of showmanship.

Captain Daniels figured they had about two hours before bivouac and told Jansen he wanted to make as many miles as possible without being reckless or taking foolish chances of unnecessary exposure. What he didn't tell Jansen was that he had come to realize there was a tragic flaw in logic marking the overall operation plan. He had put so much emphasis on getting to Neuveville in the limited time they had that he had failed bigtime in planning what they would do when they got there. The schedule they were on would get them to Neuveville at the end of the third day with no thought to what they would do overnight before taking control of the Mozelle River bridge the next day.

This bothered the captain so much now he decided he needed to discuss it with his sergeants. He stood up in the Jeep, facing backwards, and held up a hand. Henry stopped at once and the chain reaction got to the M8 in time to prevent it from rear-ending the Jeep it followed. Drivers and gunners alike stood to see what was going on.

The captain left his lead vehicle and walked back a few yards and called for a stand down. Everyone dismounted and gathered around him in a compact circle. They stood quietly and waited for him to speak.

"Well, men, it probably will come as no news to you that your commander is incompetent. I won't say this is earth shaking, but it sets us back a bit. Yours truly failed to correlate a couple of things that we are going to have to reconsider. I need to get everybody in on this."

"Say the word, sir," Shaw told him. "How can we help?"

"Okay, here's how it stands. We are on schedule to hit Neuveville just about dark. We need daylight to finish the job. The only options I see are to either do some night movement or plan to hide out somewhere overnight. I don't like either one, but I don't see any other way. Any ideas?"

There was a great deal of foot shuffling but no immediate verbal response.

"Don't everyone talk at once," the captain joked.

Gil had a question. "Sir, I'm always missing something, but why, exactly, do you think we can't do it in the dark?"

"Because we're going to have to find some intricate wiring connections on the underside of that bridge and disconnect them without blowing ourselves up with the bridge. Touchy in daylight, dangerous even to attempt in the dark."

Once again, a brief episode of foot shuffling. This time it was interrupted by Sergeant Harrison. "I'd say we do some night travel, Captain. In any case, since they know we're out here now the less time we give them to get ready for us, the better."

"That's pretty much my view," Captain Daniels said. "Anybody disagree?"

There was a chorus of, "No, sir."

"Okay, then. I want to make another thirty miles tonight. We'll stand down another ten minutes here to give everyone time to run to the bushes. Drivers, unstrap your fuel cans and gas up. And I want you gunners to check your weapons and ammo and make sure you are ready for an extended firefight. We are going to have one sooner or later."

Advancing at night with no lights led to more problems than Gil remembered. Of course, when they had done it as a three-man intel team with one Jeep and traversing the most treacherous sections on foot they had operated as a quite different force.

What he missed most, though, was returning to headquarters at the end of every mission. *Gil, get home before dark.* Yes, that was it. Getting back to headquarters was like getting *home.* He almost could hear his mother's voice reminding him when he was little not to be late. He wished he had a magic formula for staying little forever.

Once under way again, the five-vehicle column moved rapidly for a time, given just enough moonlight to make it possible to pick out farm roads and occasional short sections of real road without using lights. Jenson used the captain's flashlight once to illuminate a shallow creek crossing. He tried to be alert for spots lacking the solid ground necessary to keep the vehicles from getting bogged down again. This was his responsibility, and there was an added incentive. He suspected that if he missed an obvious barrier and got stuck again Captain Daniels would look for another driver.

Gil stood and braced himself on the machine gun mount in Henry's Jeep, which was close behind the captain's. They were on a straight, unpaved road that was uneven horizontally from time to time and very rough with occasional deep potholes. These could be bone-jarring if a driver didn't see one in time to swerve and miss it and Gil learned immediately that the swerve could be even worse. He barely missed being thrown over the side of the Jeep on the first one, and would have been were it not for the gun mount.

The road entered a narrow cut through a steep ridge and had high banks on both sides, bright with yellow broom bushes. Jensen saw a light ahead that looked like someone waving a flashlight. It was. A bright light atop a post at the edge of the road suddenly came on and revealed a German soldier, standing guard in front of a makeshift barrier waving for the captain's Jeep to stop. At the same time, of course, it illuminated the platoon's column, trapped between the high banks.

Elliott opened fire with the lead Jeep's machine gun and the guard stumbled to the side of the road and went down. Captain Daniels stood and yelled, "Gunners," and told Jensen to charge ahead. There was a single rifle shot from the top of the left bank and Gil and the other Jeep gunners sprayed the darkness as they were moving away. The M8 firepower went unused. Once again, the 2nd Intel Platoon had been lucky.

Gil's hands began to shake and his knees gave way, dropping him onto the supplies or whatever else might have filled the back seat of the Jeep. Henry heard him go down and tried to look back over his shoulder without losing sight of where he was going.

"Hey, man," he called back to Gil, "are you okay? God, don't tell me you got hit!"

"Yeah, Henry, I'm all right. Legs just had all the standing they could take for a while. That was a close one."

"Too close. Way too close."

Captain Daniels kept the column moving for another hour before looking for a heavily wooded area where the platoon could bivouac for the night—or what was left of it. He had little confidence now that he could plot their position on the map precisely. This added another complication to the end of the mission, which was the last thing he wanted.

The men virtually rolled out of their vehicles once they stopped. The captain said they would sit tight here until sunrise, but no lights and no noise. Most of the sergeants walked only a few yards into the woods and made their latrines then stretched out on the ground beside or under their vehicles and went to sleep. Henry was among them. Before he lay down, he urged Gil to do the same.

"We're not going to have long," he said, "and tomorrow is likely to be our big day. Better grab it while you can."

Gil pulled a pack of some kind out of the Jeep to use as a head rest and lay down. He didn't think he could sleep, even being almost totally exhausted. He was thinking what an easy target he had been during the shooting and was scared. Had he been hit and killed his body would have tumbled over the side of the Jeep and been left by the roadside in the middle of a German encampment and not likely ever to be recovered. Annie, his mom and dad, Aunt Gloria, none of his friends and relatives ever would know what happened to him. Was this the way he wanted to die? Did he really want to die at all? His decision that he did was a convenient way out at the depth of his guilt and shame. *That's not the Bennett way. Not this Bennett's. You have to be a man, Gil, and face the world as you are. Go home to Annie and spend the rest of your life being a good man.*

Whatever the long-term effects might be, his resolve brought immediate peace to his troubled mind. Gil joined the others in desperately needed sleep.

Captain Daniels had picked the deepest woods he saw as bivouac site for maximum concealment, of course, but in the morning it proved to be a two-edged sword. It probably was an hour later when the sun penetrated the dense forest with enough light for him to call the platoon to order and move out. This set well with the men but not with the captain, who was grasping for any possible way to make better time.

The sergeants had bought into his concerns about when the platoon should arrive in Neuveville. They finished what little reloading of the vehicles had to be done, added to the ammunition at hand for the gunners, and unstrapped the fuel cans and filled the tanks on the Jeeps and M8. Given the size of the platoon, the captain's headcount was quick and easy. They were ready to go. Tins of breakfast rations could be handled on the move.

"Henry, do you think the captain really knows where we're going?" Gil asked, intending for his query to be taken seriously.

"All I know is he did a lot of work with the compass and

believes he is close enough that whatever happens on the ground will get us there."

Gil accepted that as positive. They might be in Neuveville by suppertime.

Captain Daniels knew they were headed toward Neuveville, pinpointed on his map, and expected they would be seeing signs of that soon: marked highways, more traffic and the like. So now it became something of a balancing act. He told Jensen the challenge was to take advantage of anything that assured the most direct route while avoiding enemy forces that would be doing the same.

"Yes, sir," Jensen responded. "Kind of like eating your cake and having it, too."

So far as natural cover was concerned, it was getting more scarce. The land was flat and there were few wooded areas. Roads crossed the long stretches of well-tended farmland in both directions and moving vehicles could be seen from some distance. Their only option now was to drive straight to their target and be ready to fight their way through any enemy they might encounter. And even though they had made their presence known, at any given point they probably still would have the advantage of surprise.

"Captain, look!"

Jensen pointed to a short column of vehicles on a parallel road probably a half-mile away. There was no doubt it was a military force and there was no doubt it was German.

"If we can see them they can see us," Jensen declared. "What's our next move, Captain?"

"Stay the course."

22

THE 2nd PLATOON convoy and the Germans were on a collision course. The roads they were on intersected and at the speed both columns were traveling they would hit the intersection at about the same time. Jensen was doing what the captain ordered, maintaining the lead Jeep's speed, but surely he didn't intend for this to lead to a head-on meeting with the enemy force. He couldn't stand it any longer.

"What do you want me to do, sir?" he asked, with all the urgency he could muster.

"Stay the course."

"But Captain—sorry, sir. Staying the course."

Captain Daniels stood, so that he could study the situation with an unfettered view over the top of the Jeep's windshield. His decision now could mean the success or failure of the mission. He was confident the Germans would not have recognized yet that it was an enemy convoy closing in on them. When at some point they did, they would see nothing intimidating about this small force. The German unit looked to have at least three times the number of vehicles as his platoon but he doubted it had more firepower.

"Jensen, move over a bit so the M8 can take the lead."

He turned and called to Henry to pass the word back that he

wanted the M8 in front, cannon ready for full attack, and the Jeep gunners at the ready. He would not wait for the Germans to discover that this was an American force. He would call it to their attention with all the firepower the platoon could muster.

"Get us to the crossroads a minute or so ahead of them," the captain told Jensen. "We'll give them a little welcome party."

Jensen slowed the Jeep as the M8 passed, then pulled up close behind it. Gil was standing at the machine gun in Henry's Jeep and the gunners in the other two vehicles were doing the same. The 2nd Platoon's small but mighty arsenal was ready and waiting as the M8 got to the crossroads just ahead of the Germans.

There were no armored vehicles in the approaching German convoy and nothing that looked like troop carriers.

"Looks like a dozen supply trucks," Gil told Henry. "Not the kind of fighting force I was worried about."

"You'll get no complaints from me. I can't see around the M8. Are we about there?"

Gil didn't have to answer. Just as Henry asked his question, the M8's cannon roared with blasts at the leading German trucks. The first two trucks went up in flames with no sign of drivers escaping. Gil and the other Jeep gunners were spraying the trucks from the front of the convoy back. One evidently was loaded with ammunition or some other type of explosive. It erupted in a massive fireball with flaming debris flying in all directions and even from his distant position Gil could hear the popping sound of bullets in the cargo.

It was all over in a matter of minutes. The 2nd Platoon firepower had destroyed the enemy convoy without receiving a single shot in return. Captain Daniels had Jensen move his Jeep back in front of the M8 and signaled forward movement. They were back on track to complete their mission.

Despite the quick and easy victory in this small battle,

Captain Daniels would second-guess himself a dozen times over in the hours to come. Was it a reckless decision? Could he have overestimated the advantage of 2nd Platoon's superior firepower? The answer to the first question was possibly yes, but to the second it was clear he had not. Battalion had armed them to be a fighting force.

The captain asked Jensen to watch for a good site for a stand down so he could discuss the situation with his sergeants. It was time for some crucial decisions.

Jensen soon pulled over onto a widened shoulder of the highway alongside a field of brilliant red French honeysuckle fodder. The other drivers stopped behind the commander's Jeep and the captain soon was encircled by his platoon. Gil squeezed in between Henry and Jeff. He sensed in the other men a mix of confidence and caution that matched his own.

"You men proved your mettle back there," the captain said. "I think we know now we are the fighting force we hoped to be. Great work, gunners!"

This brought a round of appreciative, "Yes, sir!" The sergeants loosened their tight shoulder-to-shoulder ring and shuffled their feet on the roadside gravel. Their confidence had been buoyed by the quick victory at the crossroads, but how would they fare against a German fighting force not taken by surprise? They were eager to know what came next.

Captain Daniels, recognizing their vulnerability sitting here in the open, got straight to the point.

"Gentlemen," he said, "we are at a point now where we have few alternatives. We have almost reached our target. We can either look for a place with some cover and bivouac overnight and hit the city in the early morning or we can try to go straight in now. What do you think?"

The sergeants were surprised by the captain's challenge, having expected him to have made this decision. They were slow to respond.

Sergeant Shaw, usually not eager to express his opinion, was the first to speak up. "Sir, it seems to me like we don't have a lot of intel to go on. We don't know exactly what we face once we hit the city. If we need to hit that bridge in daylight like you said, wouldn't it be a little bit risky to charge on now? I guess I'd say bivouac and try to hit it as fast as we can tomorrow."

It was an easy way out for the other sergeants simply to agree with Shaw and not have to consider alternatives. At the same time, though, they all understood that the success of their mission was on the line. This could be literally a life or death choice. Gil would have liked to voice an opinion but the truth was he didn't have one. He needed more time to try and analyze the circumstances and there was no more time.

"Anybody else?" the captain asked.

No one spoke.

Captain Daniels had made his decision. "What Sergeant Shaw just said is very much in line with my thinking. We can't lose sight of the fact that our mission is to get to and save that bridge. If we don't manage that, we have wasted our time. And like he said, we don't know what kind of enemy opposition we're going to run into. So we're going to bivouac for the night a little further down the road and be ready to hit Neuveville first thing in the morning with guns blazing. So mount up, and let's go."

In minutes the 2nd Platoon convoy was moving again. Neuveville was close now. Tomorrow had just become the most important day any of the men had faced since they entered the war.

Captain Daniels ordered Jensen to go virtually full throttle. They were on a good highway through open country marked by farmland and orchards with few marked changes in the topography. The closer they got to their target today the less time it would take tomorrow. And from this point on, there was no ducking enemy forces. If they happened to run into a German unit of any size they were ready to fight their way through. Audacity had never been the captain's nature, but he had never been in a situation like this before.

Henry loved the chance to push the second Jeep in the convoy to its limits. He had one hand on the steering wheel and raised the other in the air and pumped his fist up and down to signal his enthusiasm. The Jeeps and the M8 stayed almost bumper-to-bumper and the gunners stood in position to fire at any target that might show up.

Gil had become completely fatalistic. There was a good chance he would die tomorrow. This was no longer his choice, but he accepted that willingness to have it happen was his obligation. The oath he had taken to defend the Constitution of the United States had no caveats. He had sworn his readiness to give his life.

There was a subtle but visible change in the landscape before the captain finally began looking for a place to bivouac. The large fields had given way to smaller truck-patch farming and houses were closer together, sure signs the city was close. Jensen spotted a small woods a mile or so off the highway and pointed it out to the captain, who agreed it likely was the best place they would find. The convoy moved slowly across an open field and segments of farm roads to reach it.

The woods were not nearly as thick as those they had spent last night in, and even from the center there was space enough between trees that looking out found a clear view to the edges. Sargeant Sampson surveyed the site and declared that, "If we can see out they sure as hell can see in."

It would be dark soon, though, and if the platoon had no visible lights and, of course, no fire, they probably were safe from detection. The captain called for drivers and gunners to stand down and prepare to spend the night. Given the early hour, this portended the longest period for sleep the men had enjoyed since this mission had begun. Except for guard duty, there would be no disruption.

The Three Bees huddled beside the M8. None of them wanted to talk about what tomorrow might bring. Not yet, anyway.

"Hey, I felt like I was back in Philly driving my Porsche," Henry said. "That little old Jeep's got more guts under the hood than I thought."

"You know what, Henry," Jeff said, with a note of irritation in his tone, "I just found out the other day that a Porsche is German. You can just spare us any more mention of yours. Eh, Gil?"

Gil, always one to pick his fights cautiously, chose not to comment. Henry's failure to respond made him wonder if he knew his car was a German brand. Gil, himself, had not known.

"You guys think you can sleep tonight?" he asked, partly to change the subject and partly because he really wanted to know. He had begun to worry that he might not sleep well because of the raw tension that had built up over the last several hours. He wondered if they felt the same.

"Yeah, man, I'll sleep," Jeff answered. "Like my grandma used to say, I could sleep just hanging on a nail."

Henry, still subdued, mumbled something Gil didn't understand. Then he got up and retrieved his rain cape from the Jeep and spread it, partially under the vehicle. Without saying anything more he took off his steel helmet and lay down.

"Hey, don't you want supper?" Jeff asked him. "I got a hunch tonight's rations might be something good." Henry waved off the question and rolled over, leaving Jeff and Gil to open the third meal field ration can and see what they had. Jeff was wrong. It was liver and onions. Gil wasn't sure he could eat, but Jeff swore it was one of his favorites and said he'd take an extra if Gil didn't want his. Gil was hungry enough that it actually tasted good.

It soon was completely dark. The woods were eerily silent.

Someone in the circle of platoon sergeants snored loudly, but none other made a sound and Gil assumed everybody but him was asleep. He remembered his mother complaining that his father sometimes snored and felt a wave of homesickness. He tried to think what would be going on on the Bennett farm now, but time since he'd left it was nothing more than a blurred series of events with little reference to passing days and weeks and months.

And then his thoughts turned to Annie. What was she doing now? What would *they* be doing if he were at home in southern Illinois instead of lying here in a French woods waiting for battle? This was the question he went to sleep on.

The next thing he knew it was getting light and the men of the 2nd Intel Platoon were beginning to stir. Their day of battle had arrived.

23

ANNIE HAD COME full circle. She felt foolish for her infatuation with Howard, at the same time that she was glad to have connected with him in a totally different way. She would count him as a friend—a needy friend she hoped she could help. From what she had seen he was very much alone in terms of personal relationships and she could help fill that gap.

How could she have doubted her full devotion to Gil? She loved him with all her heart and couldn't wait for him to get home. And what on earth could she say to her mother? She decided her best hope was to seek Mother White's wise counsel, even though her grandmother was a vital part of the mix and not an objective outsider. And she would go straight to the point, no beating around the bush.

"Grandmama, can I talk to you about something?"

"Of course, honey. You can ask me about anything."

Annie could feel her face beginning to flush with embarrassment. She wasn't sure she could let Mother White know about her foolish behavior. Mother White saw her discomfort.

"This is something hard for you, isn't it?" she said to Annie. "Is there any way I can make it easier?"

"I'm sorry, Grandmama. You are going to think I'm a terrible person. It's something I just hate to tell you. But I do need to talk to you about it. I don't even know where to start. I can't explain it, but I wanted to have an affair with Howard and even questioned my commitment to Gil. How could—?"

Mother White reached for her granddaughter and put a hand on her arm.

"Oh, child, that's not something terrible. It's human nature. You were lonely. Gil has been gone so long and you've had no companionship, not the kind a woman needs. Somebody who could make you feel like a woman."

"But I'm promised to Gil. And I do love him, Grandmama. How could I have doubted that?"

"I'm no expert on this, but I remember reading a magazine article about it once. It said it was human nature to want to avoid guilt. If you could make yourself believe you didn't love Gil anymore you wouldn't be betraying him. Don't you see?"

Annie did see. Maybe it was because she wanted desperately to find answers, but she believed in Mother White's wisdom and the explanation seemed logical to her. She still felt terrible about the whole situation, but talking about it with her grandmother already was making her feel better.

They sat and talked for a long time, Mother White getting up twice to make and pour fresh coffee and get a platter of chocolate chip cookies from the cupboard. She said solving big problems took lots of energy, and anyway the cookies were going to get stale if not eaten.

"It's kind of funny how I remember that article so well," Mother White said. "I guess it's because it was so interesting and maybe something I thought at the time probably all women ought to know.

"It said ever since Adam and Eve women have had to depend on men to protect and support them because the women have to be mothers and raise the children. So, whether it's fair or not, that left us in a more tricky position. You know, 'don't bite the hand that feeds you.' And I suppose a lot of women have put up with some real low-life men, Annie, because they didn't have any choice. And if they had a good man they didn't want to risk losing him by messing around, theirselves."

"I understand that, Grandmama, but—"

"I know. Get back to you and what's his name. Howard? Since I took us all the way back to Adam and Eve—nobody ever says Eve and Adam—let's get right down to brass tacks. Seems like God intended for the human race to reproduce itself—"

Annie couldn't help but interrupt. "I remember Gil telling me one time that reproduction drives everything in nature. He talked about plants producing seeds and all that and he said that's why we have summer and winter or spring and fall and all that. He sounded just like a teacher when he explained it."

Mother White smiled, and pushed her chair back from the table and stood.

"Got to stretch my old legs a little bit," she said. "But I know Gil is a bright young man. He could be a teacher or whatever he wants when he gets home. And I've seen that he understands nature right well. He could explain things a lot better than me, starting with the fact that all the plants he talked about are controlled by the seasons. Humans are not."

"But I interrupted you. You were talking about Eve and Adam. See, I can say it that way."

"Well, I forget exactly where I was going. Oh, yes. Reproducing the human race. So how does that happen? God give Eve and Adam the desire to have sex. That's what makes babies. So to make sure it happens, I guess, He made men and women attractive to each other. We're not like the cows and bulls and have breeding seasons and all that. I guess that takes too long or something. We want to do it all the time."

"This is getting embarrassing, Grandmama."

"Don't be embarrassed about human nature, Annie. It's what

we all have in common. Puts us a rung or two higher than the monkeys, they say."

By the end of the day, Annie was overwhelmed on two fronts. She felt tremendously less guilty, and she was astounded by Mother White's wisdom. She couldn't tell how her grandmother felt about their long and intimate discussion, but she felt closer for it. She hoped Mother White did, as well.

After supper, she asked about listening to the radio for a while and Mother White agreed.

"Can we try and check up on the war news?"

"Exactly what I was going to suggest. I think things are going better, but who knows what a new day can bring?" Mother White said. "It seems like this terrible war has been going on forever and sometimes I wonder why we are even in it. It's like we're fighting for France, you know?"

Annie admitted that this was one of the things that bothered her most. God forbid anything should happen to Gil anyway, but the thought of him being wounded not even fighting for America was too much. She wouldn't allow herself to think of anything beyond getting wounded.

What they heard on the radio sounded neither better nor worse so far as progress in the war was concerned. If the measure was territory, the Allied forces had made some advances. But at what cost? Whether or not the news services actually had such statistics they seldom mentioned losses. How many young American men gave their lives for a few hundred square miles of France? Mother White soon turned the radio dial to a station broadcasting music, which Annie found a great relief.

As they sat and listened, without talking, Elmo rubbed around Mother White's ankles, demanding attention. She scooped him up onto her lap, where he circled a few times seeking a perfect position then went to sleep. His purr was so loud Annie could hear it from her chair several feet away.

"You probably haven't seen much of Gil and Elmo together," Mother White said. "That's a treat you have in store. They act like the best of lifetime buddies. When Gil's around Elmo won't have nothing to do with me."

"Yeah, I know Gil loves animals. I don't think I've ever seen him with Elmo."

To her own surprise, Annie suddenly burst into tears. She dropped her face into her hands and in a moment her body was shaking with the force of her sobs.

Mother White went to her, pulled her up and into a tight embrace. "I know, honey, I know," she said softly. "It's hard."

"I'm sorry, Grandmama. It's just that every time we talk about Gil I picture him as he should be, here with us acting as his normal sweet self and doing little things like playing with Elmo. And then I remember where he really is, somewhere in France and I don't know what he's doing and is he in danger and does he have to be out in the rain and does he have dry clothes and good food and he can't even tell me. It's not fair, Grandmama, it's just not fair."

Mother White held her for a long time, wiping her tears and brushing back her hair and saying soothing words. Annie finally regained her composure to at least a limited extent and said she was ready to go to bed. She was exhausted from her emotional outpouring. Mother White took her to her room and helped her onto her bed.

"Get some rest, honey," she told Annie. "We all get a fresh start in the morning."

"I love you, Grandmama. Thank you so much for helping me today. You made all the difference."

Mother White told her good night and tiptoed out of her room. All the tension Annie had felt when she began the day had evaporated with her understanding of Mother White's discourse on human nature. Maybe she wasn't such a bad person after all.

In a few minutes she fell into a peaceful sleep.

24

GIL TRIED TO convince himself he was ready for whatever the day might bring, but he wasn't. He sensed that most if not all of the other platoon sergeants felt pretty much the same way he did, hopeful but uncertain and afraid. Their success thus far gave them plenty of reason to be hopeful, but they had very little to go on when it came to the final leg of their mission.

He remembered something the teacher had told him and other students in a high school psychology class. Miss Wilson, one of his favorite teachers, said it was human nature to fear the unknown. This struck him now as an obvious example of common sense, but apparently it had been of adequate significance to be written in a text book. Sometimes the world was not as complicated at it seemed.

But this was not the time to get into deep thoughts about human nature. Captain Daniels hurried from man to man to speak with each one individually and he came to Gil. There was no more to be said in formation, but the captain wanted to assure himself that every one of them was a dependable team player. This was the big game, his team was the underdog, and he needed it to be at full strength.

In the compact bivouac area, it had been easy for Gil to hear what the captain asked the other men. His questions were general, and yet specific when applied to an individual. He turned to Gil and asked the same: "Are you good to go physically? Are you mentally prepared for combat? Do you understand your role as gunner?"

Like all the other platoon sergeants, Gil answered each question, "Yes, sir." And he believed his answers were true.

They gulped down their tins of breakfast rations and refilled their canteens with water from a large container strapped on the back of the captain's Jeep. Drivers topped off their fuel tanks and gunners checked their weapons and ammunition. Finally, on the captain's order, they donned the heavy steel helmets and mounted up. The 2nd Intel Platoon was ready to finish its job. The Neuveville Moselle River bridge was to be saved from German destruction. Given that they no longer had any hope to avoid detection, they roared out of the woods at near full throttle, quickly reached the highway, and turned toward their objective.

By the time they had advanced ten miles toward the city the small French truck farms began to show activity. A man driving a horse-drawn wagon waited for them to pass before pulling onto the highway. Gil watched for any sign of recognition. The farmer didn't appear to notice they were American. The local French residents probably were accustomed to seeing military units moving around their streets and highways, with the German forces having occupied the region for some time now.

"He thought we were Krauts," Gil yelled to Henry.

"We're not flying any flags to advertise we're not."

Gil was holding onto the machine gun mount with both hands, trying to keep his balance as the Jeep hit stretches of rough and sometime slanting pavement. He had to be vigilant and ready for action, but at the same time his mind wandered with the small things he noticed as they sped toward Neuveville and almost certain contact with German forces.

What would it be like to be part of an occupying force? If you were a soldier in that situation would you meet people in the occupied country and even become friends, or would you be seen by them as the enemy pure and simple? Might young German soldiers meet and fall in love with French girls? *What if I'd been an occupying soldier and met Annie?* And then he was irritated at himself that he couldn't go for a single hour without thinking about Annie and worried that if he let his mind wander this way he might miss something and cause members of the platoon to lose their lives and he had to do better and he would do better.

"What do you think, Henry? We about to get there?" He had to yell to be heard over the wind noise in the open Jeep.

"Your guess is as good as mine," Henry yelled back. "But we'll know it when we do. Got that machine gun ready?"

Gil knew his gun was ready, but checked it again. He moved ammo boxes on the floor of the Jeep around with a foot to make sure he had plenty. He checked the strap on his steel helmet to make sure it was tight. Running out of any other action he could take, he pushed and pulled on the gun mount to make sure it was still tightly bolted down and wouldn't wobble with bursts of fire. And then he was back to the most difficult activity of all, merely watching and waiting.

Only a few minutes later, Neuveville came into sight. There were no tall buildings, but what probably was city hall or some similar public building had a structure on the roof with a cupola on top and there were three church bell towers. These were visible above the tree line, which by itself was evidence only that there was a settlement of some kind squatting there on the open prairie before them.

And then there was something else. Either Jensen or the gunner in the captain's Jeep saw it first and Gil spotted it at their first motion. In the distance to the right was the physical outline of some kind of military post: lots of canvas tents and two or three rows of vehicles of combat-ready design.

Gil tightened his grip on the machine gun handles. There was little hope of getting much farther without running into German forces. They would have to fight their way from here on to get to the bridge.

"You all set, man?" Henry shouted over his shoulder.

"All set! Bring 'em on!"

Gil's bravado was phony. He was not at all confident the 2nd Platoon could survive much longer. They had been lucky not to have encountered a strong enemy force and he was sure this was about to change. And he and the other Jeep gunners would be easy targets for German marksmen, totally exposed as they were. His vow to give his life for his country if necessary suddenly had become more meaningful.

Captain Daniels' reaction to the discovery of the German post was the same as before. He demanded that Jensen maintain full speed as they entered the city. So far, he told the sergeant, there was no sign they had been seen and the closer they got to the bridge before they were, the better their chances of completing the mission.

A minute later a German Army open-topped staff car, unmistakable with its sloped hood and the black cross insignia on the side, made a left turn no more than a hundred yards in front of the captain's Jeep. There were four men in it, all looking straight at the approaching 2nd Platoon convoy. That the Americans might have been discovered was no longer an open question.

The German vehicle stopped on the side street, which could be seen now to lead to the military base, and one of the men stood. Gil saw him raising binoculars to his eyes. Just at that minute, there was a burst of fire from the M8's 34 mm cannon. The German vehicle exploded into a massive fire ball. Either Shelby or Harrison had hit their mark.

"Fantastic!" Henry yelled.

Gil cheered, too, after a fashion. But he had a question that he felt was critical. Everything now would be focused on the Moselle River bridge. "Henry," he shouted, "doesn't this highway go straight through town to the bridge?"

"It does. But the captain figures that route is well guarded. He'll look to wind around town to get there. I think he expects help from the French loyalists, too."

It struck Gil as ironic that the 2nd Platoon's success, and maybe even its survival, depended on intelligence gathered by some other intel squad. And satisfying. Here was a living example of the importance of the kind of activity this platoon had been involved in before. He recalled how Captain Daniels had emphasized that the success of their work would be measured in American lives saved, though they never would get the credit they deserved. The captain knew what he was talking about.

Henry's prophecy was fulfilled almost immediately. The captain pointed to signal that Jensen would be turning the lead Jeep onto a side street. Henry and the drivers coming behind followed the captain's vehicle on a street that was perpendicular to the highway that led to the bridge and soon were several blocks from it. They were in a somewhat shabby residential neighborhood when the lead Jeep pulled to the side and stopped.

Captain Daniels was the first to have his feet on the ground, with all the platoon sergeants quick to follow. In what was a set routine now they quickly formed a tight circle around their commander.

"So who was the M8 gunner on that one?" the captain asked.

Sergeant Allison quickly pointed to Harrison and said, "That great gunner."

"That was damned good shooting. And we got it when we

really needed it. That 34 mm is going to make or break us the rest of the way, but you machine gunners will make a big difference, too. By my calculations we are about six miles from the bridge now. We can count on fighting our way the whole distance. Everybody set and ready?"

Sergeant Shelby had a question. "Sir, do you have a set route to the bridge now? I mean—"

"Quick answer is no. I'll have Jensen make lots of turns, but stay headed in the general direction of the bridge. I'm hoping we get some help from French loyalists who are in the active resistance movement, but we may not. Okay, gentlemen. Let's mount up and go save a bridge for General Patton."

Just as the engines began to start, a man dashed out from behind a house across the street and ran straight to the captain. After a quick exchange, the captain motioned him into his Jeep, then stood and gave his "advance" signal with his carbine.

"What's that all about?" Gil called down to Henry.

"Only thing it could be is he just picked up one of the French loyalists he mentioned. We've got a guide now."

In front of them, the captain and the Frenchman who had just joined them had their heads together in earnest discussion. Gil wished he could hear what they were saying, then decided he was content to be a follower and not have to make decisions on which the platoon's prospects for success probably rode. And even if they succeed in saving the bridge their fate was not promising. He wished he could stop the action for a few minutes and write Annie and tell her goodbye. And he would tell her he was proud to give his life for his country.

With the Frenchman advising Captain Daniels, the 2nd Platoon convoy made several quick turns. They raced through residential neighborhoods and passed only a few small business establishments nestled on street corners. Gil had long ago lost any sense of direction. But he was confident every block took them closer to the bridge.

When they eventually did turn back toward the main highway, they immediately found themselves blocked by an armored car similar to their M8 parked crosswise on the street. Three or four German troops stood as guards behind it.

Elliott opened fire with the machine gun on the lead Jeep and Henry turned to the side so Gil could begin shooting also. Powerful as their .50 caliber guns were, though, their bullets were bouncing off the side of the armored car or whistling by while the guards were ducked down out of sight.

The situation was only somewhat similar to those they had faced before, but the solution was exactly the same. The M8 suddenly was nosed virtually between the two Jeeps. Before it had come to a full stop its cannon had demolished the German machine and no doubt killed the guards. Captain Daniels stood and motioned Sergeant Allison to take the platoon convoy lead and drive the M8 over a curb and trimmed hedge and push down a wire fence to clear a path for them all to get around the burning roadblock. Once again they had met and destroyed the enemy.

It was clear now that they were expected by the Germans. That roadblock had been set up hastily and probably was one of many. They could expect to hit another at any time.

Based on this rationale and after further discussion with the Frenchman, Captain Daniels decided to take the convoy back onto the main highway and head straight for the bridge. With the M8 and its powerful cannon in the lead, 2nd Platoon would fight its way through Neuveville and take control of the Moselle River bridge. And it was not lost on him that the other end of the bridge rested on German soil. The success of his unit now would speed Allied invasion of the enemy's homeland.

Expectations of contact with enemy forces proved to be underestimates. There was no large German force, but single vehicles with mounted machine guns and no more than four or five troops waited at nearly every corner. As soon as they were in sight and at the same time they began to shoot, their little unit was obliterated by the powerful M8 cannon. Gil and the other Jeep gunners opened fire and swept the area in case any of the enemy soldiers survived, recognizing that their guns might be killing French civilians and doing immense damage to stores and other businesses on the streets of Neuveville. But this was war.

Henry yelled over his shoulder to Gil that the convoy had to be getting close to the bridge. The drive could be no more than a couple of miles, though he didn't remember the measure in blocks. Then he added, "Thing is, I have no idea what the hell we're going to do when we get there."

Gil confessed that he, too, was confused about their orders. Up to now, all their attention had been focused on getting there.

At the same instant they heard the shot, a bullet shattered the windshield of O'Dell's Jeep, now the last vehicle in the convoy, and no doubt killed O'Dell. By the time Gil could turn and see, he was slumped over the steering wheel and the Jeep was veering off to the side of the street. Shaw, the gunner, jumped off and ran to catch Jeff's Jeep right in front of his.

"Get down, man," Henry yelled.

Gil didn't need the prompt. He would be in the sniper's sights, too, and would be an easy target standing at the gun mount. He dropped down as low as he could manage, behind Henry's seat. Henry had jerked the steering wheel to get the Jeep to the curb and was trying to conceal himself below the dash board with faint hope that the engine compartment would block bullets and protect him.

There was no second shot. The convoy was on one of the few blocks that had multi-story buildings and one of these had come between them and the shooter. Gil and Henry held their breaths and waited, with no escape if they should be the next targets.

Jeff passed them and took the position as second vehicle in the convoy, directly behind the captain's Jeep. Henry straightened up and got his vehicle back in line but Gil stayed down. No one had thought about the Germans having snipers on rooftops or in the upper floors of buildings along the street, shooters from whom they had no real protection. Could this have been the only one?

Whatever the Germans were doing, the 2nd Platoon convoy reached the Moselle River bridge with no more shots being fired. Sergeant Allison stopped the M8 as soon as he was on the bridge. Sampson and Shelby got out and ran back to the captain's Jeep. The captain, in an intense discussion with the Frenchman, waived them back to Henry's Jeep and a moment later climbed out of his vehicle and ran and climbed into the M8.

"I think they have to get to the other end to disconnect the Germans' explosives," Sergeant Shelby said. "Allison will get him over there."

When Henry and Jeff saw what was happening, they backed up their Jeeps maybe a hundred yards and turned them sideways, nose-to-nose across the road at the beginning of the bridge approach. Gil got back into position in the gun mount and made his machine gun ready to fire. On the back of Jeff's Jeep, Sergeant Harris did the same. They would be ready to stop any enemy action aimed at preventing Captain Daniels from completing their mission.

They wouldn't get that chance.

The blast shook the ground and knocked Gil and Harris out of their respective vehicles onto the pavement. The chin strap on Gil's helmet was not buckled and it was knocked off his head. He was hit just above his right ear by a piece of flying steel. Henry and Jeff had climbed out of their drivers' seats and stood talking with Sampson and Shelby, and all four were knocked to the pavement.

Starting at the near end, the bridge began to fold, section by section, and drop to the water and disappear. The M8 went down with the middle section. Except for the approach on the German side, there no longer was a Neuveville bridge across the Moselle River.

Gil lay face-down, blood from the head wound pooling on the pavement. Though he was still semi-conscious, everything was black. He heard Henry's voice, calling from close by, and Jeff answering.

He twisted around, without trying to get up, and crawled forward. He felt a hand on his shoulder and heard Jeff's muffled voice.

"Don't try to get up. Just lie there for a minute."

"Zat you, Bennett? Come where I can reach you."

Gil crawled toward the sound of Henry's voice. He swept with his hand as he went. When he touched Henry's hand it was saturated with something he knew instinctively was blood.

"Hey, Henry, you okay, man?"

"The Three Bees, yeah, the Three Bees. Still together, eh?"

"You lie still, too," This was Jeff, whose voice seemed to come from right over Gil's ear. "And you bet we're still together. Us and Sampson and Shelby may be all that's left of the 2nd Platoon."

"For nothing," Henry whispered. "We did it all for nothing. God in heaven, it's all wrong. We did our duty, Gil. It's not fair!"

"Are you all right, Henry?" Gil asked again. "You seem a little foggy."

"It's my ears. I think it hurt my ears. I can barely hear. Your ears okay?"

Gil told him his ears had a lot of ringing but he worried more about a wound to his head. "Unless it was a bullet I think a piece of steel from the bridge hit me. May have cracked my noggin. But I'll be okay."

"It was for nothing . . . the Krauts blew the bridge . . . before we got there. It was for nothing."

There was something like a gurgle in Henry's voice, which was barely audible. Just to speak obviously took great effort.

"I'm done for. Sorry to break up the Three Bees. Tell Jeff . . . You hang on, man . . . Get home and marry that pretty girl . . . You only get one chance. Sorry . . ."

These would be Henry's last words.

Gil heard rapidly approaching footsteps and suddenly felt surrounded. There was excited conversation in French. But some man, in broken English, said they were friends and not to worry, they would shield the Americans from the German soldiers.

And then, what Gil Bennett thought might be the most beautiful words he'd ever heard: "Your army is close. Patton is coming soon."

25

MOTHER WHITE PUSHED her chair back from the table and slowly stood, brushing a strand of gray hair back from her face with one hand and grasping the back of the chair with the other. Her face was marked by weariness, but she managed a smile as she spoke to Annie.

"Honey, it don't get any easier when you get old," she said. "Take an old woman's advice and stay young. Want some more coffee?"

Annie nodded. "Can we go out on the porch, though?"

"Exactly what I had in mind."

Mother White turned and stepped to the stove and reached for the coffee pot. She barely touched the handle, jerked her hand away and put her thumb in her mouth.

"Careful!" Annie warned. "That's hot!"

"Sometimes my hands get in front of my brain, I'm afraid. Just lucky I didn't get full ahold of it and burn my hand. Probably have a blister on my thumb, but I can live with that." She wrapped the handle in a faded dish towel and brought the pot to the table and poured fresh coffee for them both. "It's a real pretty day to be outside."

Annie carried her cup carefully as she crossed the kitchen and pushed open the sagging screen door. Gil had intended to put up a new one. How many other things on his list didn't get done? Mother White, since Gil had agreed to take over the farm, had relied on him to take care of the little things needing to be fixed around the old farmhouse.

Gil had complained to Annie once that he didn't know why this was his responsibility, but he'd always been quick to respond to Mother White's requests. His absence had left many gaps that had not been filled.

The two women seated themselves in the porch swing, which hung by stout chains from a heavy cross beam centering the porch roof. Gil had painted the swing royal blue a few years back and, although the color had faded to a less commanding shade, the finish had stood up well and kept the slats smooth and splinter-free. Annie knew Mother White had found the color a bit gaudy for her taste, but she also knew her grandmother never would complain. It was not in her nature to find fault and, even if it had been, she treasured anything Gil did as if it were a gift from the Magi.

Elmo peered around a corner of the house, as if curious about what his human friends were up to. He jumped up onto the porch and walked toward them, but suddenly had to stop and scratch. Annie held out her hands, inviting him to join them on the swing. The cat studied her for a moment as if considering his next move carefully, then turned and walked away, jumped off the porch and disappeared.

"I wish I could read Elmo's mind sometimes," Annie said. "He always has that look, like he knows something we don't."

"Well, cats are right smart, no doubt about that," Mother White said. "And they've got their own individual personalities, just like us."

"I wonder if he misses Gil."

"Oh, no doubt about that. Elmo's crazy about Gil. Probably misses him as much as you and I do."

As if lost in their own thoughts, the two sipped their hot coffee in silence for several minutes. The slanting rays of the early afternoon sun, which already had moved noticeably farther north, hit at an angle that bypassed the roof and warmed the edge of the porch. It felt almost like a summer day.

"Spring's right around the corner," Mother White said finally. "I don't expect we're going to have any more real cold days. The redbud and dogwood trees on the side of the hill over there will be blooming before you know it."

Annie felt the tears welling up in her eyes. How Gil loved the spring! She remembered the delicate wreath of wild spring beauties he had woven on one of their early walks in Soloman's Woods and his disappointment that she couldn't wear it like a crown.

She had wanted to, and tried, but the little stems were too fragile and the flowers came apart before he could settle it on her head. She thought for a moment he was going to cry in his disappointment, but he laughed and made some disparaging comment about his inability to accomplish even such simple things.

Mother White, even though she couldn't see Annie's face, sensed her silent pain. She put a gentle hand on the younger woman's arm. "I know, honey," she said softly. "It's hard."

"I'm sorry, Grandmama. It's just that I think about him all the time, and how he loves the spring and the dogwood and all. He's so far away. I try to make myself believe for sure he will be home someday, but I really can't. He can't tell me anything about where he is and what's happening. But I know he's in danger, Grandmama. I know he's in danger . . ."

Her voice trailed off and she began to sob, quietly at first and then almost violently. Mother White put an arm around her shoulders and pulled her close. They sat this way for several minutes before Annie's open grief was spent and she was calm.

She breathed out in a long sigh and rested her head on Mother White's shoulder.

As the afternoon slipped away, Mother White was careful to keep their talk on pleasant topics and Annie's mood brightened a bit. They eventually went inside and she helped her grandmother fix a light supper.

"Is it okay if I turn on the radio?" Annie asked, after they'd finished washing dishes and put plates back in the cabinet and silverware in a drawer.

"Yes, but you know they are going to be talking about the war."

"That's what I want. I've not heard the news for two or three days."

Mother White smiled slyly. She knew the war was going as well as could be hoped. The Allied armies were advancing rapidly and there was a widely shared confidence the Germans couldn't hold out much longer. She would be wary of sounding too optimistic, but she felt comfortable in expressing her hope the war would be over soon and Gil would be coming home.

The newscast was as positive as she had hoped. Annie hung on every word as the man on the radio reported details of a fast strike by General George S. Patton's U. S. Third Army that led to the capture of several thousand enemy troops and was seen to have important implications when it came to a final Allied offensive. Annie's countenance brightened to the point she no longer looked like she caried the full weight of war reserved for wives and mothers and sweethearts.

"Gil will be home before long," Annie said. "Sounds like the fighting is about done and they won't have any reason to keep him over there. Don't you think?"

"Yes, I do. And that means we've got work to do."

"What?"

"Well, main thing is we got a wedding to plan. Don't you

want a big one?"

Annie threw her hands up, then jumped out of her chair and started dancing around the room. Mother White laughed, not only because of her antics but also because it was good to see her granddaughter displaying this happy excitement. It had been a long while since she had seen much of a display of anything except nearly total dejection. She stood, too, and stepped quickly over to the radio.

The newscast had ended and made way for a commercial for some brand of beer, said to be available "wherever you buy your beer." They were playing music now. It was a song by Frank Sinatra, evidently something new, and she would like to hear it. But she reached and switched it off. *Last thing I want her to hear is a bulletin with some bad news about the war!* But she tried to make the move casually, hoping Annie wouldn't notice.

Annie had stopped dancing. Her expression warned she was about to say something serious.

"You know what, Grandmama? I don't care what kind of wedding I have. I just want my Gil home and everything back to normal. Seems like a hundred years since I saw him."

Mother White, even though she was hoping for an extravagant ceremony, would not disagree. "Well, honey, you know what I say: Everybody to their own likin'. You'll be just as married, big fancy to-do or just stand under a tree and have the preacher tie the knot. But right now it's about bedtime, don't you think?"

Annie said yes. Although she really hadn't done anything all day, she suddenly felt very tired. She was emotionally drained after their talk about Gil and ready for sleep. And though it was early, it was nearing their usual bedtime; except for the radio there was nothing to entertain them and they always got to bed not long after supper. And anyway, Mother White still got up very early in the morning and couldn't stay up late and expect to get the sleep she needed. Annie realized she simply was keeping the schedule she'd grown up with as a girl on the farm.

Annie was asleep in no time. She slept soundly through the night, in spite of the loud thunderstorm her grandmother told her about in the morning. She woke feeling refreshed and almost eager to get up and face whatever the day might bring. Mother White already had finished her breakfast and was sitting in front of the radio drinking coffee when Annie got to the kitchen.

"Any news?" Annie asked.

Mother White, who switched off the radio as soon as Annie appeared, was noncommittal. "Don't sound like anything's changed much. I think that's good. It seems like a while since you've got a letter from Gil. Think he might be on the move? I'm kind of thinking they might be getting our boys out of the field some and bunched up where they can get 'em home real fast. Don't you think that might be what's going on?"

"Gosh, I hope so. I hadn't thought about that."

Elmo rubbed against Annie's ankles in a show of affection. He was always up even ahead of Mother White and eager to start his day with a bowl of meaty cat food. He had finished his morning meal well before Annie made an appearance in the kitchen.

"Cat, sometimes you are in the way," Annie complained. "You're going to trip me before I even get my first cup of coffee."

Mother White opened the back door and Elmo went out.

Annie was more hungry than usual for breakfast, and readily agreed to her grandmother's offer of a generous plate of bacon and eggs. She sat and enjoyed her coffee while the older woman got her food ready.

Her eagerness surprised and pleased Mother White, who had worried about her lack of appetite but understood it. She actually had marveled at times at Annie's strength; having Gil off at war for so long had to be almost unbearable and going for weeks at a time having no communication with the man she loved was enough to dishearten even the most valiant. It had been hard when John was called to duty in his war and he hadn't even left the States. She knew her situation then was nothing like Annie's now. She never had worried that her husband might be killed in action.

"Uncle Ben ought to be starting the spring plowing pretty soon," Annie said, as her grandmother brought her a plate of steaming bacon and scrambled eggs. "He's getting pretty old. How much longer do you expect him to be up to all the hard work?"

Her question offered Mother White an opening she was hoping for. "He won't have to do much more," she said. "Gil will be here to take over before it's time to get the planting done. And I'd been meaning to ask, you think there's any chance Gil might have changed his mind about taking over the farm? I'm still counting on that but you know what they say, 'how you gonna keep 'em down on the farm . . .'"

"After they've seen Paree," Annie interrupted and finished the lyric for her. "I don't worry about that. He can't wait to get back and begin. How about Grandpa? Did he have any problem coming back?"

"No, but then he didn't see Paris or any of the rest of the world beyond Camp Jackson."

She went on to explain that Annie's grandfather had spent his entire period of service at Camp Jackson, where he became a drill sergeant training new troops. She said he wasn't thrilled with his assignment but glad he didn't have to get into combat in Europe.

"But we weren't married yet then," she added, "and so I don't know a lot about his time in the Army."

Annie finished her breakfast and, when Mother White got out her sewing kit and began to stitch up a loose hem on one of her dresses, went to her room and picked up the book she had started reading three weeks earlier. Dalton Trumbo's novel, *Johnny Got His Gun*, had received a lot of attention when it was published just a few years ago and she remembered it when she saw the title on a shelf in the library. She checked it out and brought it home, planning to read it at once. Now it no doubt was overdue, and she needed to get it back but wanted to read at least a bit more.

She was not prepared for the horrible description of war wounds she soon was reading. She knew she couldn't handle much of this but at the same time could not make herself put it down. She was lying on her bed reading when Mother White knocked on her door, then pushed it open without waiting for a response.

"You got a letter from Gil!" she announced, making no effort to hide her own excitement. "Mr. Jacob knew it was so important he brought it to the door. I'll let you read it in private, but I can't wait to hear any news."

She handed the letter to Annie and left the room. Annie ripped open the envelope and began to read:

My dearest, sweetest Annie,

You probably will notice right off the bat that this is not my awkward scribble. We have the most wonderful nurses and Red Cross volunteers who do so many things for us and one of them, this young Irish girl named Erin, is writing this for me. She says she can write as long as I can talk. Well, we'll see about that because I have a lot to tell you.

First thing is, the war is over for me. I'll be home before you know it. I will explain later. And I think it will be over soon for everybody because the Germans are whipped.

Annie jumped off the bed and ran to the living room where Mother White was waiting for whatever information she had to share. Tears were streaming down her face. "He's coming home, Grandmama," she called as she came through the door. "Gil's coming home!"

She held out the letter and Mother White took it. Soon she was reading what she assumed Gil had written.

After reading the first few lines, she paused. "It's wonderful news, honey," she said. "Can I go ahead and read the rest of it."

"Yes, please. Read it out loud. I didn't get far."

Mother White began to read again, raising her soft voice so Annie could hear:

And I think it will be over soon for everybody because the Germans are whipped. God in Heaven it's terrible to see the damage it's done and I'll bet nobody ever knows how many people have been killed. And for what? I think I'll wonder for the rest of my life unless somebody can tell me that.

I guess I'll have a guilty conscience, myself, knowing we did a lot of the destruction. I didn't do it but I am part of the U. S. Army that did. I talked to a chaplain about that once and he told me always to remember we were the good guys and we set free a lot of people and all that. He made me feel better. But, boy, our bombing raids just about wiped a lot of German towns off the map.

I didn't see it, but some of the guys were talking about a horrible experience I'm just as glad I missed. Right outside this little German town they found camps filled with starving prisoners and dead bodies everywhere. They said you could smell death from a mile away. And the prisoners still alive were little more than skeletons, like they hadn't eaten for days or weeks. All the German guards had pulled out when they heard we were getting close and just left everybody locked up in their cells.

Mother White paused and looked at Annie as if checking to see if what she had just read was too hard. When Annie didn't say anything she went on.

I know this is a terrible story and I'm sorry I even started it but believe it or not it has kind of a funny ending. Colonel Davies took a squad of MP's up to the town and made the people who lived there come down and see it and start picking up bodies.

They said the colonel ordered all the bakers in the town to start baking round the clock to feed the prisoners still alive. A few of them refused and he had tanks parked in front of their bakeries and told them to start baking or he'd have the tank gunners open fire. They all started baking. Kind of wish I had come to know Colonel Davies.

Some of the guys were so messed up by what they saw they had to go to chapel and pray or something. As far as I know, Captain Arnold is still our battalion chaplain. I like him, but I only saw him once. There's nothing pretentious about him and he doesn't claim that God will take care of all our problems if we just ask.

Annie, do you ever think about those Sunday nights we used to go to Walnut Creek Church and set and hold hands and try to talk through that code we made up? I remember some of the code, like hooking thumbs or little fingers or three squeezes or two half-squeezes or whatever.

Mother White stopped reading and smiled at Annie. "Sure you want me to go ahead with this? Sounds like it may get a little personal."

Annie laughed and told her to go on. She started reading again:

We never listened to the preacher. It's a wonder we didn't get caught and get thrown out. But I can tell you honestly it wouldn't have mattered if we listened to the preacher then, because whatever faith in God I might have had has been pretty much lost in this war. I have seen too many terrible things, and I don't know how if God could control things they would have happened.

Well, I was about to wrap this up, but Erin says I should go on and say everything I want to say. Isn't she great? She told me she is a legal secretary in a big law firm in Ireland which is why she can write what I say and keep up with me. Oh, now she said she writes it in shorthand and will have to write it out later for me to sign.

But, Annie, to say all I want to say would take me all day. And besides, you know I'm not a real eloquent talker. I forget something important and have to come back to it later just like I do when we are face to face. And speaking of that, I don't know if I ever really told you what a beautiful girl you are. I guess I kind of took you for granted when we were together, but boy that all changed when I had to leave you. But even if the Army dragged my body away, in my heart I never left southern Illinois. Please know I've never left your side in spirit. Right now I can even imagine I'm holding your hand.

I've been trying to think how long we have known each other. I remember I was crazy about you when we were just little kids. Okay, you don't have to admit it, but I know you didn't like me all that much in the beginning. Which I understand. It's a miracle you can love me now because I know I don't have a lot to offer. But I don't need to ramble on about myself because you know me very well.

I've seen some amazing things since I left southern Illinois, Annie. I'd never been in a big city before, and I'd never even dreamed of places like I've seen in Europe. All the old castles and that kind of thing. It's a big world, Annie, with lots of beautiful places. But I can honestly say I have not yet seen any place I'd rather spend the rest of my life than right there at home.

And I guess this brings me to the really important thing I have to tell you. I hate to tell you this, but I would rather you hear it from me than somebody else. The real reason I have to have somebody else write this for me is, I am blind.

Mother White gasped and Annie screamed, "No, no! Oh my God, no!" She fell into her grandmother's arms, her body wracked by her uncontrollable sobs. Mother White was crying, too, and they clung to each other for desperately needed support.

It was almost an hour before both regained their composure to the point they could get back to Gil's letter. Her voice quaking with emotion, Annie took up the reading where Mother White had left off:

The doctors gave me hope for a while that I might see again but not anymore. And I can't bear the thought that I will never see your face again. Oh, I'll always see it in my mind and in my dreams, but I'll never again be able to look into your beautiful blue eyes and feel the joy I get when I see your smile. I would give my life for just one more chance at these but I know if there is a God He is not going to offer me that deal.

But, Annie, this is the most painful part of all. Please forgive me, but I can't marry you now. I will always be a burden to whoever is close and has some responsibility to help take care of me and I would never want to burden you. You have so much to offer. You will make some other man a wonderful wife and be a wonderful mother to his children. I wish that steel fragment or whatever it was that took my sight had killed me so that I never had to face this situation, but then once again if there is an almighty God He didn't choose to play the game that way. I want you to have a long and happy life and maybe, somewhere down the line, we can have a chance to visit and talk about all those happy times we had together.

Despite her anguish, Annie's voice had grown stronger and she clearly had regained her self-control. She finished reading:

And no matter what, I want you to know that I will always love you.

My deepest love for eternity, Gil.

Now Mother White was the one barely able to express her thoughts, her face wet with tears and her voice quivering when she spoke. "I'm so sorry, honey, so very sorry. If there was anything I could do . . . ."

The heartbreaking news in Gil's letter left both women in nearly total despair. There was little they could say or do to break through the agony. How could a loving God permit this to happen to Gil, who never in his whole life had intentionally hurt another human being?

Annie was physically ill and twice ran out on the porch and vomited over the railing. Mother White, contrary to her normal disposition, felt both helpless and hopeless, as if all the light in her world had been extinguished and she was destined to live in darkness.

With hardly any conversation, they went about nighttime routines mechanically. Mother White was still crying softly when they went to bed, but Annie's tears were spent. She fell into bed crushed emotionally and completely exhausted physically, devastated by a sense that her whole being was as lifeless as if all the blood had been drained from her veins. Her loving Gil had been robbed of his ability to see the beautiful world around him and nothing else mattered.

26

IT WAS THE middle of the morning before Annie woke. She had tossed fitfully almost all night, until her worn out body finally gave in to the demand for escape. And at some point she began to dream. The dreams could have been real life, as she felt cool breezes on her face and smelled lilac and honeysuckle and relished the soft touch of Gil's hand holding hers. They walked in the woods and listened for songbirds and Gil wanted to take the path that went along the bank of the gently flowing creek but said he couldn't because his eyes didn't see.

"But I'll show you the way," she coaxed him. "Take my hand and we'll walk as one."

He did and they skipped along the path like children, swinging their arms and trying to remember the songs they used to sing. It was as if Gil had never been away. They stopped and stood against one another. She could feel the beat of Gil's heart as he embraced her and whispered in her ear, "You are my eyes now, sweet Annie, and through you I will see all the beautiful things."

She got out of bed and stepped to the window and looked out, and was stunned by the beauty of the meadow before her on a sunny day. The scene was calming and offered a sense of renewal. It was almost as if she were two people, one standing at the window still in the throes of yesterday's agonies and the other strolling across the meadow ready to accept all the possibilities offered by a new day.

She went to the kitchen and poured a cup of coffee, decided she wanted to add cream and sweetener, and did this in small increments and sampled after each until she had achieved the perfect taste. Yes, simply pouring coffee and drinking it black was much faster and easier but the delicious brew in her cup was worth the extra time and effort.

Mother White was on the porch, sitting motionless in the swing. She looked haggard, her face unusually drawn and pale. For the first time Annie had ever seen it, Elmo was curled up beside her.

She managed a slight smile in greeting her granddaughter. "Did you get any rest, honey?"

Annie grasped her hand. When she spoke she expressed herself calmly, in a matter-of-fact tone that belied the painful circumstance she was about to address.

"Grandmama," she said softly, "we're overlooking the main thing. Gil's *alive*! And he's coming home. His body's damaged in a terrible way but his mind is still good. He expressed his feelings as strong as ever. We will be married and I will take care of him. I'll be at his side for the rest of his life. My eyes will be his eyes. He will be the father of my children.

"Yes, I will hurt for him. Every day I will hurt for him. But I will be thankful he is here, that he is alive."

Mother White took a moment to respond. "But he doesn't want to marry you now, Annie. He made that very clear."

Annie smiled, her face no longer marked by last night's distress.

"That's my Gil," she said. "That's out of compassion for me. He's afraid he would be a burden. Give me ten minutes with the big dummy and I'll fix that."

Annie stepped to the porch railing. Elmo jumped from the swing and nearly entangled himself rubbing around her ankles. She reached down and scuffed him behind the ears. He rolled onto his back and fawned, and she tickled his belly.

"Oh, sure," she teased, "you are the most beautiful kitty in the whole world. But you're getting a little wide around the middle. Maybe we need to cut back on the chow a bit and see if we can get you in a little better shape for Gil. He'll be here soon."

She turned back to Mother White and lowered herself into the swing beside her. As they sat, gently swinging, Annie looked into the distance to the north. Across the valley, the greening seemed to boast of a new season's coming as if it were something miraculous. And, well, maybe it was. *Spring means the renewal of life, a chance for everything old to be young again.* And my sweet Gil will have seasons of renewal, too, she thought. *And I will have my sweet Gil and there will be no more war and we'll never be separated again.*

"We'll stand under a dogwood tree and let preacher Maxwell tie the knot," she said to Mother White.

Her grandmother turned to face her. For a moment, Annie was afraid she was going to resist that idea. But Mother White's smile was an unmistakable expression of approval. "You are a beautiful person and you will make Gil a wonderful wife," she said.

Mother White's countenance was pensive. She seemed to be lost in thought for a moment before she went on. "I won't be around all that much longer, Annie, but I will be here at the beginning and I will rejoice in seeing the two of you together. And I'll get to hold that first baby and tell that child how lucky he or she is to have roots in such a strong family."

Annie said nothing in reply. She simply had no words. If there was such a thing as an overflowing heart, she felt one.

Yes, Gil would be her lifelong companion, to have and to

hold and to help adjust to his new limitations. And she would never feel sorry for herself. She would lead Gil into the woods and make a chain of spring beauties for his head and he would smell the sweet fragrance and laugh as the delicate flowers pulled apart and fell around his shoulders.

Gil's spirit, his strength of character, and his determination would help him come to accept his limitations and move on. The lack of physical vision could barely diminish the vision within his conscious mind and would be bested by the ideas spawned in his vivid imagination. How she would relish listening as he gave these voice and such rewards she would reap merely knowing her approval was all the encouragement he needed to set new goals for himself and press ahead.

And, yes, what a privilege she would have, helping him view in his mind's eye the beautiful world around them when the red-bud and dogwood trees bloomed in the spring and the golden-rod brightened the hillside at the approach of autumn. *I am the most fortunate woman in the world.* So many husbands, so many sons, so many brothers would not be coming home. Her Gil would be. She could ask for nothing more.

THE END

Author's Notes and Acknowledgments

I have been a journalist almost all my adult life, beginning on my high school newspaper in Carmi, Illinois. This gave me a rather gentle start because there was very little bad news in *The Bulldog Barks.* Later, as a journalism student at Southern Illinois University, I wrote for and served a term as news editor of the student newspaper, *The Egyptian.* Here again, although we dealt with occasional controversies on campus, there was little really "bad" news.

But I would soon learn that high school and college reporters usually live in a small, somewhat sheltered world and that negative stories about things happening to fellow human beings abound in the pages of most newspapers. This is good. News is inherently reports of the *unusual*; God help us if unfortunate things negatively impacting the lives of people become the common occurrence.

As I explained to my journalism students at the University of Illinois, "It is not news that you made it to class this morning without incident. It would be news if you had been hit by a bus and didn't make it."

Newspaper reporting tends to make realists of the reporters. One of my worst days at work on *The Granite City Press-Record,* a powerful medium on the Illinois side of the Mississippi River opposite St. Louis, began with a call to a local family regarding the death of a child. She was only a toddler, and our sketchy information made clear it was accidental but we couldn't piece together the details. I found myself talking with the child's father and had to force myself to ask him what happened.

After a long pause, he told me, somewhat angrily, "She was playing in the driveway and I backed over her with my truck. Okay?"

I often told my students about this, urging them never to forget that things they reported were things which affected the lives of fellow human beings. This is the maxim that spawned the adage, almost always attributed to a journalism teacher, "If it bleeds, it leads." This has been used cynically as an indictment of newspaper sensationalism, but the intended message to would-be reporters is an emphasis on the rule that, no matter what other destruction, if a happening leads to personal injury this is the most important thing to be reported.

I implied earlier that reporters tend to become realists, and I count myself as no exception. Life's tragedies seldom come with happy endings. This view has prevailed to some extent in my novels, and I suppose this one—my ninth—is a ready example. But I hope to help readers recognize that something good often grows out of something bad. Surely the story I've just told ends with that option.

I believe strongly that the indomitable human spirit prevails. There are personal models for this belief but I'd rather not cite any one in particular. If you have just finished my story, let me assure you that I am fully confident that Gil Bennett, with support from his loving Annie, is a model too.

As always, I am indebted to a great many people whose support is very much appreciated. Foremost among these is Michael Thomas. His *Good Living in West Frankfort* magazine story about an area man's experiences in World War II offered insights that helped me structure my story. Michael not only gave me permission to make use of his superbly told piece, but encouraged me to do so. I am grateful.

I owe words of thanks to members of my former writing group in Champaign, Illinois, and the novel-reading discussion group at the Carmi, Illinois, Public Library, too great in number to name here. Two people whose names I must mention, though, are my sons, Alan Hays and David Hays. While I dedicated this book to them solely because of my fatherly love, I need to cite them here for their general support and encouragement which compel me to keep writing. I can always ask for and get constructive comments from them and in addition I often call on David to apply his experienced journalist's eye for a bit of proofreading.

As always, I must thank my marvelous Thomas-Jacob publisher, Melinda Clayton. If there is a model for everything a publisher ought to be, she surely is it. And I thank you, reader, for your time and interest. Without you my writing would serve no purpose. I hope to see you again in one of my other stories.

About the Author

Robert Hays is a U.S. Army veteran and a newspaper reporter turned teacher who is professor emeritus on the faculty of the University of Illinois. He is the author of eight previous novels, three of which gained nominations for the prestigious Pushcart Prize literary award. His non-fiction works include his collaboration with General Oscar Koch, *G-2: Intelligence for Patton*, a standard reference for military historians published in 1971 and still in print. He also authored a biography of General Koch, who as intelligence chief for General George S. Patton Jr. was one of the true unsung heroes of World War II.

Other Books by Robert Hays

Fiction

Darkening of the Light
An Empty House by the River
An Inchworm Takes Wing
A Shallow River of Mercy
Blood on the Roses
The Baby River Angel
The Life and Death of Lizzie Morris
Circles in the Water
Equinox and Other Stories
Early Stories from the Land (editor)

Non–Fiction

Patton's Oracle
A Race at Bay
Editorializing "the Indian Problem"
State Science in Illinois
G-2: Intelligence for Patton (with Gen. Oscar Koch)
Country Editor